Healing Promise

Windsor Peak: The Monahans
Book 1

Denise Latham

ISBN: 979-8-9888952-9-9

www.deniselatham.com

Windsor Peak Series

Coming Home
Staying Home
Finding Home
Forever Home
Holiday Home
You're Home
Our Home

Windsor Peak: The Monahans

Healing Promise

Broken Promise

Dedication

5

To my fellow nurses especially, and to all who work in healthcare. No matter how big or small you see your position, you make the world a better place. I know how hard you work, and what you sacrifice to help the community around you, and I am thankful for you. Even if we haven't worked together in the thick of it, we've walked the same path and felt the same joys and heartache, and I am proud to be a part of a community of healers.

Chapter 1

"Who put this order in?" Dr. Evan Lincoln's voice boomed across the nurse's station, causing everyone sitting there to cringe and duck their heads. He glanced around, seeing patients with concerned expressions on their faces, and lowered his voice. "Who did this?"

"What is it?" Sandi, the charge nurse, stood to walk to where he was looking at the computer. She typically oversaw each new order that came through and made sure it was entered correctly.

"Here, for Mrs. Lee," he said, pointing at the screen. "She's allergic to this. It's noted everywhere on her chart."

Sandi frowned and clicked on the order, which brought up more information. "It was entered by Dr. Howard," she said. "And confirmed by a nurse who works with him. They must have put it in for the wrong patient and not realized. Perhaps the names are similar."

"Are you serious?" He stared at her in shock. "And no one thought to double-check before giving it to her?"

"Med errors happen, Dr. Lincoln. We are only human," Sandi said calmly. "It was recognized almost immediately, and she was sent to the emergency department to get medication and to be monitored for reaction. The pharmacy should have caught it as well, but they sent it up for her. I can't answer questions as to why it was given without checking her allergens, but I will address it with the nurse and offer some further training."

"Who was the nurse?" He glared across the oncology unit to where Finley Monahan was talking to a different patient and his wife. Of course it would have been her. She was probably gossiping and not paying attention to what she was doing.

"It was Abby," Sandi said. "She's a new graduate and has only been on her own for a week. I should have double-checked the new medications with her, so it's my fault."

He deflated, seeing that Sandi was telling him the truth. Abby was a sweet young nurse who appeared terrified of him every time he stepped on the floor, so there was no way he could yell at her. "Please make sure it doesn't happen again."

Evan turned to walk back to his office and had just taken a seat when Finley appeared in the doorway. "Got a minute?" She asked just before slamming the door closed, with her on the wrong side of it.

"Not really," he said. "I need to go to the emergency room to follow up with Mrs. Lee. And I have a family meeting in half an hour."

"You were out there ready to light me up for the mistake, right?"

"I was simply trying to find out who had done it," he explained. "You are usually assigned patients who are under my care, so I assumed she was under your care."

"Do you know what happens when you assume?"

"This doesn't seem productive," he said, starting to rise from his chair. "If you'll excuse me."

"No, I will not." She stood with her arms firmly crossed across her chest, glaring at him. She barely came up to his biceps, but her fury was intimidating enough to cause him to sit back down.

"I understand she wasn't your patient today," he said. "Why weren't you the one in charge of administering her treatment?"

"That's none of your business," she replied. "I want to know why you were out there yelling when you thought it was my fault and then left it to Sandi when you found out the truth."

"I don't know," he said, sighing. He pulled off his glasses and wiped them on his white jacket before putting them back on.

"I thought you had been busy socializing and hadn't paid attention."

"I always pay attention," she shot back. "I could recite my patient's allergies the same way I can their family member names. It's possible to be chatty and thorough."

"I think we could focus more on the professionalism, and less on the chatter," he said. "As I've told you several times now."

"But you aren't my boss," she fired back.

"Aren't I? I'm the doctor in charge of this unit. I believe you ultimately report to me and perform the tasks that I have ordered for the patients."

"First of all, you aren't the only doctor," she pointed out. "Second, half the time you're writing orders for things that I've suggested or requested. I pay attention to what they need and ask you to treat their side effects. I notice when things aren't working, or when someone is struggling. Don't act like you're out on the floor, in touch with what the patients want, when you barely know their names."

He watched as she stormed out of the office, and half rose to chase her down. Realizing it would be futile, he sat back in the chair and glanced at his watch. Thinking he had a few minutes, he sighed when the phone rang, and the receptionist told him that his next appointment was there. Put this away for now, he told himself, and focus on the person coming in. They deserved his full attention, especially given the news that he was about to break.

***

Because the universe was cruel and he hadn't already suffered enough, Finley was in line in the cafeteria when Evan went to grab a cup of coffee. Pretending to look at his phone, he hoped she wouldn't turn around, but that lasted roughly ten seconds.

"You should probably go ahead of me," she said with a sarcastic note in her voice. "After all, you're the most important person in the hospital."

"I just want some coffee," he said quietly, hoping to avoid a scene. "I don't want to fight with you right now."

"No, that would tarnish your image, wouldn't it?"

He grabbed a large cup from the stack and filled it with black coffee, snapping a lid on and resuming his stance behind her. Although he could go around the people waiting with their trays for hot meals, he felt rude doing so, and instead relegated himself to waiting.

"Aren't you going to eat something?" Finley asked, glancing at the cup and lack of tray in his hands.

"I'm not hungry."

"Black coffee on an empty stomach isn't a great idea," she continued. "Even just some of those peanut butter crackers would be good."

"I said I'm not hungry," he snapped.

She sniffed and turned her back on him once more. He listened as she started chatting with the nurses in front of her, who he didn't recognize. They were talking about a new show that depicted life in the hospital, and he tuned them out. There was no show that could convey what he did each day. It would never last if it put the viewers through the emotional roller coaster that he rode every day.

Once he had paid for his coffee, he headed toward the exit, frustrated to find Finley matching his steps. When he glanced at her, she shrugged and held up a paper bag. "I got mine to go," she said. "I have a patient coming in any minute."

"You don't, actually," he said. "I just met with him and his wife. There's no further treatment regimen that will help him. He's going on hospice."

"What?" She stopped walking and stared at him. "Are you serious?"

"Yes."

"He's so young," she said. He saw tears gathering in her eyes, and she swiped one away with the back of her hand when it fell. "They just had a baby six months ago."

"I know."

"How can you be so cold?" She jabbed him in the arm with a pointed finger, making his hot coffee slosh onto his hand. "He was my patient for the last year. I've gotten to know him and his wife. I went and met the baby when he was born. Why would you tell me like this? Why wouldn't you have had me be a part of the meeting?"

"Because of this," he said, gesturing to her tears. "You get so emotional. I needed to focus on him and his wife, not deal with your feelings on the matter."

"You didn't even give me a chance to say goodbye to him," she said. "Or to soften the blow. I can't imagine how hard it was to hear those words with no compassion at all."

He stiffened, then avoided her gaze. "I'm sorry you feel that way."

"You're sorry I…" Her voice trailed off, and she shook her head. "I don't know why I bother. You're never going to get it. I can't believe you did that to him, and to me. It's obviously less horrific that you're blindsiding me, because I'm just his nurse. But I hope you had more tact when telling him he was going to die."

She stormed away, and he let her go. What would be the point in telling her that he had fought off tears after the young couple had left his office? That he had sat alongside the couple, not behind his desk, so he could be a shoulder to lean on as they got the worst news of their lives? That he had spent his entire weekend researching clinical trials and what the hospitals outside of the United States were doing, to see if there was any hope to be found. And that he had offered his own money to send them to Switzerland to try the one option he had found, but they had gracefully turned him down. It had nearly broken him when the thirty-three-year-old had turned to his wife and said all he wanted was to enjoy the time they had left, not to be part of a medical experiment. And that even though he could see how devastated his wife had been, she had nodded and reached for him, putting her own emotions aside for the person she loved.

Instead of chasing Finley down to share all that, he turned and walked to the emergency room. It was on the opposite end of the hospital from the Oncology unit and was a hive of activity. Gurneys were flying down the hallways, ambulances were arriving at the back doors, and medical staff rushed in every direction. They all ignored him as he checked the board behind the nurse's station and then headed to the bay where his patient was listed. Fortunately for both of them, it was a quieter room where the door could be closed, and he found Mrs. Lee resting with the TV playing on low.

Earlier she had been given a medication that she was allergic to, warranting the rush to the emergency department for treatment. The IV bags hanging above her contained medication to treat the reaction, as well as fluids because he had noticed that she appeared dehydrated as they rushed her down the hall. She was alone, and they usually had a volunteer sit with her for her treatment but hadn't thought to send anyone here. Instead, he settled into the chair at her side and watched as a home renovation was performed on the TV screen above them. When she woke up, she would at least have a familiar face at her side. It wasn't a lot, but it was something he could do.

A nurse appeared in the doorway and looked startled to see him. "Hi," she said. "Are you her family?"

"No, I'm Dr. Lincoln from oncology," he replied. "That's where she was when she had the reaction. I'm just keeping an eye on her."

"Oh," she said. She appeared stunned by the news and stared at him for a minute longer than was comfortable before shaking her head. "I just need to check her vitals."

"Please," he said, gesturing for her to come in.

After she had turned on the machine and the blood pressure cuff filled, Mrs. Lee woke up. She glanced around in confusion before seeing him sitting next to her. "Dr. Lincoln," she said.

"Mrs. Lee," he replied. "Do you remember what happened?"

"I do," she said, nodding. "I just didn't expect to see you here."

"I didn't want you to be alone," he said. "Especially when you woke up in an unfamiliar place."

"I may be old as dirt, but I'm not senile," she said, laughing softly. "At least, not yet."

"You are neither," he said, patting her hand. "Young as a spring chicken and just as bright."

"You are sweet to lie. And to sit here with me. But I always knew you had that inside you," she said.

"What?"

"The capacity to care. You hide it well, but you always ask the right questions, which shows you do see me as a human. So many doctors think of me as a number, or a checklist to complete. Especially as I've gotten older, I've felt more and more invisible," she said. "But not with you. I always felt safe with you."

"That's very flattering," he said. "I'm not sure I deserve it, but on a day like today, it was what I needed to hear."

"Not to mention, having you at my bedside means these nurses will be jumping twice as fast when I ask for something," she said with a laugh. "Handsome doctors tend to get more attention than little old ladies."

He laughed and pointed to the TV. "I don't know, with carpenters walking around like that, I pale in comparison."

"All you have to do is take your shirt off," she said, with a mischievous glint in her eye. "Then the playing field will be even."

He laughed and sat back in the chair, happy to spend his afternoon with her. The work would likely pile up on his desk, and he would have to keep an eye on his phone for notes to come through, but it was worth it. From the smile on her face, he knew he had turned her day around, and nothing else mattered.

Chapter 2

"He is the most infuriating man on the planet. I honestly can't stand him," Finley Monahan slammed her work locker closed after making the statement, turning to her coworker Audrey. They worked as nurses together in the oncology unit of a small hospital just outside Windsor Peak, Vermont. Their days were filled with emotional and difficult situations, so the bonds between them were strong.

"Are we talking about our favorite doctor?" Audrey asked as she pulled on her sweatshirt.

"Who else?"

"What did he do now?"

"Today, he made a point to lecture me on how I needed to send him direct messages about his patients, rather than just charting, so he can respond quicker. It was humiliating to be lectured in front of Sandi and Abby like that. And yesterday, he put one of my patients on hospice without me," she said. "Blindsided me with it after the fact. I didn't even get to say goodbye."

"That's weird," Audrey said, frowning.

"I know, right?"

"No, not about you," Audrey said. "That he did it himself. If anything, it's usually the opposite. The doctors put it on us and a social worker to break the news. He did it himself?"

"Yes," Finley said, feeling the air leave her sails slightly. "And it must have been hard. The patient was in his thirties. Married with a baby at home."

"Oh, that's terrible," Audrey said with a sigh. "I know I couldn't have handled that. We celebrate the wins so often, it's easy to forget the heartbreak when we lose."

"But don't you think he should have included me?"

Audrey shrugged. "I guess, if you really would want to be there. But I wonder if he thought he was sparing you the pain?"

"There's no way he's sensitive enough for that," she said with a sniff.

"How would we know? He keeps to himself. I barely know anything about him," Audrey said. "Even when we had literal movie stars in the room, he was in his office, not socializing with the rest of us. And that was a celebration."

Finley thought back to several weeks before, when her patient Stella had completed her treatment. Her son was one of the biggest movie stars on the planet, and he had accompanied her on the last day at the hospital. Patrick had been generous enough to pose for pictures with all of the staff and charmed everyone in sight. He had also brought along two co-stars, who had recently moved to town, who had done the same. Between Patrick, Natalie and Liam, the star power in the hospital had never been stronger, and yet Dr. Lincoln had simply congratulated Stella and disappeared.

"Speaking of Stella, last Saturday night was the celebration for her. You wanted to be my plus one until you realized it was your mom's birthday, remember?" When Audrey nodded, Finley continued. "He was invited because he was her primary doctor here. Not only did he not respond, but he didn't show up. Can you imagine?"

"I can," Audrey said with a laugh. "I can't picture him at a party. Although he is handsome, don't you think?"

"No," Finley said with a sniff. "No one who acts like that can be considered handsome."

They started walking out of the locker room towards the parking lot, both carrying tote bags filled with their lunches, extra clothes, and whatever else they dragged to and from work daily. "I don't agree," Audrey said. "If you just looked at him, it's hard to deny he's gorgeous. The dark eyes behind those glasses, I can just picture him taking them off right before kissing me. I kind of want to go back and hit on him just to see if reality is as good as my imagination."

"Good luck," Finley said. "He's the last person I would ever want to kiss."

"Speaking of people I'd like to kiss, want to go by the Palace and see your brother?"

"That's even worse," Finley said with a groan. "Why do you have to flirt with him?"

"Because it's fun," Audrey said, laughing. "And I know nothing will ever happen. It's just to pass the time."

"I don't know. I'm exhausted," Finley replied. "Today was long. I kind of want to just put pajamas on and watch a movie."

"You literally live above the bar," Audrey pointed out. "And you need to eat dinner, anyway."

"Fine," Finley said with an eye roll. "But I'm going upstairs by seven, no excuses."

Audrey waved as she pulled out of her parking spot, and Finley followed her. When they arrived at the downtown area, Audrey parked on the street while Finley pulled into the parking lot behind the building. Living above the bar meant private parking, and she was able to dash upstairs and drop her bag before heading down to the bar.

Audrey's blond ponytail was bopping at the far end of the bar as Finley entered, clearly talking animatedly to the person next to her. Desmond, Finley's twin brother, was helping a guest closer to the door, so at least she had found another person to flirt with. Des waved as Finley walked by, and she knew he would get her a drink without needing to be asked. She pulled out the empty chair next to Audrey and then caught sight of who was on her friend's other side and froze.

"Look who's here!" Audrey declared, bringing unnecessary attention to her companion. "Dr. Lincoln finally ventured out of the hospital."

"Hello," he said, nodding at Finley briefly.

She slid onto her chair and glared at Desmond, sending him a twin-powered mental message that he needed to hurry with her wine. He glanced her way and held up a finger, at which she scowled.

"Dr. Lincoln was just telling me that he went to Harvard," Audrey continued. "Isn't that great?"

"He's mentioned it once, or a hundred times," Finley said dryly. She saw the doctor tense up and felt bad as soon as the words left her mouth. "But yes, it's very impressive."

"Where did you go to school?" he asked, and she couldn't tell if it was genuine interest or a veiled barb.

"University of New Hampshire," she replied.

"That's a good school," he said, nodding at her. He glanced over her head and pushed his stool back. "You'll have to excuse me; my dinner companions have arrived."

Finley turned to look and saw Ben and Stella Burrows walking into the restaurant. Her head snapped back, and she surprised herself by grabbing Dr. Lincoln's arm as he tried to walk past. "So, you blew off her party and demanded a private dinner?"

"That's not exactly accurate," he said slowly, removing her hand. "But she was gracious enough to accept my invitation to dinner. She seems less upset about my missing the party than you do."

He walked away, and she found herself watching until her brother loudly coughed from behind the bar. She flushed and turned back, only to find Des and Audrey laughing at her.

"You have a thing for the good doctor?" Desmond teased. "I can call him back over for you."

"Knock it off," she said. "I do not."

"He's not a bad guy," Desmond went on. "I expected him to have horns or be cruel, based on how much you complain about him. We had a chance to chat for a few minutes, and I liked him."

"Maybe you can work with him," Finley snapped.

"Hi, honey," a woman's voice came from behind her, so Finley turned again. Her sister-in-law, Zoe, stood behind her. Zoe was the head chef at the Palace and had partnered with the restaurant owner to open a business next door. Palace Plates specialized in catering, cooking lessons, prepared meals, and special events. She had married Finley's brother, JJ, which was the first smart thing her brother had ever done.

"Hey, Zoe," Desmond called over. "Finley's just embarrassed herself with the good doctor."

"Oh, is he here? Where?" Zoe turned and glanced around the restaurant, causing Finley to groan.

"This is so embarrassing," she said. "You can't all stare."

"Just tell me who he is," Zoe demanded. "The guy eating alone by the window?"

"No, he's with the Burrows," Finley said.

Zoe grinned at her. "That's convenient, because that's who I was on my way to see. Now I can meet him."

"Please don't embarrass me," Finley begged. "I've been so excited to finally have a sister , and I would hate to have to stop talking to you."

"You'll love me no matter what," Zoe said. "I make JJ normal. Which reminds me, he'll be in when he finishes for the day, so that's a bigger problem for you."

"I need to go upstairs," Finley said. Her brother was the town sheriff and had a tendency to be extremely overprotective of his little sister.

"Colin's coming too," Desmond called out. "He texted me a few minutes ago, and I told him you and your gorgeous friend were here."

"You're so sweet," Audrey said, smiling at him.

"Obnoxious," Finley said, correcting her friend. "He's obnoxious."

"I'm going to say hi to the Burrows," Zoe said. "Then I'll make you some dinner. You seem cranky."

"This is a disaster," Finley said as Zoe walked away. She watched as she shook Dr. Lincoln's hand, her eyes darting over to Finley's as she did. "I think I need to move. I don't know why I felt the need to leave Boston."

"You're not moving," Audrey said.

"Travel nursing, then," Finley replied. "I could go back to switching locations every six weeks. It would be perfect."

"You know as well as I do that you would never leave your patients in the middle of their treatment," Audrey said. "Stop this foolishness."

"I'll have you know I did just fine when I traveled," she argued. "Granted, most times I got put on different units and was happy to leave, but still."

Finley had started at the hospital as a travel nurse, thinking she would try it before making the move permanent. During that time, she floated to several units, and when she saw the job posting for oncology, she had jumped on it. She loved working with Audrey, Sandi, and their newest nurse, Abby. The position allowed her to really bond with the people she cared for, in a way no other role had. As much as she hated to admit it, Dr. Lincoln's suggestion that they be assigned to patients as they started the treatment, when they were terrified and unsure of what was happening, had been beneficial to both the staff and patients. Seeing them go through the process and ideally ending treatment in remission was the most gratifying part of her job.

The hardest was when she had to sit and hear the doctor explain that all treatment options had failed, and when she lost those patients.

"You're right," Finley said to Audrey. "I'm just going to have to live with this humiliation."

Desmond walked away to answer a customer who was waving for him, leaving the two women alone. Audrey turned her full attention back to Finley as he left. "You'll be fine," she said. "It's really not as big a deal as you think. And I don't know that Dr. Lincoln is even aware of what's going on."

"I hope you're right," Finley replied. The door opened, and her brother JJ came in, thankfully out of his uniform. In jeans and a flannel shirt, he could be any local, although anyone who lived in Windsor Peak knew who he was. He went immediately to his wife's side, kissing her on the cheek before shaking hands with the two men at the table and hugging Stella. "Great, now JJ is with him. When will this end?"

"Let's talk about something else," Audrey suggested. "Are you going to Harvest Festival?"

"Of course," Finley said. "I live in the middle of it, after all. Are you?"

"I plan to," Audrey said. "A few of us were making plans for Saturday, if you want to meet up with us."

"It's still a few weeks away, but I'll let you know," Finley promised.

They chatted about the upcoming town activities until Zoe walked by, waving as she went back into the kitchen. JJ was a few steps behind and stopped to wrap his sister in a hug. "How's it going?" He asked her and Audrey, nodding hello to her friend.

"Good," she said. "Are you going in to wait for Zoe?"

"No," he said. "She'll be here for a little while, and I need to get home to the dog. I'm just going to grab my dinner."

"Okay, see you later," Finley said.

"I feel like you're trying to get rid of me," JJ said. "I met your doctor friend. Nice guy."

"I saw," Finley said. Audrey laughed behind her, hiding it with a sip of her drink.

Desmond appeared again, pointing at JJ. "Colin is on his way. Want to sit and I'll grab you a beer?"

JJ looked at his watch and shrugged. "I guess the dog can wait half an hour," he said. "Sure."

"I see two seats down there," Finley suggested, pointing down the bar.

"Why are you trying to get rid of me?" JJ asked, laughing.

"This was supposed to be a relaxing drink with a friend after work," Finley said. "And all of a sudden, my entire family is getting involved in my work conflict."

"I can go back over," JJ offered. "Make it clear that he needs to go easy on my baby sister."

"No," she said quickly. "Just go sit and have a drink with Colin. This is a work issue, not something for you to get involved in."

He grinned at her and went to claim the seats where Des had placed two bottles of beer, anticipating Colin's arrival. When her third brother arrived, Audrey's eyes popped even wider. "Wow, he's even better looking than Desmond."

"Don't let Des hear you say that," Finley cautioned her. "They are all so competitive."

"Where have you been hiding him?"

"Nowhere. Colin is just always busy," she replied. "No idea what he's been doing since he moved up here, but I've barely seen him."

"Shame, because he is nice to look at," Audrey said. "Is he dating anyone?"

"No idea," Finley said with a shrug. "He's very private."

Finley worked to redirect the conversation to topics other than her brother or their coworkers. By the time she finished her glass of wine, she was utterly exhausted. Her brothers were still talking midway down the bar, and a quick glance told her that the Burrows and Dr. Lincoln were still at their table.

"I'm going to head upstairs," she said. "I'm sorry, but I'm so tired."

"I am too," Audrey said. "I want to go sit and get to know your brother, but I think it's better to head home."

Finley waved Desmond down, who came right over. "Another round?"

"No," she said, shaking her head. "Can we get our check?"

"Oh, the doctor took care of that," he said, smirking at her.

Audrey laughed and elbowed her. "Now you'll have to be nice to him."

"I'm leaving," she said, pushing her barstool back. "Drive carefully."

Finley slipped through the kitchen door, careful not to bump into any servers carrying trays. Zoe was back in her zone, directing traffic in the busy workspace. She glanced up and saw Finley and pointed at a covered plate. "That's for you."

"Thanks," Finley said. She didn't question what the meal was, knowing that Zoe was more familiar with her taste than anyone, and that whatever it was would be exactly what she needed.

Chapter 3

Evan said goodbye to Stella and Ben Burrows outside the restaurant before starting the short walk back to his new house. He had purchased it six months prior, but was still adapting to the idea of having this home of his own. He needed to find the time to make it a place he was proud of, but work tended to exhaust him. Besides, what more did he need other than a bed, a couch and a TV? Other than his well-stocked bookshelf, that is.

The house was just a few blocks outside of the downtown area, and a short drive to the hospital. When he had been shopping with the realtor, he had first wanted to be closer to work. Thankfully, she had the good sense to steer him away, reminding him that a separation between work and home was a good thing.

After hanging his coat and placing his shoes in the closet, he wandered into the kitchen for a glass of water. The book he was reading was still in its spot on the end table next to the couch, so he sat and opened it, hoping to get a few more chapters done before bed. He barely made it through the first line before thoughts of Finley Monahan made it difficult to focus on the words.

Seeing her outside of the hospital tonight had thrown him off balance. He was used to their professional relationship, poor as it may be. She appeared as unhappy to see him as he was her, so ideally, they would be able to avoid each other in the future.

A part of him wished there had been a particular incident that had set them on a path of mutual dislike, so he could just avoid her and think of whatever the insult was. However, nothing specific had happened that he knew of. One day she just appeared to hate him, and he found her to be off-putting, so there they were. Which didn't explain why her image kept popping into his head as he tried to read his murder mystery novel.

***

"Dr. Lincoln, can I speak to you a moment?" The medical director of the hospital, Dr. Neil Collins, was in the doorway to his office.

"Of course, come in," Evan said, jumping to his feet.

Dr. Collins handed him a folder across the desk as he sat down. "There is a conference I'd like you to attend," he said. "I know you usually choose your own over the year, but this is to represent the hospital and take my spot. I apologize for the short notice, but I'm able to cover your shifts here and will be indebted to you if you can make it work. You'll have an opportunity to hear some great speakers and learn about some research in the oncology field, while also meeting with some professionals I'd like to lure here for a stint."

"I'd be honored," Evan said. His role at the hospital was usually with patients, and he rarely even saw the other heads of department, never mind the Medical Director. Being asked to represent their small hospital was exciting, and doing so in place of Dr. Collins made it even more so. His boss had an upstanding reputation in the community

"It's in Boston, and I know you're familiar with the area," Dr. Collins continued. "There will be a large contingent of graduating Harvard students, so obviously we'd love for some of them to come here for their fellowships. We're also facing a nursing shortage, so I'd like to try to entice some new graduates to come up this way."

Evan frowned, looking over the paperwork. "I'm not sure I'm the best candidate to speak about the nursing roles," he said. "I haven't spent much time in the other departments, and I'm sure we need more than just nurses in oncology."

20

"Correct," Dr. Collins said. "That's why a nurse will be attending along with you. She worked in several units when she first started, in addition to having been a travel nurse prior, and has the experience to share."

"Excellent," Evan said, relieved that he wasn't being set up to fail. He was still new at the hospital and wanted to set a good impression on the first task specifically handed to him, not fall flat on his face.

"She works in your department," Dr. Collins continued. "Finley Monahan. She already agreed to go. I've left the information about the hotel reservations there in your packet, and you can choose if you want to drive or fly. Either way, the hospital will reimburse you. If you opt to drive, perhaps you can ride together."

Evan nodded, his throat feeling tight. It was a four-hour ride to Boston on a good day, five when traffic was bad. That many hours trapped in a car with Finley, who would likely feel the need to talk the entire time, was too much. "I'll probably fly," he said. "More efficient use of my time."

"Either way is fine," Dr. Collins said as he stood. "Sorry for the short notice on this. In full transparency, I'll share that I was slated to attend myself, but then realized it's the week of my granddaughter's birthday. And although she may not realize, since she's only two, the rest of my family won't be quick to forget if I miss it."

"Understood," Evan said, nodding. If his boss had noticed the stress that was likely showing on his face at the thought of several days alone with Finley, he didn't say anything. Instead, he slapped a hand on the doorway as he walked out, as if that was his goodbye.

Evan sank back into his chair, trying to wrap his head around the plans. Even if they were at the same conference, there was a good chance they would never see each other, right? She would be busy with the nurses and attending seminars appropriate for her, and he would be schmoozing with doctors and new graduates. Certainly, there would be no occasion for them to cross paths, he thought with relief.

***

His shift ran long, plagued by issues. One patient had an adverse reaction to the chemotherapy and needed to be rushed to the emergency room. A new patient had struggled, requiring frequent reassurance from him that he was in the right hands. Communication between himself and nursing seemed to be more strained than ever, after he had asked the day before to be tagged in notes that were concerning so he could react faster. He had thought it would improve things, but Finley had taken it as an insult, and now he felt even more on the outs.

Evan felt worn out as he left the hospital, for once dreading his empty house and lack of companionship. At the last second, he changed directions and parked in front of the restaurant he had been at the night before. Finley's brother had welcomed him like an old friend, and the entire experience had been pleasant. Locals that he recognized from town had greeted him as if they had known him for years, and he needed that company tonight.

The bar was only half full when he entered, so he was able to grab a seat without crowding any of the groups already in place. The bartender saw him when he turned around and grinned. "Doc," he said, reaching across to fist bump him. "Nice to see you again."

"Thanks," Evan said, feeling his innate shyness trying to claw its way up his throat. He forced himself to continue, meeting the other man's eyes. "I had a rough day and thought it was better to be around friendly faces than alone."

Desmond nodded. "I get that," he said. "That's why I love doing this. I work full time, but from home. It's lonely, and this gives me a chance to talk to another human."

Evan nodded, unsure how to answer. Ask about his work? Order a drink? Why did it have to be so overwhelming for him? "At least it's convenient for you," he finally said, feeling foolish even as he said it.

"Sure is," Desmond replied. "And I get to eat my sister-in-law's amazing cooking every day. What more could I ask for? Now, what can I get you?"

Evan ordered a glass of red wine, then kicked himself for not getting a beer like most of the other men at the bar had. A few had short glasses that probably contained whiskey or a similar liquor, and he was here with his fancy wine. Even something as simple as a drink he got wrong.

"Want to look at a menu?" Desmond offered, holding one up. "Zoe also has a special tonight, a wild mushroom risotto that is out of this world. It's served with roasted chicken, and it's flying out of the kitchen."

"That sounds great," Evan said, relieved to have a decision taken out of his hands.

Desmond turned and typed into the computer behind the bar, then returned to lean on the bar in front of Evan. "Mostly locals here tonight," he shared. "Do you know the Burrows?"

Evan looked down the bar where three men were sitting with beer bottles in front of them. He had met them when their mother had gone through chemotherapy, and one of them raised a beer in acknowledgement. He waved back and then averted his eyes so they wouldn't think he was hoping for an invitation to join them.

"Then we have a couple local teachers down there," Desmond continued, pointing in the other direction. "And Piper, who owns the bakery. All locals, so I'm sure you'll get to know them. Did you hear about the Harvest Festival?"

"I've heard people talking about it," Evan said. "But can't say I've paid much attention. I tend to avoid large crowds if I can help it."

"I hear that," Desmond said. "But a Vermont crowd outside in the square isn't quite like Times Square at midnight on New Year's Eve. Know what I mean?"

Evan nodded and was saved from answering when Desmond moved away to take an order from a new arrival to the bar. It gave him a chance to sip his wine and really take in his surroundings. Although the building was huge, it was divided up so that each space felt warm and cozy. The bar ran the length of one wall, curving at the end where the Burrows brothers sat. The door to the kitchen was visible behind them, and a further space held dart boards. The other end of the bar sat in front of the main entrance, which opened regularly to let in new customers. Behind him, the tables were set around the room with enough space between them for private conversations, and a small stage sat at one end. The opposite end, the front of the building, had an area with large club chairs, encouraging friends to sit and chat together.

It was nothing like what he had encountered in Boston, where he had attended college and then medical school. Nor was it like anywhere else he had lived, not that he had been frequenting bars during his youth. But even a dinner out was a luxury during those years and tended to be in a place where you ordered at the counter. His hometown was even smaller than this one, and didn't have the beautiful main street filled with stores and restaurants. Even the coffee shop in Windsor Peak was charming, offering plenty of space to sit and relax with a book, while the staff kept his coffee mug full.

A large crowd came in together, filling the bar with their laughter and loud voices as they debated a drink at the bar or sitting at a table. Evan was relieved when the hostess encouraged them to take their seats at the table until he caught a glimpse of who had come in behind them.

Finley was at the far end of the bar, talking to the woman that Desmond had said owned the bakery. Piper, if he remembered correctly. She hadn't seen him yet, so he averted his eyes and pulled out his phone, hoping to appear busy enough to have missed her entrance.

"What are you doing here?" Her voice broke through his thoughts as she slid onto the stool next to him. Unlike him, she was clearly comfortable in the setting, as she continued to smile and wave at those around them.

"Last time I checked, this was a business in the town I live in," he replied. "I didn't realize I wasn't welcome."

"Of course you're welcome," Desmond said from behind the bar, shooting a look at his sister. "Don't let my twin tell you otherwise."

"I didn't mean it like that," Finley said, looking somewhat contrite. "I've just never seen you here, and now two nights in a row. I was surprised, that's all."

"I needed some company after the day I had," he said. "Going home to an empty house was undesirable."

"Undesirable," she repeated slowly. "Yes, that's what I felt too. It was a bad day."

"Yes, it was." Silence fell between them, broken when Desmond handed his sister a drink before vanishing again.

"Dr. Collins told me that you'll be replacing him at the conference," Finley said.

"He asked me today," Evan said with a nod.

"We'll both be there," she replied. "But it's not like we have to hang out. I know you don't like my company."

"It's not that—"

Desmond appeared and placed down a plate of food in front of each of them. Evan's contained his risotto and chicken, while Finley's held a shrimp scampi that looked equally delicious.

"I'm going to eat upstairs," she protested, trying to push the plate back to Desmond.

"Tough," he said. "You can either carry your plate upstairs and let it get cold on the way or eat here. It would do you some good to have company for a while."

She sighed and picked up the fork that Desmond had slapped down next to her plate. "Having a twin is the worst," she said. "Especially when he thinks he knows everything."

"I'd have thought it was the opposite," he replied.

"What do you mean?"

"You have someone who clearly loves you and looks out for you," he said. "He knows you well enough to know that you had a bad day and shouldn't be alone. That's nice."

They ate side by side in silence, the conversations from those around them washing over their quiet. When she finished and placed her silverware across the plate, she leaned back in her chair. "I hate to admit it, but he was right."

"About what?"

"I needed food," she said. "And it was less lonely to eat here. I'm sorry if I was bad company. Or if I irritate you in general. I hope we can find a way to get along while we're in Boston."

"I hope so too," he said. "Are you driving or flying?"

"Driving," she said. "I tend to over pack. You?"

"Flying."

"I'd like to address something while we're on slightly friendly terms," she said. "Kyle had been my patient for months, and you told him that chemo wasn't working without me. I really wish you had included me in that conversation. I got to know him and his wife well and supported them through his treatment. I should have been there for them. I should have been able to say goodbye."

He frowned, glancing around to make sure no one was listening to them. "It's really not appropriate to be talking about it here," he said. "We can discuss it at work if you want."

She stared at him, and he saw her eyes shutter as she did. "Of course."

"We do have laws we need to follow, Finley," he said, sighing. "It's not like I'm personally attacking you."

"No one is even near us," she argued. "And I was expressing how I felt. Have you heard of human emotions?"

"It's a slippery slope and I'm not willing to discuss patient information in a public setting," he said, his tone stiff. "If you want to meet with me in the morning, that's fine."

She nodded and pushed back from the bar. "I guess I'll see you at work, Dr. Lincoln?"

"Yes," he replied. Before she left, he turned quickly, catching her off guard. "I'm sorry if I just upset you. I would really like to talk about it in my office tomorrow, if you're willing. It wasn't an intentional slight. I thought I was sparing you a brutal conversation. It was a rough day for both of us. But I thought I was looking out for you, and I apologize that I clearly handled it wrong."

She looked him in the eye for a long minute before he nodded once and turned to walk away. But not before he caught the emotion in her eyes, and knew that despite their many differences, they at least shared the same feelings about their work.

Chapter 4

"This particular type of cancer is very difficult to treat," Evan told the couple sitting across the desk from him. They were older, in their early seventies. Newly retired, enjoying life and anticipating becoming grandparents for the first time. And he was destroying them word by word. "I don't want to get your hopes up. At most, we will be buying you a few months with your family. Chances of remission are less than one percent."

"But we do see miracles happen every day," Finley said, smiling at the couple and reaching for the woman's hand. "There's no telling what might happen when we start treatment, things could change."

"Not of this magnitude," Evan said, his tone annoyingly even as he glared at her. "This is an extremely difficult cancer to treat."

"Nothing is impossible," Finley raised her voice, forcing a happy tone and a fake smile on her face even though it hurt. "We have so many experienced doctors here, and our affiliation with other hospitals expands that reach. Maybe there's a trial somewhere that we could find."

"I've already examined every possible avenue," Evan said to the couple, who were watching the two of them like a tennis match. One moment they looked hopeful, the next devastated. Evan watched as the woman let go of Finley to add another hand to the one her husband was tightly clasping.

"I'm just saying, maybe there are things you haven't thought of that someone else might," Finley said.

Evan's face turned red and the pen in his hand was so tightly gripped she was surprised it didn't snap. When his eyes met hers, she saw how furious he was and she had to force herself to stay calm.

"Nurse Finley, would you please excuse yourself?"

The words were so sudden, it took her a minute to absorb them. The couple was holding each other now, crying softly, and Evan was glaring at her across the desk. She stood stiffly and walked out, leaning against the door once it closed behind her.

Once her legs worked again, she made her way to the staff lounge to cool off. After pouring a cup of coffee, she abandoned it on a table to pace, her fury building with each step. How dare he?

"Oh, boy," Audrey's voice came from behind her. "You look like you're about to kill someone. You know our jobs are the opposite of that, right?"

"Do you know what he just did?"

"No," Audrey replied, pouring a coffee and adding creamer as she looked over at her. "Who? And what?"

"I can't even tell you," she said, changing her mind about sharing. "It's so humiliating and infuriating."

"Dr. Lincoln?" Audrey asked, blowing on the hot coffee and looking gloriously unbothered by Finley's life falling apart.

"Of course, Dr. Lincoln," Finley snapped. Audrey's eyes widened and then narrowed, and Finley knew she had gone too far. "I'm sorry. He's got me so wound up. You wouldn't believe how he just talked to me. And in front of patients!"

The door was thrown open suddenly, causing both nurses to jump. Evan stormed in, looking furious. His eyes scanned the nearly empty room before landing on Finley and pointing at her. "My office," he practically growled. "Now."

"Happily," she spit out the word, storming past him toward the doctor's suite. Her steps faltered when she saw Dr. Collins in the hallway outside Evan's office, but he was talking to another physician and only nodded at her.

When Evan nearly slammed the door behind her, she jumped. "Did you call him to come in here?"

He glanced around the small room, as if to point out they were alone. "Who?"

"Dr. Collins," she hissed, pointing at the hallway.

"No," he said. "If I was going to call anyone, it would have been the director of nurses to tell you how out of line you are."

"Me out of line? Are you serious?"

"Very," he said, his voice like steel. He was standing behind his desk, the chair kicked back like it had insulted him as well. "What right do you have to give them false hope? To negate everything I'm saying with your Pollyanna version of life?"

"I did no such thing," she said, crossing her arms. "I was trying to offer them some hope. If they don't have that, it makes treatment far harder."

"Hope doesn't exist in this case," he said. He put both hands flat on his desk as he leaned across towards her. "Do you know how hard that is for me to sit and tell someone that? To tell them they are dying, and my best chance is to get him three months so he can see his first grandchild? Do you think I want to look him in the eye and say those words to him? Or to see the devastation in his wife's eyes?"

Finley started to feel her anger seep out of her at his words but stiffened her spine as she did. He had humiliated her in front of a patient she was trying to care for, and she couldn't forget that. "And you think he'll enjoy these three months, counting the minutes? Without any hope that it could be longer, or that he could survive?"

"I'd rather they be shocked and thrilled when they get more than three months than be looking at me in horror when they realize their time has run out. It's cruel to give them hope when there is none. To let them think that they could have years left together, when there's a clock ticking. They deserve a chance to enjoy these days together, and to say what needs to be said to each other," he said, sighing heavily. "They deserve the chance to say goodbye on their own terms. Not be blindsided when things take a turn and suddenly time is up. This is why I told Kyle without you. You have no idea the weight that sits on my shoulders while you run around like a cheerleader."

"That's insulting to me and my degree," she snapped back. "I'm an experienced, competent nurse. I take care of every part of my patients and don't just see them as a name on a chart."

"When have I ever treated someone like that?" He was staring at her as if he was in shock, and she faltered again.

"You do it all the time," she said, choosing stubbornness again. "Talk to them clinically without any emotion, any regard for them as humans."

"That's categorically false," he said.

"Do you know the names of their children? Their grandkids? How long they've been married, or when their spouse died? Do you know how many of them come in here alone, afraid, and needing a hug?"

"While I commend you for that," he said. "I do need to focus on the finer details. I can't spend hours sitting with them chatting, because I have a stack of files for people who I need to try to save. I spend hours, most of it my own free time, researching when I can't find a solution for someone here. So, no, I may not know their grandkids names. But I do know every clinical trial in every other country, and I know every doctor in this field and what they specialize in."

Finley found herself suddenly battling tears. How had that happened? She was supposed to be mad, not upset. She swiped angrily at her cheeks as she glared at Evan some more. "That was humiliating," she said finally, when he was just watching her cry. "I would never put you down in front of a patient, no matter what."

He sighed heavily and pushed a box of tissues across the desk. "I wasn't trying to embarrass you," he said. "You just wouldn't let me do my job."

They stared at each other for a heavy beat before she turned to the door. She stopped, her hand on the door handle, and tried to catch her breath. "I'm just really disappointed in you," she said. "I know we don't like each other, but that was low."

"And I wish you wouldn't give false hope to people who would rather believe that than what I'm telling them. Or make me feel like a jerk for being honest with patients," he responded from behind her, his voice weary. "I care about them more than you think."

***

The rest of her shift passed in a blur. Fortunately, her last two patients were stable and near the end of treatment, so they were in a better mood than their nurse. They both had family with them and if they thought Finley was behaving oddly, they didn't say anything. Evan stayed out of sight for the rest of the day, so one positive thing had happened.

When she dragged herself through the back door of the restaurant, with the sole purpose of grabbing as much sugar as possible before retreating upstairs, Zoe caught sight of her. "What's wrong with you?" Her sisters-in-law faint French accent made the words feel softer than her tone implied.

"Nothing," Finley lied. "I just hoped you had some cake lying around."

"I made cookies for the staff," Zoe said. "Here, I'll put some in a bag for you. Go see your brother."

"I have no patience for Des right now," Finley argued. "I had a terrible day."

"Good thing I was talking about Colin," Zoe answered, a laugh in her eyes as she took Finley's tote bag and pushed her toward the door. "I'll put this and the cookies on the stairs for you. Go see what's wrong with him."

"I'm not the best—" Finley was cut off by the kitchen door closing in her face, so she sighed and turned around. Sure enough, Colin was at the bar, staring into a pint glass and looking more sullen than usual.

"What's your problem?" she asked, taking the barstool next to him. His mood had chased any other guests to the opposite end of the bar, so at least she hadn't needed to scramble for a seat.

"Nothing."

"Real mature, Col," she said. "I had a horrible day, and now I'm in charge of fixing you. Lay it on me."

"Why was your day bad?"

She sighed, knowing he wouldn't tell her anything until she shared first. "I had a fight with the doctor I work with. Your turn."

"The one that was here the other night? I thought people liked him," Colin said.

"Maybe they do, but I sure don't," she answered. "He was a jerk, and we had it out."

"Enough of a jerk that your brother should go have a word with him?" Colin turned to her, looking all too happy at the thought of having it out with the other man.

"Grow up," she snapped. "It was a disagreement at work about how a patient was handled. Not worth a fight in the alley."

Colin leaned back in his chair and almost cracked a smile. "I don't do that anymore," he said. "It's easier just to scare people."

"You haven't been in a fistfight since tenth grade," she reminded him. "When Mom grounded you for a month. Knock off the tough guy talk and tell me what's wrong."

"Absolutely nothing," he said. "Other than having the most annoying sister on the planet."

"Fine," she huffed, pushing her chair back. "All I wanted was some sugar and the TV remote. You don't want to talk? That's fine with me."

"I hurt someone I care about," he said, his voice so soft she almost didn't hear it. "And I have no idea how to fix it."

"Care about, like a woman?"

"Does it matter?"

"Well, you've never come to me for love advice," she said.

"You aren't exactly a study of the science, are you? You've been single for how long now?"

Desmond came and put a glass of wine in front of Finley. "I can answer that," he said. "This is easy."

"Go away." Finley and Colin both snapped at him at the same time, making Desmond laugh as he walked off.

"Come on," Finley prodded. "Give me more information. At least then I can focus on your problems instead of mine."

"It's someone I knew a long time ago," he said. "I hurt her feelings. And I don't know how to fix it."

"Did you say you were sorry?" Colin glared at her, and she shrugged. "Okay, if you tried that already, maybe if you give me more details I can help."

"No," he said. "I should probably just let it go. Move back or go somewhere new."

"Wait, she lives here? Who is it?"

"Drop it, Fin," he ordered. "I'm done."

They sat in silence for a few minutes while she racked her brain, trying to think of any woman that she had seen Colin with in the last few months. No one came to mind, and she rarely even saw her brother. Who knew what he was up to on his own? "For what it's worth," she said finally. "I hope you don't move. I can't imagine that whatever you did was bad enough that it can't be forgiven. Sometimes we just have to keep showing up and prove ourselves, you know? Admitting you were wrong is hard, but not as hard as knowing you hurt someone."

He nodded and pushed his empty glass away before slapping a twenty on the bar and standing. He kissed her on the head before moving towards the door. "Thanks," he called over his shoulder. "You might be able to take some of that advice yourself."

She took her wineglass with her as she went to collect her belongings off the stairs. Cookies and wine would be the perfect dinner, and then she could wallow in her thoughts. Colin's words followed her as she went, and she knew he was right, although she would never admit it to him. But maybe it was time she practiced what she preached.

Chapter 5

Evan found himself still at the hospital when midnight hit. He hadn't had dinner or even a drink of water in at least five hours. Once everyone else left for the night, he hunkered down in his office and begun researching again. He went through the entire process he already went through before delivering the news to the patient earlier. He even tried a few new angles, before determining he had been right the first time. At most, their patient would last six months. And that was with a miracle. The three months he had suggested was the kindest approach. Promising six and seeing them only get four would be even more devastating, and he couldn't do that to them.

He stood and stretched, then started packing up his belongings. Returning in six hours was going to be difficult, but nothing he hadn't done before. As he was locking his office, a doctor passing by in the hallway paused.

"Long day?"

"You could say that," Evan replied with a tired smile. "Have a good night."

"I hate to say this, but you might want to know," the other doctor said, looking unsure. "Unless you'd rather leave now, and we never saw each other."

"No, tell me," he said.

"We have a patient of yours who just came in from the emergency department," he said. "Edna Lee?"

"What happened?" Evan asked, suddenly wide awake.

"A neighbor called 911. Apparently, no one had seen her for a few days, and when the neighbor went to check on her, she was out of it. Not able to answer questions appropriately, didn't know where she was."

"Stroke?" Evan asked, starting to walk next to his colleague.

"Negative so far. She came in with equal strength bilaterally and answering questions appropriately. I'm waiting for the CT scan results to confirm what happened. Right now, the only concern is the change in mental status."

"How are her labs?"

"Still waiting on them. I can send you an email when they come in, along with the CT results?"

"I may be in her room," Evan said. "But yes, please do. You have her treatment plans in the system, right? You know what she was on?"

The other doctor nodded and then stopped to talk to a nurse. Evan continued walking, checking the board behind the nurse's station for the room number. Once he had it, he went straight there, knocking lightly before going in.

Edna was sleeping, her tiny figure barely visible in the dim light. Her white hair blended with the sheets, and her skin was almost as pale. He pulled the hard chair closer to her bed and got as comfortable as possible.

He must have nodded off somehow, because when he felt a hand touch his, he jumped almost a mile. Glancing around, he realized he was still at the hospital, and Mrs. Edna Lee was staring at him.

"Mrs. Lee," he said. "I'm so sorry. I must have drifted off there. How are you feeling?"

"Well, I'm not too sure," she said. "I thought I had gone home, but now I just woke up and find myself in the same place I was a few days ago. In a hospital bed with a handsome doctor sitting watch over me."

"You were at home," he said. "But a neighbor found you. You were disoriented, and they called for help. The labs are relatively normal, other than dehydration and an electrolyte imbalance. I know we've talked before about how important it is to stay hydrated."

"I know," she said, waving her hand. "All of you doctors and nurses wanting me to drink more. Why can't it be gin, I say. Then it wouldn't be a problem."

"That would have the opposite effect," he said.

"Oh, I know," she said, laughing lightly. "But wouldn't it be more fun?"

"Do you have any family around here, Mrs. Lee?"

"You should call me Edna," she said. "After all, you're seeing more of me than most people. And no, unfortunately not. My husband, Hank, passed away over twenty years ago. We weren't blessed with children, so it left me all alone. That wasn't how we had planned our life, I'll tell you."

"It never goes the way you plan," he said softly.

"It sure doesn't," she agreed. "We had some cousins, but they've all faded away by now. We were both only children, so no nieces and nephews floating around. Just lonely old me."

"Not so old," he said, winking at her. "Do you feel like you can get some more rest?"

"At my age, if you sleep for too long, you start to think you're dead," she said. "Hence the hospital stay. You should get home. Get some sleep yourself."

He checked his watch, seeing it was already four in the morning. No point in going home now, but he didn't want her to worry about him. "I'll do that if you're sure that you're okay here."

"I am, I promise," she said. "Maybe you can tell Finley to come visit me."

He nodded quickly, not willing to discuss his issues with a patient. He could leave a note in the computer, that would save him from any conversation with Finley. At this point, anything he tried would end up in an argument, anyway.

"There's something between you two that I can't quite put my finger on," Edna said suddenly.

"What two?"

"You and Finley," she said with a laugh.

"Oh, there most definitely is not," he said firmly.

"Remind me to tell you about how I met Hank," she said. "Another day, when you're not rushing around."

"I'll do that," he promised. He gathered up his belongings and headed toward the door. "You sure you don't need anything before I leave?"

"Nothing," she said. "And I have nurses and a doctor here if I do. You go sleep now."

Evan left the small room and nodded at the nurses before going to the doctor's lounge. He could grab a quick nap there, and then take a long, cold shower to wake him up. It was only fourteen hours before he could go home, he could do that standing on his head if needed.

***

Evan should have been exhausted by the time his shift was over, but twelve hours of avoiding Finley had done the opposite. He had been spared passing the message from Edna on by a phone call from the attending doctor on her floor. She was being discharged home with visiting nursing services and could continue her treatment plan under his care.

Once home, he was restless, so he tied on his running sneakers and set out. Since moving to town, he had discovered several trails around the mountain base, as well as through town. Since it was getting dark, he opted for the more populated town area, weaving through the pedestrian traffic of locals and tourists heading out to dinner. His feet faltered as he passed the Windsor Peak Palace, wondering who was sitting at the bar, before he shook his head and kept going. He had spent all day avoiding Finley, and now he was looking for her through windows? He needed to get his own head examined.

As he cooled down, he caught a whiff of something delicious coming from the small shop next to the restaurant. He had picked up a few meals there over the months he had been in town, and they had all been wonderful. His stomach gave a loud growl, reminding him of the hospital food diet it had been on for the day, so he headed in.

The shop offered a selection of hot and cold meals packaged to go. He could even stock his freezer with ready to cook trays and made a note to come back when he had his car. Choosing two hot meals, because he couldn't decide between them, he paid and turned to leave, running smack into the town sheriff.

"Evening, Doc," JJ said, grinning at him. "How are you doing?"

"Fine, thank you. And you?"

"Great," JJ glanced out at the street. "Good day so far. Tourist season is kicking into high gear, so that will change soon."

"I thought most people came to ski?"

"They do, but we also get a good number of leaf peepers." At Evan's confused look, JJ laughed and continued. "People who come to see the foliage as it changes colors. We have a beautiful town and plenty of trees, so it's a popular spot."

"I see," Evan said.

"You don't get out much," JJ said.

"No, I guess I don't," Evan said, a little surprised at the statement.

"It's a friendly town. I would say you'd be welcome anywhere, if you wanted to get to know people."

"That's nice of you, but I work a lot," Evan said.

"I hear that," JJ said, laughing. "But think about it. Fun is good for the soul."

JJ nodded and shifted the bag of food to his other hand while trying to figure out what to say. The sheriff appeared open and friendly, but he was also carrying a gun and was the size of a small tree, so things could change on a dime.

"I hear Finley has been giving you some trouble," JJ said suddenly.

"I wouldn't say that," Evan responded. "We just seem to clash. Oil and water, you know?"

JJ nodded. "She's a strong personality. But she's a good person at her core. Keep that in mind."

"Will do," Evan said.

"I'll let you get off to eat your dinner," JJ said, gesturing to the bag. "My wife would kill me if she knew I was talking your ear off and making the food go cold."

"Have a good night," Evan said, heading towards the door.

"You too," JJ called out. "And remember what I said."

Evan walked home quickly, trying to process JJ's words as he did. Was there a hidden warning there about Finley? Or was he reading too much into it? He hadn't faced these issues when he lived in Boston. Being an anonymous face among thousands might be preferable to this small-town life, where everyone knew your business.

His mood got darker after he got home to his empty house and ate his solo dinner. He flipped through TV stations as he ate, hoping to find something to distract him, before throwing the remote onto the couch. His cell phone sat on the kitchen table, as if it was taunting him. Rather than give in, he put his dishes in the sink and left the device on the table as he went up to bed. No point in making a bad day even worse.

***

Normally after a sleepless night at work, Evan fell into a deep sleep and felt refreshed the next day. That was not the case as he dragged himself out of bed the next morning. He felt as though he had tossed and turned all night, ghosts from the past mingling with current worries to keep him awake.

His phone was dead, so it wasn't until after his shower, when he plugged it in, that he saw his missed calls and text messages. It was as if he had conjured up trouble with his thoughts the night before, he realized as he scrolled through them. Sighing, he shoved the phone into his pocket without reading any of the messages and headed to his car. The reason he had made the choice to move to a small town in the middle of nowhere had reappeared, and he needed time to decide how to respond.

One thing he had learned from his time so far in town was that his life had been unusual. Families here seemed close and appeared to share a great deal. They even enjoyed each other's company, choosing to spend time together. It was the opposite of his life in every way.

His parents had chosen work over family, and he had been raised in childcare and with babysitters until he could be independent. They had provided for him with material goods, but not the security that love would have provided. Even their own relationship had never seemed to be born of anything other than convenience, and he and his brother felt like tasks that had been checked off a list, rather than the desire to build a family.

He shook off the thoughts of the past and forced himself to get into a better mood for the day. Work had to be better than it was the day before, but the only way to make that happen was to have a better attitude. The lack of sleep and phone messages had gotten him off to a bad start this morning, but his early morning run and cold shower, combined with the bucket of coffee he planned to consume, should hopefully turn things around.

Chapter 6

"What's wrong?"

Finley sighed as her mother's voice came through the phone. She had just arrived home and slipped on her favorite pajama pants before settling on the couch. Although she had been craving more sugar, she had taken the plate of healthy food Zoe had waiting for her. And the large slice of chocolate cake that had been next to it.

"Nothing's wrong," she said. "Which one of my annoying brothers told you something is?"

"None of them," Maggie Monahan said, too fast to be telling the truth.

"Was it Zoe?"

"I don't reveal my sources," Maggie said with a laugh. "But I heard that your dinner last night consisted of wine and cookies, and that you were in a foul mood."

"So was Colin," she said, wanting to shift the focus.

"He always is," her mom countered. "You are usually a ray of sunshine."

"Everyone has a bad day once in a while," she said, digging into her dinner as she talked. Grilled salmon and asparagus, two things she had never thought she liked until she met Zoe.

"Tell me about it," Maggie prodded.

"I just don't get along with the doctor I work with," Finley admitted. "I don't know what do about it. Or him."

"Why don't you get along?"

"I don't know," she said. "I annoy him."

"That can't be true," her mom said, ever loyal.

"Oh, but it is. My very being sets him off," Finley said. "But it's mainly how much I talk. Or when I talk."

"What do you mean?"

"He thinks I'm too social with the patients," Finley said.

"He told you that?"

"Pretty much."

"Finley," Maggie said with a sigh. "How many times have I asked you what happens when you assume?"

"But Mom," she said, hating the childish whine in her voice. "You would know I'm right if you saw how he reacted to hearing my voice. And he made a big stink about not talking to the patients about our social lives."

"That can't possibly be what the problem is now," Maggie said. "Something else must have happened to make you upset."

"Okay, fine," she said. She shoveled a bite of food into her mouth to stall, chewing slowly before taking a deep breath. "I may have stepped out of line during a conversation with a new patient."

"In what way?"

"Evan, I mean Dr. Lincoln, was telling him he only had a few months to live at best," she said.

"That's terrible," Maggie said.

"I know, right? I just wanted to soften it a little. Give the guy and his wife some hope."

"What did you do?"

"Just that. I said miracles happen, and maybe we were being shortsighted on the timeline," Finley said. Saying it out loud to her mom made her feel ashamed, and her anger switched to embarrassment.

"And obviously the doctor wasn't happy with that," her mom said. "I can see why, Fin. If he was trying to be honest with them, I'm sure that was already difficult for him, without you giving false hope."

"He's a robot," she said automatically. "I don't think he has emotions."

"Or he's well versed in hiding them," Maggie said softly. "Not everyone has a safe place to land when they feel vulnerable. Still waters run deep, you know."

"He was horrible to me," Finley said, trying to get the anger back.

"It sounds like you might have deserved it," Maggie said. "As long as he wasn't out of line. Did you feel unsafe?"

"No, nothing like that. He would never hurt me."

"I'd say you have some thinking to do," Maggie said. "I love you forever, and as much as one person can love another. But even with all that love, I know you aren't perfect. No one is. And being able to admit our mistakes is part of life."

"You're saying I should apologize to him."

"No, I'm saying I know you'll do the right thing," her mom said. "Once you think it over and get the mad out."

"I think it's gone already," she admitted.

"Sugar will do that," Maggie said with a laugh. "I hope you're having something healthy to eat along with the sugar tonight."

"Zoe made sure of that," she said. "Now I feel a little bad that I avoided him all day. I probably should have just apologized and gotten it over with."

"No, because you wouldn't have meant it," Maggie said. "And besides, you needed the wisdom of your mother to help you get there."

"Always," Finley said with a laugh. "Love you, Mom."

"Love you back, sweetheart. Now let's talk about your brothers."

Finley laughed and got more comfortable, gossiping about the three men who varied between being her best friends and her biggest nuisances. Despite Colin confiding in her the night before, she played dumb and didn't share. Her mom wasn't great at keeping information to herself, and she wanted Colin to feel safe talking to her. It was so rare that he did, the last thing she wanted to do was immediately ruin that trust. Instead, they spent a long time talking about Desmond's multiple flirtations, and whether JJ and Zoe were ready for a baby.

By the time she hung up, she realized how exhausted she was. No longer interested in a movie, she headed to bed with a book. The night before had been filled with fitful sleep, likely because of her subconscious trying to tell her she had been wrong. Now she had to try to put that out of her mind, and not get anxious about her upcoming apology, so she could get sleep.

***

Stopping at the bakery before getting into her car for work had been a last-minute decision, but as soon as the smells hit her nose, Finley decided it was the best one she had ever made. Piper grinned at her from behind the counter. "Hey, stranger," she said. "How's it going? You haven't been here forever."

"I know, I'm sorry," Finley said. "I'm trying to lower my carb intake. But I need an apology pastry."

"Apology pastry?" Piper's eyebrows went up. "This sounds like a section I need to establish. Who are you giving it to?"

"A doctor I work with," Finley said.

"Not the handsome one from the bar the other night?"

"The very one," Finley answered.

"What did you do?" Piper asked, crossing her arms on top of the bakery case and looking ready for a long story.

"It's too much to get into right now," Finley replied. "Maybe another time. With a drink in hand. But the short version is that I was a jerk, and I need to make it right."

"I made cinnamon rolls this morning," Piper said. "Those feel very apologetic. Or maybe a selection of donuts?"

"I should probably do both," Finley said, looking at the options in the case. "I was that bad. And we have to go to a conference together, so I really need to get back on better terms."

Piper started packing the boxes. "Where is the conference?"

"Boston," Finley said. "Close to home at least."

"Nice," Piper said. "I haven't been there in forever. Or anywhere, for that matter."

"You work too much," Finley said. "You need to find some help here."

"I know," Piper said, sighing. "Easier said than done. I have enough help when I need it, but a vacation would be a dream come true."

"For me too," Finley said, thinking of sandy beaches and tropical drinks. "Maybe we could do a girls trip."

"That would be amazing," Piper said quickly. "Let's meet up tonight and discuss. Bar or my place?"

"I'll meet you at the bar," Finley promised. "Then if Des is annoying, we can move on. But I'll need a stiff drink after this day, I know that already. And food."

"Deal." Piper slid the two boxes into a bag and took Finley's credit card to swipe. Another customer came in, so Finley waved as she headed back out. As she climbed into her car, she realized Piper had stuck a small box in the bag with a single cinnamon roll. Her friend, looking after her in little ways, made her smile as she drove to the hospital, enjoying the sweetness as she did. With the bakery detour, Finley was the last to arrive to the department, rather than the usual first. She hurriedly stuck her belongings in a locker and carried the bag of treats toward the doctor's offices. After taking a deep breath, she approached Evan's open door and saw him hunched over a stack of lab results.

"Good morning," she said, knocking lightly to get his attention.

"Morning," he said warily, studying her. Although it was early, he looked as though he was already worn out. She hadn't noticed before how strained he was, or how tired he looked behind the glasses.

"I brought you a treat to say I'm sorry," she said, holding up the bag. "I'm hoping some sugar will make my overstep yesterday better. And maybe improve our overall work relationship."

"I appreciate the gesture," he said. "I've been concerned about our upcoming trip. And in general, we need to find a way to work together. I'm on your team, Finley."

"I know that," she said. "I just struggle with the losses."

"Maybe oncology isn't the right fit," he suggested. Although he said it with kindness, it rubbed her the wrong way.

"What's that supposed to mean?"

"You just said you have a hard time with the losses," he said, looking baffled. "Another type of nursing maybe wouldn't have as many. We work with terminal illnesses every day. It's always life or death here. With something like ortho, you wouldn't have to deal with that."

"You want me to go work on ortho?"

"No," he said. "I thought you might like the change."

"But I like what I do," she said. "And I think I'm good at it."

"I didn't say you weren't," he said, removing his glasses and rubbing his eyes. "I was responding to what you said."

She placed the bag on his desk and crossed her arms. "Enjoy your breakfast," she said stiffly. "I apologize for my behavior yesterday."

When she arrived at the nurse's station, Audrey took one look at her face and laughed. "What happened?"

"I was determined to have a good day," Finley replied, fuming. "Which is why I shouldn't have started it by trying to be nice to Dr. Rude."

"Dr. Rude? That's a new one," Audrey said. "What did he do now?"

"Breathe," Finely snapped, then sighed. "No. I brought him breakfast to apologize for yesterday. And he told me I should go work in ortho."

"I didn't say that," Evan's voice came from behind her. "I was making a suggestion based on what you said. And I do appreciate the breakfast. In fact, it's way too much, so I was going to come out and share it with everyone."

Audrey looked delighted at the drama and sat back in her chair. The other nurses, who were setting up their stations, all paused to listen. Finley straightened her spine and met Evan's gaze. "I suppose you want me to apologize again?"

"Absolutely not," he replied with an easy smile. "After all, Dr. Rude understands bad behavior."

With that, he placed the two bakery boxes on the counter, nodded at Audrey, and retreated to his office. Finley sat heavily, glad there was a chair behind her. "I'm the worst," she said. "But also, so is he."

"I just don't see it," Audrey said. "I think he's swoony. All handsome and mysterious. And he's the best with the patients, of the doctors."

"I'm going to get ready for my first patients," Finley said, standing up. "I thought I was going to have a good day, but now I'm reconsidering."

"You don't want some sugar?" Audrey asked, looking up from the boxes. "These look amazing."

"They are," Finley called over her shoulder. "I ate a cinnamon roll that was as big as my face on the way to work. If I eat anything else, I'll pop."

Audrey's laughter followed her as she pulled out blankets and water to put at each of her stalls. She would have two patients coming in first, who had been there before. In an hour, a new one would arrive, and it would take longer to get him settled. Going through the routine of arriving and easing their anxiety for the first treatment took time, so she was grateful the other two wouldn't require much of her.

***

"How did the apology pastries work out?" Piper asked as she slid onto the barstool next to Finley, who was already halfway through her first drink.

"He accepted them, and then we immediately got into another fight," she reported. "I don't know why I tried."

"Yes, you do," Piper said gently. "Because you're a nice person, which means you're upset that you hurt someone's feelings."

"Well, he hurt mine today."

"You sound like a kindergartener," Piper said with a laugh. "Actually, I take that back. A preschooler."

"How am I supposed to get along with someone who just doesn't want to get along with me?"

"Categorically not true." The voice came from behind her, and she felt herself tense up as she turned around. Once again, Evan had overheard her talking about him. The man should wear a bell around his neck.

"How can you say that?" she fired back, seeing Piper's eyes dart between them as if she was watching her favorite reality show. "You've been against me since the day you arrived."

"You've taken it that way," he said quietly and slowly, infuriating her even more that he wasn't getting upset. "But I'm just trying to provide the best experience for our patients. You didn't have an issue when I requested that nurses be assigned to oversee a patient for their entire treatment, right?"

"No," she said sullenly. "That was a good idea. We all like that."

"I just asked if we could have a more peaceful environment," he continued. "And you took that as an insult."

51

"Well, it is," she shot back. "You're saying I talk too much. That I'm too loud."

"I agree with Doc." Desmond reached across the bar to fist bump Evan, and Finley glared at him.

"Not your business, Des," she said. "But thanks for the support."

"I'm not trying to put you down or make your life more difficult. I responded this morning to something you said, and it came out wrong. I apologize," Evan said.

"Come down here, Doc, and I'll introduce you around," Des said, pointing down the bar. He talked over his shoulder, meeting Finley's eyes as he did, as he walked away. "To some *nice* people."

"He's—"

"Don't say it," Finley cut Piper off. "If you're about to comment on his looks, please don't."

Piper laughed and took a sip of her drink. "Alright, what should we talk about?"

"Our getaway," Finley said.

"I thought about that," Piper said. "And I'm afraid I had second thoughts. Nothing good happens when I leave this town."

Finley couldn't help but notice that Piper's eyes were following a certain man as he made his way through the bar as she spoke. A man that happened to be her brother, who hadn't stopped to say hello. Colin settled on the barstool next to Evan, pointed there by Desmond, and avoided looking in her direction.

Before she could dig into the oddness of it all, Piper pushed her seat back. "I'm exhausted," she said. "I'm going to head home."

"What? I thought we were going to have dinner at least?"

"Another night," Piper promised.

"I can get takeout and come to your place?"

"No, I think it's better if we wait until I'm not so tired," Piper said. She was pulling on her jacket and inching away already. "I'll text you."

Finley glanced around the bar, full of friends and couples laughing and talking, and felt lonely. She knew most of them, but the idea of inserting herself into any of the conversations felt fake. Opting for pajamas and Hallmark, she left money on the bar for their drinks and slipped out the front door to walk around the building. Not that she was avoiding Evan, she told herself. Just that it was easier than going through the busy kitchen.

Chapter 7

"Sorry about my sister," Desmond said after Evan sat down. "She can be tough if she doesn't get her way. What are you drinking?"

Evan ordered a local IPA and didn't respond to the comment about Finley. It felt both too familiar and yet disloyal to join forces with her twin. The thought itched at his brain, as if he should spend time examining why he felt that way. Before he could, Desmond returned with the beer.

"Do you play poker?" he asked, leaning against the bar.

Evan was surprised at the quick change in topic, but grateful. "I try."

"Why don't you join us Monday night? We have a regular game," Desmond said. "The next is at Mike's house, he has the best set up."

"I don't think I know him," Evan said. "Would I be imposing?"

"Not at all," Desmond assured him. "We can ride up together if you want. Mike is the big dude that dates Natalie Cloud? He's an ex-NFL player, and his entire basement is a man cave like you dream about."

"Natalie Cloud, the movie star?"

"Man, you must live under a rock," Desmond said with a laugh. "Yes, she's a good friend of Patrick Burrows. You know he lives here, right?"

"Yes, I met him when I treated his mother," Evan said.

"Okay. He used to be our only movie star. He grew up here and became famous young. Anyway, Natalie came to visit Patrick and then fell for Mike, so she stayed. And Liam Dorsey came for Christmas and never left," Desmond shared. "It's fantastic for business, because all the tourists come in hoping to catch them. But they're all good, down-to-earth people. You'll like them."

Evan laughed, not able to picture himself hanging out with a bunch of Hollywood elite. "I'm sure."

"Here comes Colin, he'll keep you company," Desmond said, looking at the door and waving. Evan couldn't help but notice that Colin hesitated behind his sister and Piper but didn't stop to say hello. Instead, he put his head down and barreled through the crowd to the empty seat next to Evan.

"Hi," Colin said, his tone curt. "Hope you don't mind if I join you. I'm starving, and this idiot won't stop harassing me to come in to hang out."

"Is it so wrong that I want to see my big brother?"

Colin made a show of looking around the bar before answering. "Where's JJ?"

"Home with the dog," Desmond replied. "That's why you're my favorite brother tonight."

"You're exhausting," Colin said with a sigh. He turned to Evan. "Don't get dragged into his nonsense. He wants me here to wingman for him."

"Don't ruin it," Desmond called over his shoulder as he grabbed a bottle of beer to put in front of his brother. "I was hoping that having a doctor here would draw in more lovely ladies."

"You've already met them all," Colin said. "It's probably time to actually start dating and stop flirting from behind the bar."

"Don't worry about what I do," Desmond said. "You're so much older, we should get you settled down first."

"There's no reason for that," Colin replied, his tone firm. "Don't fix what isn't broken."

Desmond frowned at his brother but looked at Evan. "What about you? Want me to keep an eye out for someone to introduce you to?"

"No, thank you," Evan said quickly. "I don't even have time for a dog, never mind a date."

"We need to work on that," Desmond said. "No wonder you're fighting with my sister."

Colin looked at Evan. "You're having issues with Fin?"

"Who doesn't?" Desmond laughed before Colin quieted him with a look, and then he disappeared to take someone's order.

"We've had some growing pains since I came to town," Evan admitted. "I wouldn't call it fighting. More like disagreeing."

Colin sipped his beer and stared straight ahead for so long that Evan was convinced the conversation was over. When he finally responded, Evan barely heard him. "It's not worth it."

"What?"

"Fighting over work. Prioritizing work over relationships," Colin said. "By the time you realize what you've done, it's too late."

Evan frowned, unsure where this had come from. "Finley and I don't have a relationship," he said. "We struggle to get along."

"Isn't that the same thing?" Colin asked, beer bottle halfway to his lips. "They say there's a fine line between love and hate."

***

The following Monday evening, Evan found himself rushing through a shower to be ready when Desmond arrived to pick him up. He had planned to leave work a little early, but that plan went out the window. Instead, his shift had run very late, as if the universe knew he was trying to socialize and wanted to keep him in line. Rather than having the time he needed to plan out some conversation topics and convince himself that he would survive this attempt at making friends, he was rushing around to be ready on time. He saw headlights pull in his driveway as he was pulling on a shirt and ran down the stairs barefoot to open the door.

"Sorry, I'm just about ready," he said as Desmond came onto the porch.

"No worries," Desmond said. "Nice spot you have here."

"Yes, I like it," Evan said. "Close enough to town to walk, but nice and quiet."

"I'm a little jealous," Desmond said, wandering around and looking at the books on the shelves that lined the walls. "And not just because I couldn't read this if you offered me a million dollars."

"Well, that's a medical textbook," Evan said with a laugh. "Even I wouldn't enjoy reading that. I'm ready if you are."

They headed out to Desmond's truck, a well-loved Ford model that looked ready to handle Vermont's snowy winters. Desmond drove away from town, seeming to know where he was going. He pulled onto a street that held large houses, very spaced apart, and Evan whistled.

"So, this is the nice side of town, huh?"

"You could say that," Desmond said with a laugh. "Huge lots, big, beautiful houses, and mountain views. Can't get much better."

Apparently, they were going to one of the nicest, Evan realized, as they came to the end of the street to a house tucked far back from the neighbors. The house was glowing with light, and several cars were in the driveway, indicating they were one of the last to arrive.

Desmond knocked when they got to the front door, and Evan had to stop his jaw from dropping open when Natalie Cloud herself answered the door. She was in leggings and a sweater, hair in a ponytail and face fresh, looking like any of his neighbors. Any of his gorgeous neighbors, that is.

"Nat," Desmond said, kissing her on the cheek. "This is Dr. Evan Lincoln. He has the misfortune of working with my sister at the hospital."

"Oh, you were part of the team that treated Stella Burrows," she said, hugging him. "We were all so grateful that she got through okay."

"Me too," he said, feeling like a fool. How do you talk to a movie star like she's just a normal person? "It's nice to meet you."

"Don't worry," she said, leaning in to speak just to him. "It wears off after a while, and I'll just seem like anyone else."

He laughed and felt himself blush, realizing she had seen right through him. "Sorry, I didn't see many movie stars in medical school. I'm not sure how to act."

"Well, don't let Patrick and Liam know that," she said. "They'll take full advantage of you during the game. I'll be up here hanging out with their girlfriends. If you get sick of male bonding, feel free to come up."

Evan waved to the two other women, who he assumed were the girlfriends Natalie mentioned, before Desmond led him down a flight of stairs. At the bottom, the room opened up to be the ultimate man cave, as promised. A bar took up one wall, a few arcade-style video games on another, and one entire wall was covered in TVs. In the middle, comfortable-looking couches faced the screens, and a poker table sat just behind them.

"Evan, this is Mike, who lives in the sweet house," Desmond said. A monster of a man stood to shake his hand, less imposing because of the smile on his face. "You know JJ and Colin. This is Patrick and Liam. You might recognize them from some cologne commercials they've done."

"Nice to see you again," Patrick said with a grin. "I'm the nice one here."

"He's trying to take your money," Liam warned. "Thinks if he plays nice, you won't realize he's bluffing."

"Don't give away all my secrets away," Patrick complained. They started laughing as they talked, a sign that their friendship had been around long enough for private jokes.

As Evan looked around the room, he saw the same thing everywhere. These men had known each other for a long time and were at ease around each other. Mike was taking snacks out of Patrick and Liam's hands to replace them with vegetables, while JJ and Colin talked quietly across the table.

"Are Jake and Dan coming?" Mike asked, shuffling the cards in front of him.

"Let's just start," Patrick said. "When I talked to them earlier, they didn't think they'd be able to. If they aren't here by now, I don't think they are coming."

"They both have babies at home," JJ told Evan. "We see them less and less."

"Just wait until the next one comes, we'll never see Jake," Patrick said. "But it's nice that he's back in Windsor Peak and settled down. I'll take it."

"Speaking of settling down," JJ said, pointing across the table. "You three are on the clock now."

"Whoa," Liam said, hands in the air. "I moved in with Holly. If you knew me in California, you would see how out of character that is. Let's take it slow."

"I'm more than ready," Mike said. "I've had a ring for months. I'm just waiting until I think she's ready."

"You think you'll be able to tell?" Patrick asked, laughing at his friend.

"Hey, I live with her," Mike said. "When she was thinking of getting a new Peloton, she talked about it for weeks before deciding. Plus, she'll talk to Emma and Holly, and they'll tell you two. Who will then tell me. It's foolproof."

"I can't wait for this to play out," Liam said. "What about you?"

Everyone looked at Patrick, who shrugged. "Maybe it's coming. You'll find out when Emma does."

"Man of mystery," Mike said with a laugh. "Are you worried we'll tell the tabloids?"

"No," Patrick said. "But I want it to be natural, not something she's waiting for or that I feel pressured to do. If I tell you guys that I have a plan, that adds pressure."

"Enough of this chat," Colin said, his normal surly mood seeming darker than ever. "Are we playing cards?"

"Who brought sunshine?" JJ asked, then elbowed his brother. "Lighten up."

"We could always dissect your love life," Desmond offered. "We even have a doctor here, I'm sure he knows something about dissection."

"Not of that," Evan said quickly, not wanting to get on Colin's bad side. "And mine is probably worse. I'm in no place to offer advice on relationships."

"You're single?" Mike asked, placing cards down in front of everyone.

"Perpetually," he answered. The men at the table all laughed.

"That's what I thought," Liam said.

"Me too," Mike replied. "Although not for lack of trying."

"You want to talk about trying?" JJ asked, picking up his cards. "It took me years to convince my wife we were even dating. And it took daring her to marry me for that to even happen."

"Mom's still mad about that," Desmond replied. "Eloping without all of us?"

"If you had all shown up in Vegas, Zoe would have known," JJ said. "And it was hard enough to get her to give me a chance alone. Add all of you freaks in, and there's no chance."

"Hey," Colin objected. "Don't lump me in with Des."

"What I heard was you calling mom a freak," Des replied. "And I will be telling her that."

"You're the worst," JJ said, but with affection in his tone. Although the three brothers appeared different in every way, Evan could see the genuine affection between them. They bickered, but with kindness, and shared a closeness he had never experienced.

By the time the night was over, he was down two hundred dollars but felt like he had made some new friends. Desmond drove them back to town, chatting away with the ease that made him successful at bartending. He didn't even need another person to participate in his conversations, Evan realized.

"Thanks for the ride," Evan said as they pulled into his driveway. "And for the invitation. That was a lot of fun."

"We do it every week, unless too many of us are busy," Desmond replied. "Liam and Patrick travel a lot, and Mike goes with Nat when she leaves. But we can usually get at least six people together, especially when the other Burrows are around. And now you'll add to our numbers."

"I appreciate that," Evan said. "I'm off to Boston tomorrow, but I'll see you when I get back."

"Sounds good," Desmond said. Just before Evan closed the door, he heard his friend's voice again. "Go easy on Fin while you guys are in Boston, okay? It would be nice to know you're looking out for her."

Evan ducked his head back down to look Desmond in the eye as he responded. "I'll always look out for her, even if we're at odds. But I'll do my best to make peace. Hopefully, being in another environment will help."

Desmond reached over to fist bump before Evan closed the door, heading into his empty house. Just a few hours before, he had been appreciating the quiet and solitude he found here. Now, it felt empty and slightly lonely after a night spent getting to know new friends. He pushed the thought out of his head as he brushed his teeth, choosing to think about the upcoming trip instead.

He hadn't been back in Boston since he had moved to Vermont a few months back, but it felt like a lifetime. Most of his time at Harvard, he had been forced to spend studying or working. He hadn't found the free time that some classmates did to enjoy the city, because he really needed to apply himself. If his grades had slipped even a little, he worried he would lose the scholarships he had won. Now, he got to return to enjoy the time with colleagues and hopefully enjoy some of what the city had to offer. And ideally, avoid any of the trouble that had helped him choose Vermont in the first place.

Chapter 8

The conference was kicking off with a cocktail reception at five p.m., and Finley was still sitting on the highway with less than half an hour to get there. She still needed to check in to the hotel, change her clothes, and get her badge from registration. Somehow, the other drivers on 93 South didn't seem to understand her situation, because no one was parting ways to let her pass through. Even once she finally got off the highway, she was stuck in traffic through the city streets until she finally reached the hotel. It was conveniently located next to the convention center, and she decided to splurge on valet parking rather than battle her way into the garage.

After completing check-in and grabbing her registration packet from the desk in the hotel lobby, she had less than five minutes to get her dress on and apply a quick swab of a mascara wand. Her dove-gray dress fell to mid-calf, with a slight poof to the skirt. The bodice was fitted and had a deep V-neck and plunged in the back as well. She grabbed the shimmery blue sweater that she might need for the weather before flying out of the room back to the elevator.

Doctors, nurses, pharmacists, and scientists mingled with salespeople from various companies. At the conference, the companies peddling services or wares for the medical and scientific community would be set up in the grand hall of the convention center, while the smaller rooms held speakers and workshops. Finley knew no one in the room but was greeted warmly by fellow nurses and nodded at by a group of doctors talking by the bar. She ordered a glass of white wine to calm her nerves and had just turned to rejoin the crowd when she felt something wet hit her back.

"Oh, I'm so sorry," a voice from behind her said. That it was one she recognized had her turning around twice as fast, finding Dr. Lincoln with an empty wine glass and a remorseful look on his face. "Let me get some napkins."

She watched as he grabbed a handful from the bar and approached her, indicating for her to spin around. He patted her bare skin with the napkins and tried to do the same with her dress, hesitating when he reached her lower back. Sighing, she turned back around.

"It's okay," she said. "I think you got most of it."

"It's red," he said, his face blushing the same color. "I'm afraid I ruined your dress."

"Nothing the dry cleaner can't handle," she said. After handing him the glass of wine she held, she pulled on the sweater. "That should cover the worst of it."

"Will you please let me handle the dry-cleaning bill? Have the hotel do it in the morning, and I'll have them add it to my room charges."

"I will," she said, agreeing with a nod. Without her home remedy of vinegar and baking soda, she would need to take advantage of the services the hotel offered, and it was likely to be outside her budget.

"I should let you get back to it," he said, starting to retreat.

"Wait," she called out, reaching for his arm. The action surprised both of them, but she kept with it. "I don't know a soul here other than you. Do you?"

"A few," he responded. "People from Harvard, and some researchers I got to know during medical school. There are a few medical journals here that I've submitted to, so I know those editors."

"Oh," she said, feeling deflated. "Okay then. I'll let you go."

"No, it's fine. I can introduce you to some people, if you'd like," he said. He leaned closer, and she had a quick sniff of his aftershave or cologne. Cedar and something else she couldn't put her finger on, but nothing she had ever noticed before. "I owe you one after essentially pouring a glass of wine down your back."

He led her around the room, introducing her to some doctors he had attended Harvard with, and a few of the people from the journals. When they were approached by the head of the nursing department at Finley's alma mater, he gestured he was going to talk to someone else and disappeared. She tried to focus on the conversation and eventual introductions to nurses that she could try to persuade to move to Vermont, but Evan's presence made it difficult.

He moved around the reception with the same quiet grace he did in the oncology unit. Smiling and occasionally stopping to shake someone's hand and have a brief conversation but always seeming to be on the move from one group to another. By the time she finished handing out cards to the prospective nurses and scheduling times to chat the following day, she had lost sight of him. As the reception ended and groups drifted out in search of dinner, she searched for him again with no luck. There was no explanation for the sense of disappointment she felt, when it should have filled her with relief.

***

She changed into jeans and a sweater before heading back to the lobby, refusing to order room service on her short visit to Boston. Although they only lived a few hours away, it was rare that she would make the trip down, never mind staying at one of the nicer hotels in the Seaport district. Determined to enjoy the time, she headed out and towards the water, where she knew all of the restaurants would be found.

Her phone rang as she walked, and she pulled it out to see her mom's face on the screen. "Hi, mama," she said into the phone.

"Hi, baby," her mom responded. Maggie Monahan was easily Finley's most trusted confidant, and she often referred to her as her best friend. But she was a mom at her core, and worried about her children no matter how old they were. "You forgot to text me when you got to the hotel."

"I'm sorry, I was so late," she said. "I threw on my dress and ran down to the cocktail reception. Although maybe I should have taken my time."

"Why? You didn't enjoy yourself?"

"I did, somewhat," she said. "But you know that doctor that I'm always complaining about? He spilled wine all over me within two minutes of me arriving."

"Oh, no," her mother gasped. "Was it an accident?"

"Yes," Finley said. "He's not malicious. He's just not that nice."

"You two have been on the wrong foot with each other since he started working there," Maggie said. "Maybe you just need to get to know each other. This conference might be just the thing to get you on the same page."

"I don't know. I'm a little off my game here. I'm so used to knowing everyone and feeling confident in my work, and here I don't know a single person and am feeling insecure," she admitted.

"But you know him," her mom pointed out. "And maybe he's feeling the same way."

"I don't think so," Finley replied. "It's almost like we flipped roles, and I'm the shy one while he's Mr. Social. He was talking to everyone at the reception and seemed just fine. It's just me that he would rather avoid."

"When your father and I were first introduced, I thought he was the rudest man on the planet," Maggie told her.

"What? Dad is so nice and outgoing," Finley said with a laugh.

"Now he is," she said. "But that night, he wouldn't talk to me and couldn't even look me in the eye. We were stuck sitting across the table from each other through an entire dinner and barely said a word. Our friends were dating, and they thought it would be fun to fix us up. The next day I told my friend thanks but no thanks, and she was shocked. Said he had been raving about me all morning."

"And we all know how it turned out," Finley said. "All these years of marital bliss. How is this relevant?"

"He was nervous," Maggie replied. "Said I put him off his footing, because he was so uncomfortable."

"And?"

"And maybe the same could be true here," Maggie said. "Perhaps you're more alike than you think, or he's nervous around you."

"He's not attracted to me, I promise."

"How do you know? You're a beautiful girl, it's entirely possible."

"You're my mom, you have to say that," Finley said with a laugh.

"Do you think he's attractive?"

Finley thought of the too-long black hair that was constantly sticking up around his ears where his glasses sat. The brown eyes nearly hidden behind those glasses, and the long lashes that brushed his cheek when he looked down. When her mind drifted to his trim frame and wondering whether he was hiding a six pack under his loose-fitting scrubs, she pulled her thoughts back. "No."

"Finley, you are not a good liar," Maggie said with a laugh. "I can hear the lie through the phone."

"He's good looking, of course," she admitted. "But that's all. There are a lot of handsome men around here."

"Well, maybe you'll meet another one and this conversation will be forgotten," Maggie said. "All I'm saying is to give him a chance, even if it just improves your work relationship. Don't shut down a friendship because he's a little shy."

"It's more than that," Finley protested. "He clearly doesn't like me. Maybe he didn't do the wine thing on purpose, but at work, he's constantly making it obvious. I think the sound of my voice alone makes him crazy, he can't stand being around me."

"Didn't you have dinner with him just a few nights ago?"

"Desmond and his big mouth," Finley fumed. "That was his fault, and now he's making it seem like something it wasn't."

"He thought you two got along well," Maggie said. "Even suspected there might be a spark between you."

"There's no way Des said that," Finley said with a laugh.

"Okay, maybe I asked. Or it could have been Zoe," Maggie admitted.

"I knew I should have moved to Chicago," Finley said.

"Oh, it's not that bad. We love you and want you to be happy," Maggie said. "And to be safe in the city. What are you doing tonight?"

"I'm walking around now looking for somewhere to eat," she said. "I can't believe how busy all the restaurants are. All the ones that I've walked past have had people waiting outside."

"I don't like the idea of you walking around by yourself after dark," her mom fretted.

"I'm a big girl; I can handle myself," Finley said. "Don't forget, JJ had me take that self-defense class last year."

"Be safe, and text me when you're back in your hotel room. No matter how late, okay?"

"I will," Finley agreed. "I'll talk to you later. Love you."

Her mom repeated the words and then hung up, leaving Finley feeling lonelier than she had before the call. Life in a small town meant knowing almost every person who walked past her, and now she was in a city with people rushing every which way, and not a familiar face in sight.

She found a small cafe that looked like it had open tables and was able to enjoy a quiet dinner overlooking the waterfront area. Her waitress was friendly and chatty, sharing some locations that Finley should try to visit if she had time. By the time she finished her meal, she was feeling more relaxed and better about her time in the city.

The walk back to the hotel was now in darkness, other than the city lights. Fewer people were milling about now, most were settled into the busy bars and restaurants in the area or climbing into waiting Ubers. Each time she had to pass an alley, she steeled herself, thinking of her mother's warning, and it was a relief when she finally caught a glimpse of the hotel down the street.

Quickening her pace, she was all but running down the dark street when she felt a hand on her arm. Turning and swinging without looking, she felt her fist hit a solid wall of muscle and heard the responding grunt from her attacker. Stomping on his foot, she was about to raise her knee and finish him off when she happened to glance up and see his face.

Chapter 9

"I'm so sorry," Finley's voice came from above him, since he was doubled at the waist. "I thought you were attacking me. My mother got into my head. Are you okay?"

He rubbed his abdomen where she had punched him and leaned his weight onto the foot that hadn't been stomped. "You can really throw a punch."

"My older brother is a cop," she said. "Did you think he hadn't trained me to protect myself?"

"I wasn't trying to hurt you, or even scare you," he said. "You were running and looked like something was wrong, and I wanted to check on you."

"Like I said, my mother got into my head. She was worried about me being in the city alone, and it spooked me. I was just hurrying to get back to the hotel."

"Makes perfect sense," he said. "In the moment, it just looked like maybe someone was chasing you, or something was wrong. I'm sorry I grabbed you."

"No, I'm sorry I hurt you," she replied. "Are you okay?"

"Nothing bruised but my pride," he said, laughing softly. "I never thought someone so little could beat me up, but I've learned my lesson."

"Are you sure you're alright?"

"I'm fine," he said. "I'll walk in with you, if that's okay?"

"Sure," she agreed.

They walked side by side for the remaining half block to the hotel entrance, where he opened the door and gestured for her to go through. She walked into the lobby, thanking him quietly, and he felt off balance again. She was normally animated and lively, and now she seemed too quiet.

"Are you okay?"

"Yes," she said, looking at him sharply. "Why?"

"I've just never seen you be so quiet," he replied. "It seems like something must be wrong."

"First my talking makes you crazy, and now me being quiet does? That means everything I do is annoying to you," she said.

"Not everything," he said without thinking. When she stared at him, he shrugged. "You're a really good nurse. One of the best I've ever worked with. You show compassion and genuinely listen to every single patient. Even when they might get frustrating, you never show it. I've seen you go to battle with doctors and family members to get them what they want. Including me. You're their champion. I respect that."

She stared at him for so long, he was sure he had put his foot in his mouth again. Then she nodded once and turned to head to the elevators. "Good night," she called over her shoulder. She paused after a few steps and halfway turned back to him. "And thank you for that. I happen to think you're a pretty great doctor yourself. Despite your horrible bedside manner."

He stopped to buy a bottle of water before going to his room, not wanting to be trapped in an elevator with her. After chatting with a doctor he recognized from the earlier keynote speech for a few minutes, he headed to his room. He swore he could smell Finley's perfume as he got off at his floor and realized that she was just behind a half wall at the ice machine. She glanced up and looked surprised to see him again.

"Are you following me?" She asked, walking towards him with her full ice bucket.

"No, just going to my room."

"That was a joke."

"Oh. Well then, good night." He turned and then gestured for her to walk ahead of him, then kicked himself when he couldn't help but notice the sway of her hips as she walked. "You really shouldn't walk around barefoot. You never know what you could step on out here."

She rolled her eyes at him. "My shoes were killing me, and I just needed some ice. It's not like I was going outside."

He sighed and bit his tongue, stopping when he reached his door. Then immediately got tense again when he realized that she was going into the room next to his. The one that connected to his room with a thin door. "You're right there?"

"Yup," she said, grinning at him. "Looks like I'm harder to avoid than you'd like."

"Good night," he said again, swiping his key card and opening the door.

"I'll try to keep it down!" She called out as his door closed behind him. He could hear her laughter as her own door opened and then clicked closed.

After a long, hot shower, he slipped on a pair of pajama pants and stretched out on the bed with his book. He read the same paragraph three times, then gave up, staring at the door that connected his room to Finley's. Surprisingly, he couldn't hear anything from her room. He had expected the TV to be blaring and her to be talking on a speaker phone at the same time, long into the night. The silence was even more unsettling, because it left him with his own thoughts. Which was unfortunate, because they were dominated by her. And her hips.

***

He had obviously dozed off at some point, because he was jerked awake by a loud alarm. He fumbled for his cell phone and knocked it to the floor before realizing that it wasn't the one he had set for morning, but the fire alarm on the wall. Moving quickly, he slipped his feet into sneakers and managed to find the phone under the bed so he could turn on the flashlight. He grabbed his key card from the bureau and headed to the hallway, hesitating when he saw Finley's door still closed and no sign of her in the group waiting to go down the stairs.

He ran back down the hall and banged on her doorway, stepping back when it was flung open. Finley was disheveled, her hair sticking in every possible direction and a sleep mask on her forehead. Thankfully she was dressed, but her shorts and T-shirt exposed far more than he would have liked. Her widened eyes made him realize he was also significantly underdressed, as he had forgotten a T-shirt.

"Let me just grab a shirt," he said, pointing to his door. He swiped his key with no response, trying again and again with the same result.

"The power is out," Finley said. "The lock won't work. We need to go."

"You're right," he said. He gestured down the hall to the stairwell, where the crowd had disappeared. A fireman came through the doorway and frowned when he saw them.

"You all need to get down to the lobby," he ordered them. "Do you need help?"

"No, thank you, officer," Finley replied quickly, starting towards the stairs.

"Officer?" Evan said under his breath as they raced towards the lobby.

"I was flustered," she said. "Man in uniform and all that."

He followed her down the rest of the stairs, then hesitated as he saw the large crowd gathered in the lobby. Most of the conference attendees were mingling, and there were more people who looked like solo business travelers mixed with families. Everyone looked worried, and most were in some form of pajamas. He regretted not grabbing a shirt as he looked around, seeing that most people had managed to cover up somewhat.

Hotel employees were helping to organize guests into small groups, explaining that if the building needed to be evacuated, they would need to stay with their leader. Evan was assigned to a concierge, in the same group as Finley, the minute they came out of the stairwell. She ushered them all to a corner of the lobby, inviting everyone to get as comfortable as possible in the limited chairs available. Their group of twenty included a family with three young children, who were watching the scene with wide eyes. The concierge explained that they all needed to partner up, as they would use the buddy system if they were to leave the building.

"Want to be my buddy?" Finley whispered to him. He hadn't realized she had moved back to his side until that moment, but at her whisper in his ear, the hair on the back of his neck stood up.

"Sure," he said. "Unless you want to go with that guy over there who's staring at you like he's never seen a woman before."

"That's exactly why I wanted to be paired with you," she said. "Considering I did not know you had the physique of Captain America under your scrubs, you seem the most logical person to protect me if he were to try and drag me back to his room."

"He looks like a scientist who rarely leaves his lab," Evan pointed out. "But more importantly, I think you'll be the one protecting me. I have never felt so objectified in my life."

"Well, I assume it's not often you walk around shirtless," she replied, looking him up and down. "Which is a shame, I have to say. Would you mind if I took a picture to show the staff at home?"

"I would mind, very much," he said. "This is wildly inappropriate."

"It's hard to remember that you're my boss when you're looking like that," she said. "And knowing it makes you uncomfortable only adds to the fun. Let's not forget, you have been a source of misery for me."

"Misery?"

"Okay, maybe that's a little strong," she said. She put her hand on her chin and tilted her head to the side, causing the wild hair to bounce to the other side of her head. "Grief? Unhappiness? Is there a word for when you question your self-worth?"

"Is that what I've made you feel?" he asked, horrified. He felt sick suddenly, after hearing the description of what she had been feeling.

"Is it awful if I say yes?" she asked, looking down at her bare feet. "I don't want to make you feel bad, but it's been pretty rough."

"I don't know what to say. I'm sorry doesn't seem good enough," he said. "What I said to you earlier about your strengths as a nurse? I meant every word of that. You're very good at what you do, and I'm lucky to work with you."

"Even though I drive you crazy," she replied, the question in her eyes.

"Maybe we just got off on the wrong foot," he said. "Or we're so different, it made it hard to find a path to getting along. I don't know what it is. The heaviness of our jobs…"

"What about it?"

"It gets to me sometimes," he admitted. "The desire to be perfect doesn't work when you're a doctor in an oncology unit. I can't save everyone. But I shouldn't put that pressure on everyone else."

"We feel it too," she said. "We grieve every person we lose. It always hits us hard. But the fun we have, that's what gets us through. The friendships and laughs we share make the hard times easier."

"I never thought of it that way," he admitted. "I just thought you were goofing off."

"We do that too," she said with a laugh. "And we talk about reality TV way too much and get caught up in pop culture crazes. We've done the TikTok dances and all the trends during the pandemic. It just helps to lighten the mood."

"It doesn't come easily to me," he admitted.

"What doesn't?"

"Social stuff," he said. "I get nervous. I always say the wrong thing or do something dumb. Like spilling a glass of wine on a lady during a cocktail party."

The alarms turned off suddenly, and everyone sighed in relief. The concierge asked them to wait while he went to get an update from the fire department, and he returned a few moments later with the news that they could return to their rooms.

Evan was pushed along with the crowd making its way to the elevators. Seeing the number of people waiting, he opted to climb the ten flights of stairs and was wide awake by the time he got back to his room. It was two in the morning, well past his regular bedtime, and between the exercise on the stairs and Finley's words, he knew he wouldn't sleep.

After another hot shower, he flipped on the TV, hoping to find something that would lull him back to sleep. The fact that his eyes kept going to the door connecting his room to Finley's was a pure coincidence, and not something to think about. But he probably should make sure she got back upstairs safely. Right?

He walked to the door quickly, before he could talk himself out of it, and knocked softly once he opened his side. Just before the door started moving, he wished he had put a shirt back on, but her disheveled appearance made him forget.

"Are you okay?"

"I think so, but why are you looking at me like that?"

"You just look," he hesitated, then waved a hand at her hair. "A little frazzled."

"Well, I got trapped in the elevator line with the creepy scientist," she said. "Who I think was trying to ask me to go out for a drink, but I ducked away in time. I ended up helping that couple carry their kids up, since they all fell asleep waiting for our turn."

"That was nice of you," he said.

"It was less kind than self-motivating, if I'm being honest," she said. "As soon as I was holding a toddler, the guy found other things to interest him."

"Okay," Evan said. "I just wanted to make sure you had gotten back all right. I felt bad that I had ditched you."

"I was just about to put a movie on," she said, gesturing to the TV. "Want to watch?"

"It's the middle of the night," he reminded her.

"And yet we're both standing here, wide awake. I promise I won't do anything to jeopardize our professional relationship," she said. "I just don't trust that the alarm won't go off again. And I know I won't be able to sleep."

He hesitated and then nodded. "What are we watching?"

Claiming the chair in the corner, he watched out of the corner of his eye as she got settled into the bed. Once she had the remote back in hand, he focused on the TV, which was already signed into Netflix with a romantic comedy selected. She clicked play and then snuck a glance at him, as if expecting him to object, but he leaned back in the chair and crossed his arms.

Within half an hour, she was sound asleep, snoring softly. He managed to sneak the remote out from under her hand and turn the TV off before pulling the blanket up to cover her. Resisting the urge to push that wild hair back from her face, or worse yet, kiss her on the forehead, he went back to his room.

He flipped the lock on the door, as if that would also lock up the unknown feeling he had in his stomach.

Chapter 10

"My twin powers tell me that something happened last night." Desmond's voice blasted out of the speaker of her phone, which was propped up in the bathroom so she could FaceTime him while putting her makeup on. A decision she regretted immediately.

"Shhh," she said. "No."

"Why shhh? Is someone asleep in your bed?"

"Des. Knock it off."

"Don't make me call mom," he said. "Or worse, JJ."

"You wouldn't dare."

"Try me."

She sighed. "I may have spent a little time with Dr. Evil. But not like that."

"Walk me through it," Desmond said. She watched as he poured himself a cup of coffee and then sat at the kitchen table.

She ran through the events of the night before quickly. "And then I woke up this morning. Drooling on myself, I'll have you know, so that was quite a sight for him."

"Was he still there?" Desmond's face looked shocked as he asked.

"No! Don't be ridiculous. I'd say we're just friends, but I don't even think we're that," she said. "Not quite the enemies we were, but somewhere weird in between."

"I knew there was something between you two," he said. "Working at the bar has honed my senses."

"You're an idiot, you know that?"

"And you love me anyway," he said. "Plus, you know I'm right. You have a thing for him."

"When they were handing out twins, they really couldn't give me a twin *sister*?"

"Imagine the bloodshed that would have occurred," he said. "You love being the only girl."

"I thought I did," she retorted. "But I've changed my mind. I should be talking to Zoe about this, now that I finally have a sister."

"You should," he said, his face lighting up. "Think about how long she pretended she didn't like JJ. Let me add her to the call, hold on."

"No—"

She was put on hold while he attempted to add their sister-in-law to the call. If she had any sense in her brain, she would hang up. But if she did, her entire family would start calling almost immediately.

Desmond's face came back on the screen, and a new box, showing Zoe still lying in bed. "Oh, Zoe. I'm sorry Desmond is an idiot and woke you up."

"Be sorry he woke me up," JJ's voice came from off the screen. "He's going to pay for this."

"Shouldn't you be at work?" Des fired back. "It's after eight."

"I have the day off," JJ said. "I wanted to enjoy some quiet time with my wife, which you have now ruined. Get to why you're calling this early."

"Fin has a crush on her boss," Desmond said. "And she's denying it. It's like when you were in love with JJ but didn't want to admit it, Zoe. What can we do to snap her out of it?"

"I am not in love with him," Finley interjected.

"See what I mean?" Desmond said, grinning at the phone.

"He seems like a nice man," Zoe said. "I got to talk to him when he had dinner with Stella and Ben. I didn't think you were particularly friendly."

"We aren't," Finley said. "Or we weren't."

"This sounds like a you problem," JJ said. "We should leave you to it."

"JJ," Zoe slapped him on the shoulder. "Be nice."

"I just don't see what we can do about it," JJ said. "Unless we all want to fly to Vegas and trick her into marrying him?"

"That only works once," Zoe said. "Give him a chance. That's all you can do for now. Don't get caught up in what you think, let your feelings come through."

"Excellent advice," JJ said. "And now I'm hanging up so my feelings can come through."

JJ and Zoe disappeared from the screen, leaving Desmond in a fit of laughter. "Hang on, let's add Colin. This is fun."

"No! I'm hanging up," she said. "I'm already late."

She swiped on some lip gloss and grabbed her badge and then hesitated at the door connecting her room to Evan's. It was still weird to call him by his first name, after so many months of only thinking of him as Dr. Lincoln. But one middle of the night fire alarm and a movie session seemed to have moved them to a new place, and he had insisted she call him Evan. Her falling asleep and drooling all over herself was probably one step too far into familiarity, but she was trying to forget that happened. Focusing on what he looked like in just his plaid pajama bottoms, hair ruffled as if her hands had been running through it, was a better thought. Although twice as distracting, she realized, shaking her head and moving towards the hallway.

***

The day was filled with informational sessions, meetings with nurses interested in making the move to Vermont, and visits to the booths in the large convention center. Her feet were killing her, the tote bag she had gotten as swag was filled with even more swag from all the companies with booths, and all she wanted was a hot shower by the time the conference closed for the day. Groups were milling about the large hallway, making plans for dinner or sightseeing, but Finley was intent on getting back to her room.

They had one full day remaining in Boston, and Finley planned to drive back the following night. The hospital had offered to pay for the additional night in the hotel, but she had figured there would be less traffic in the evening, and she could sleep in her own bed. However, now that she had done one full day of events, she was less certain about driving back after dark.

Once she entered the hotel, she stopped at the front desk. The clerk smiled sweetly at her and asked how she could help. "I wanted to see if I could still add tomorrow night to my stay," Finley said.

The clerk typed on the computer and frowned at the screen. "I'm so sorry, but it looks like we're full tomorrow. We have a large convention coming to town that starts checking in tomorrow, and many of the current guests are staying. The weather is going to get bad in the evening and through the following morning. Most guests have already added on that night in anticipation."

"Okay, thanks for checking," Finley replied, smiling to put the other woman at ease. It wasn't the clerk's fault that Finley was late to the game on adding the extra night. She should have kept the reservation as it was and changed it after she arrived. Instead, she had acted without thinking, as usual, and dropped it before she knew how tired she would feel.

She lugged her tote bag to the elevator bank, surreptitiously scanning the crowd around the hotel bar to see if Evan was around. Despite her best intentions, she had spent most of the day looking for his face among the attendees. Knocking on his door seemed like a bad idea, as if she was trying to become his best friend instantly. But when she got off the elevator and walked past his room, her steps slowed down and then stopped. Before she knew what she was doing, her hand was rapping on his door, while her brain was telling her to move quickly and get into her room.

The door swung open, revealing Evan in a pair of dress pants, a button-down shirt half undone, and a tie undone but hanging around his shoulders. His glasses were crooked, and he was shoeless. The entire image somehow made her mouth dry and her heart race. What was happening?

"Hi," he said, when she stood there mutely. "How was your day?"

"Exhausting," she admitted. "I just wanted to make sure you were okay. I never saw you."

"I left early this morning to do a tour at Dana Farber, and meet with some doctors there," he said. "I was hoping to convince a few to move, but that's not likely. They did have some names of doctors who were looking for a spot, though, so I spent the rest of the day tracking them down in between sessions."

"That's great," she said. Not knowing what else to do, she held up the tote bag. "I got a lot of stuff."

"I see that," he said. She could be wrong, but it looked like amusement on his face as he looked at the overfull bag. "I have to pack light, I'm flying back."

"That's right," she said. "But you can always put stuff in my car, if you want. I'm driving back tomorrow."

"I'll keep you posted," he said. He leaned against the doorframe, one arm up so his wrist was against his forehead. "What are you doing tonight?"

She had to bite hard on her tongue to stop herself from the completely inappropriate answer that almost snuck out. "Not sure," she said. Her cheeks were flaming red, no doubt, and he probably could see straight through to her thoughts. But he didn't seem fazed, so she powered through. "Do you feel like grabbing a bite to eat?"

"I can't," he said. Almost too quickly, but he did look slightly disappointed. "I already made plans to meet up with some Harvard friends. Do you want to join us?"

"No, thanks," she replied. "Maybe I'll just order some room service and rest my feet. I'm still exhausted from the middle of the night events."

"Same," he said. "I was debating a nap, and I haven't done that in years. I'll probably just get another coffee after I shower, that should keep me awake for a few hours."

"Alright, then," she said, trying to hide her feelings. Which was easy, since she couldn't even clearly identity what they were. Disappointment seemed weird, considering she had planned to avoid him the entire stay. "Have fun. Hopefully, I won't be seeing you in the middle of the night."

"Seriously," he said with an easy grin. "I'll see you in the morning."

She moved to open the door to her room, noticing that he lingered and didn't let the door close immediately. Once she dropped the bag on the floor and removed her shoes, she started to pull off her dress, pausing first to make sure the door between their rooms was firmly closed.

***

The morning came too fast, considering she felt like she had only slept for an hour. Despite her best efforts to distract herself from the man next door, nothing had worked. She had tried a movie, a good book, and playing games on her phone, all to no avail. The movie and the book were both romances, and she blamed them for the thoughts that were swirling every time she tried to close her eyes.

Less than a week ago, she had wanted to avoid Evan at all costs. Now he was all she could think about, it and it was unnerving. Nothing had really changed between them, other than maybe her realizing that he wasn't the monster she had

88

assumed. In reality, he was nice. A little funny, even when he wasn't trying to be. And Audrey had been right. He was handsome, although he was either trying to hide it with his messy hair and glasses, never mind hiding his physique, or completely unaware of what he looked like.

She forced herself to get out of bed and shower, then packed up her suitcase. Since she had to be out of the room at check-out time, it was easier to just lug everything down to the lobby before breakfast. The schedule didn't allow for many breaks, and the last thing she needed was to realize an hour too late that her stuff was still all over the room. After carefully packing, she headed out into the hall, only to come face to face with the source of her sleepless night.

"What happened?" she gasped, taking in the sight of him. His left eye was covered in a massive black and blue, which looked like it was still developing. There was a scrape along his jaw line too, that looked like it had been carefully cleaned but was probably painful.

"Oh, it's nothing," he said, glancing away from her.

"It's not nothing," she said, taking his chin in her hand and pulling his face closer so she could look. "This looks terrible. Did someone punch you?"

"No," he said. "I was an idiot."

"You did this to yourself?"

"No," he admitted. "I was up early, I couldn't sleep. I went for a run outside, because the weather was perfect for it. I should have known better."

"What do you mean? What happened?" She released his chin and stepped back, realizing how close she had been to him.

"I got lost in my own head, which happens a lot when I'm running," he said. "And I guess I went outside of what would be considered a safe area around the hotel. At least, that's what the police told me."

"The police?" she gasped, staring at him.

"Yes," he said, nodding. "One second I was running along, and the next I was hit in the face with something and then hit the sidewalk."

"Oh no," she said, feeling sick at the thought of it.

"They were trying to rob me," he continued. "But I only had my hotel key with me. Not even my phone. Well, I guess I had one thing of value that they took."

"What was it?" she scanned his body, as if that would solve the mystery.

"My sneakers."

"Your what?"

"Yes," he said, half smiling as he nodded. "They took my sneakers right off my feet as I lay there. I was too dazed to even try to fight back."

"They could have hurt you even worse if you did," she pointed out. "I'm so glad they didn't."

"The police came within a few minutes and drove me back," he told her. "They took what little information I could give them, but it wasn't a lot."

"I'm so sorry," she said. "This is terrible. Did you go to the hospital?"

"Not sure if you noticed," he said, leaning close and whispering in her ear. "I'm a doctor."

"Right, but you can't see inside your own brain or bones," she fired back. "You could have an orbital fracture. Or a concussion. What if you have a brain bleed?"

"I don't," he said calmly.

"But you don't know that for sure," she said. "How many times have you seen patients who waited too long to be checked out? And now you're one of them? We need to go to the hospital."

"There are hundreds of doctors right here in the hotel," he argued.

"But not a CT scan," she said. "Let's go. My car is at the valet, we can take that."

"We have a full day of sessions," he said. "I promise, I'm okay."

She crossed her arms and studied him, then shook her head. "We make the worst patients," she said. "I'll let it go for now if you promise to check in with me every hour. And you need to cancel your flight. You can't fly if you have an unknown head injury."

"There are no more rooms left for the night, and I really want my own bed," he said.

"Good thing I have my car here," she said, smirking at him. "You'll ride home with me."

Chapter 11

The headache was getting worse by the second, but he knew if he admitted it to anyone, he would be in an ambulance within minutes. He had gotten a concussion once as a kid when he tried to play soccer, which had convinced him to switch to running. Even with that experience, he didn't remember it being this severe. Coffee, a pain reliever, and even a quick catnap in the lobby had done nothing to relieve the pain. Seeing Finley walking towards him with a determined look on her face had him straightening his spine. If she knew what he was feeling, he knew what she would do.

"How are your sessions?" he asked once she was closer.

"Fine," she said, waving a hand to dismiss the question. "More importantly, how are you feeling?"

"Fine," he said, repeating her response to her.

"You don't look it," she said. "You're paler now than this morning, and you keep grimacing."

"I am not."

"Yes, you are. I've been watching you for ten minutes," she said. "We need to go get you checked out."

"I promise, it's just a headache," he said. Admitting that was a compromise he had to make and hope she would go with it. "If it was worse, I would tell you. I think I have a mild concussion, and there is nothing they can do for me at the hospital that I don't already know."

"What are you taking for pain?"

He showed her the bottle, and she nodded. "I'm also drinking plenty of water."

"The lights are too bright in here for someone with a concussion," she said, frowning at the ceiling. She glanced around, and he could picture her tracking down a maintenance person to dim the lights.

"They're fine," he lied. "Most of the rooms are a little darker."

"No, they aren't, but nice try," she said with an impressive eye roll. "And you shouldn't be going to the sessions, that's too taxing on your concussed brain. We have two choices."

"Which are?"

"We can go to the hospital," she said. "Or we can head home. You can rest in the car and even wear my sleep mask if you want to. But this setting is too much."

"I can find a place to rest here," he said. "You should finish the day."

"I'm not putting you in a corner somewhere, hoping you'll still be alright in a few hours," she insisted. "You need to be monitored with a head injury. Certainly, they taught that in medical school."

"Honestly, I'm fine."

She crossed her arms and glared at him. "I think you're forgetting that I'm the only girl in my family. I'm used to dealing with stubborn, foolish men. And I promise you, I always get my way when they act like that."

He sighed, knowing she was telling the truth. He had been working with her long enough to see that she dug in when she wanted to get her way. "Fine," he said. "We can leave."

As they walked back to the hotel to get their bags and her car, he realized he had never even agreed to ride back with her. She had just assumed, rightfully, that he wouldn't argue with her. Fortunately for her, his head hurt too badly to do it, anyway. He waited while she talked to the bellman about retrieving their bags and then followed them out to where her car was waiting at the curb. He slid into the passenger seat, realizing at once that he was even more exhausted than he had thought. The leather seat felt cool but comfortable, and once he put his sunglasses on, his head started to feel better.

Finley glanced at him as she pulled away from the curb. "Are the sunglasses enough? I have the sleep mask if that would be better."

"This is fine for now," he answered. "Especially if I have my eyes closed."

"Tilt your seat back if you want," she suggested. "I'm going to wake you up every hour if you fall asleep, but then you can go right back."

"I swear, I'm fine," he insisted.

"I'm not going back to work explaining why I brought Dr. Lincoln back as a vegetable. Or worse," she said. "Just go with it."

"It almost sounds like you would miss me," he teased her, seeing her cheeks get pink at the words.

"Don't be silly," she said. "I'm just thinking of the extra work that would put on everyone else. Now go to sleep."

He put the seat back and immediately drifted off, lulled to sleep by the motion of the car and the quiet music she had put on. He wasn't someone who could normally sleep in cars, because he rarely trusted someone else to be in control. That he felt this comfortable with Finley was something he would need to examine later.

***

Later, he could remember being gently awoken along the ride, with Finley fulfilling her promise to check on him hourly. He had mumbled a response to whatever question she had asked and then fallen immediately back to sleep, so the car ride passed quickly. He woke up on his own as the car slowed and then came to a stop. With one eye open, he saw they had just entered the main street of Windsor Peak and Finley had pulled over.

"Is everything okay?" he asked, making her jump in surprise.

"Oh! I didn't realize you were awake. Yes, I just don't know where you live," she said. "You still had fifteen minutes until I needed to wake you again, so I was going to wait."

"You could have woken me," he said. "But thank you. I live on Colchester, just past the library."

"Okay, I know where that is," she said, putting the car back in drive. The few blocks passed quickly, and he was soon pointing out his house on the street.

"It's the blue one," he said.

"Is your car at the airport?" she asked as she pulled into his empty driveway.

"Yes," he said. "I wasn't even thinking of that."

"We can get it tomorrow," she said, opening her car door.

"I can get inside fine," he replied, meeting her at the back of the car to grab his luggage. When she took her own small bag out of the car as well, he looked at her in confusion.

"You aren't staying alone," she said. "Hourly checks, remember?"

"We aren't past that yet?"

"No," she said. "I either stay here, or you can come to my place. But since I live over a bar, and have Des as a roommate, I would recommend option one. Unless you have a friend or family member who could stay with you? Maybe a girlfriend?"

"No," he said, shaking his head and then regretting the motion. "No girlfriend. And no family."

"Looks like you're stuck with me," she said, grinning at him. "Fortunately, I happen to be a good nurse. As you've so kindly told me."

"Come on in," he said, too weary to argue with her. Not that he thought he could win, she was the most stubborn woman he had ever encountered. He flipped on lights, revealing the open kitchen and living room that had drawn him to the house.

A two-story colonial, he had first thought it was too big or elegant a house just for him. Then he had walked in, seeing the warm kitchen and living space, the cozy but bright office tucked behind the stairs, and he had fallen in love. It had reminded him of the family comedies he had watched on television as a kid, and had always dreamed of living in. Somehow, the house gave the impression that it was happy. His childhood home had been solid and safe, but lacked any charm, and when he saw this house, he knew it was exactly what he wanted.

"This is beautiful," Finley said. "I don't know what I was expecting, but it's not this."

"A messy bachelor pad?"

"Maybe," she said. "A townhouse, maybe. Something where you don't have to deal with the lawn. I can't see you pulling weeds or mowing."

He laughed softly. "I have a landscaper who comes and does that for me."

"I'm glad I wasn't totally wrong in my impression of you," she said.

"A little wrong," he said. "I'm not a monster, after all."

"I never thought you were a monster," she said. She yawned loudly and laughed. "I'm exhausted. And you should get rest."

He picked up both of their bags and then laughed when she pulled hers out of his hand. "So much for trying to be nice," he said.

"I can carry it myself," she said, her tone stiff before she shook her head and offered him a small smile. "Sorry. That was rude. I should have said that I didn't want you to overextend yourself. I'm here to take care of you, not the other way around."

"I hurt my brain, not my arm," he reminded her. "And you're not getting paid to be here. Unless I said something in my sleep?"

"As a matter of fact, you offered me a million dollars to be here," she teased, a mischievous glint in her eye.

"I hope you accept Monopoly money," he said. "If you saw my student loan bills, you would know that million isn't coming in real dollars."

"We can work something out," she said lightly. "Now show me the upstairs, please."

He gestured for her to precede him up the stairs and then cursed himself as he watched her hips swing with each step. Forcing himself to stare at the ground in front of him, he almost tripped when he reached the landing. Catching himself, he tried to cover it by pointing down the hall. "That's my room," he said before pointing again in the opposite direction. "Three guest rooms down there, you can take your pick. The bathroom is here in the middle. I have one in my room, so you don't have to worry about me needing it."

She peeked in the bathroom and then into the first guest room. "Very nice," she said. "Housekeeper?"

"Just once a month," he said, not sure why he felt defensive. "She gets the things I miss. But no one really uses those rooms, so they should be fine. And the bathroom should have everything you need. But if it's missing anything, just let me know."

"I have my bag," she reminded him, holding it up. "I should be fine."

"Alright," he said, feeling very unsure of himself. They had barely spoken before this week, and now he was trying to find a way to say goodnight to her in his own home. "I guess I'll see you in the morning."

"I'll see you in an hour," she said. "But hopefully you'll sleep well enough to go right back to dreamland."

"I feel bad that you'll be up almost all night," he said.

"I won't," she said. "I grew up with three brothers in a very loud house. I can get to sleep in any situation in under two minutes."

"That's impressive," he replied.

"Go get some rest," she ordered him. "If you're up before me in the morning, I take my cream with a little coffee."

He laughed. "Noted."

***

When Finley came into his room, just after the sun had come up, he was already awake. She jumped when she saw him standing, making his bed. "I'm up," he said. "And I'm okay. You can sleep now without worrying."

She nodded sleepily and left without a word, which was unlike her. That meant she was more tired than she thought she would be, most likely.

His head pain had dulled to a mild headache, far improved from the day before. After he showered, he opted not to shave, noting the cuts along his jawline. His eye was swollen almost shut and hurt more than his head. He pulled on a pair of jogging shorts and a long sleeve T-shirt before making his way to the kitchen to start the coffeemaker. A quick glance in his refrigerator had him realizing he was grossly unprepared for an overnight guest, so he pulled on his sneakers and headed out the front door. It was a quick walk to the bakery downtown, and the owner, Piper was behind the counter. Her smile faded when she saw his face.

"Doc, what happened?" she cried.

JJ Monahan, Finley's brother and the town sheriff, had come in behind him and leaned against the bakery counter to see what

99

had shocked Piper. "Man, that looks painful. Did that happen here?"

"No," he said. "In Boston."

JJ's spine straightened. "My sister was there with you. Is she okay?"

"She's fine," Evan promised. "I went out for an early run, and someone attempted to mug me. Unfortunately for them, all they got were my sweaty old sneakers. Fortunately, I had left this new pair at home to break in later."

"Did you file a police report?" JJ asked.

"I did," he replied. "They don't think much will come of it."

"That's terrible," Piper said. "Why do people do things like that?"

"Who knows," JJ said. "I saw it all the time when I worked down there."

Piper turned back to Evan. "What can I get for you? Some sugar will probably make that feel better."

"That's what I was hoping," Evan said. He realized suddenly that ordering two coffees might raise JJ's attention and second guessed himself. Until the other man's gaze narrowed, as if seeing right through to his brain. "I'll take a box of assorted pastries and two coffees, please."

"Two?" Piper asked, eyebrows raised. "I know how to make one. Do you want them both the same?"

"No," Evan said. "One with extra cream. Like more cream than coffee."

Piper appeared to smother a laugh as JJ's eyebrows shot up this time. "That sounds a lot like my sister's coffee order."

"It is," Evan admitted. "She was nice enough to drive me back last night, and then she stayed the night to make sure I was okay. She was in the guest room. But she had to wake me every hour because of the concussion."

"Okay," JJ said, his tone sounding anything but that. "She's my baby sister. My only sister. Just keep that in mind."

"Nothing is happening," Evan assured him. "We really don't like each other. Or we didn't."

"Why?" Piper asked as she filled the box. "She's a doll."

"One of the best people I know," JJ agreed. "I can't imagine anyone not liking her."

Evan felt himself start to sweat and regretted his decision to even get out of bed. "I don't know," he said. "We work together, and that can cause conflict. And she tends to talk a lot, and I prefer quiet."

JJ laughed and nodded. "She does talk a lot, I'll give you that. But she's also the kindest person I know, and a natural nurturer. Maybe you want to go easy on her."

Chapter 12

Finley woke slowly, relishing the comfort of the bed. She stretched and rolled over, debating going back to sleep, before realizing where she was. Her eyes snapped open, and she glanced around the guest room to make sure she wasn't imagining it. Sunlight was streaming in the window, indicating she had slept later than usual. Her bag was open on the bureau, and her phone was charging on the bedside table. When she had last gone to check on Evan, he had told her he would stay awake and she should sleep, and apparently, she had taken him at his word.

When she slipped out of the guest room to the bathroom, it was so quiet in the house she worried he had fallen back to sleep. But his door was open, and the bed was made, so she took a quick shower and dressed before going down the stairs with her bag.

Evan was sitting in a club chair in front of the fire, feet propped up on the hearth. He had his glasses on, and a book on his lap, but wasn't reading as she came down. His beard had grown in overnight, making him almost look like a different person. She filed the mental picture away for later, clearing her throat to make him aware of her presence.

"Hey," he said, opening his eyes. "I wasn't sleeping, I promise. I was trying to read, but it hurt my head, so I thought just sitting was better."

"How are you feeling?"

"Much better," he said. "The eye hurts worse than the brain, so that's a good step."

"Very," she said.

"I have good news and bad news," he said. "What would you like first?"

"Good," she said instantly.

"I have coffee and pastries from Piper," he said. He stood and led the way to the kitchen counter. "I put your coffee in this mug so it would stay hot, but if you want to heat it up, you can."

She took a sip and smiled at him. "It's perfect. You even got the cream ratio right. Most people assume that it's too much."

"Well, that kind of leads to the bad news. I saw your brother there, and he was able to help with the coffee."

"Which brother?"

"JJ," he said.

"Okay, so almost worst-case scenario," she said, laughing at the look of horror on his face.

"What's the worst?"

"Colin," she said without hesitation.

"Worse than your brother, who is also in charge of our town police?"

"Yes," she said, nodding. "You never know what Colin's thinking or what he might do. JJ will just tell you right away if you're stepping out of line."

"Oh, he did."

"What?" she looked at him, her turn to be horrified. "What did he do?"

"Just made sure I knew you were his little sister, and I better stay in my lane," Evan said. "And that I was wrong to dislike you."

"You dislike me?"

"Not anymore," he said quickly. "At least, I don't think so. I feel like we've turned a corner?"

She nodded and felt herself smiling. "I agree. That's not such bad news."

"Oh, that's not the news," he said. "A tree fell last night, right across the end of my street. Apparently, there was a storm overnight, although I slept right through it. I saw the tree when

I was walking to town, and I asked JJ about it. He said he's trying to get the town crew out to move it, but since it's the weekend, it might take a while. So, you're kind of stuck here."

"Oh. I guess that is a problem." She peeked into the pastry box and smiled at him. "But at least we have sustenance. And really, I can walk home and come back later for the car. That way, you won't be stuck with me all day."

"I didn't think of that," he said. He almost looked disappointed, which surprised her. Had he actually been looking forward to more time together?

"But I'm in no rush. You have all these treats, and it's still early."

He brightened up at that, so she had read him right. "I found a puzzle," he said. "I figured that was an easy thing for me to do, since I shouldn't be reading or watching TV. Any chance you like jigsaw puzzles?"

"I haven't done one in years," she said. "But that sounds fun. Should we do it here on the kitchen table?"

While he went to get the puzzle, she moved the pastry box and her coffee to the table. When he came back in, she was caught off guard again at how different he looked with some scruff on his chin. Somehow, the look softened him, when on most men it did the opposite. But he was always so put together, seeing him in sweats and unshaven made him more approachable.

He dumped all the pieces out and they began sorting them. As he made a pile of edge pieces, he glanced over at her. "Tell me about your family," he said.

"Well, you know I have three brothers. Des and I are the youngest, with me truly the baby since I was born two minutes after him. They all like to say that it set me up for a life of being late for everything, but I disagree," she said. "My parents are the epitome of the happily married couple. They are enjoying retirement and hoping that Zoe gets pregnant soon so they can be grandparents. You know that JJ is married to Zoe, right?"

"Yes, I heard that," he said. "I think you all mention her more than anyone else in your family."

"Well, for good reason. She feeds us," Finley said with a laugh.

"You grew up here?"

"No," she said. "We grew up in Massachusetts, but when JJ moved up here, my parents fell in love with it. Since they were empty nesters, they sold the house and followed him, and we slowly all ended up here. Colin was last, but that's not surprising. Well, I guess it's shocking that he moved here at all."

"Why?"

"He's the most difficult of us," she said. "Tends to go against the grain and do everything the hard way."

"Is he the oldest?"

"No," she said, shaking her head. "JJ is."

"It can be hard to compete with a successful older brother," he said. He had shadows in his eyes as he said it, and she couldn't stop herself from prying.

"What about you? What's your family like?"

"My parents are divorced," he said. "Classic overachievers in every way. They are both very devoted to work and will probably never retire."

"Any siblings?" His hand fumbled a few pieces of the puzzle as she asked, and she couldn't tell if it was the question or just clumsiness.

"A brother," he answered. "We don't see much of each other."

"I might be jealous," she said, trying to lighten the dark clouds that had formed over his head. "I have one or two too many to ever get a break from them. Maybe three too many."

As if on cue, her phone rang, showing Desmond's face on the screen. In the craziness of the day before, she had never thought to tell him that her plans had changed. She clicked accept on the FaceTime and waited until he appeared before she said hello.

"Hello? That's all you have to say for yourself? I've been here, wearing the carpet out with my pacing, and you just say hello?"

"Were your ears ringing, Des?"

"What do you mean?"

"I was just talking about you," she answered. "And you weren't up all night worrying about me. I forgot to text you when my plans changed, but it just took you twelve hours to realize I might be missing."

"Not true," he said, a smug look on his face. "I was tracking you on Find Friends. Watched you drive all the way back to Vermont, only to stop moving once you reached the good doctor's house. And I'm not one to intrude on romantic time, as much as it pains me to think of my sister in that way."

Evan choked on his coffee, and Finley turned the screen to show him. "Say hi to Evan, Des."

"You're supposed to do that signal when you aren't alone," Desmond said with a sigh.

"You made that up, and I've never known what it is," she argued. "Obviously, you know I'm still here."

"I didn't think you would answer if you were still, you know," Des said, covering his eyes with his hand.

"You know what?" Evan asked, causing Des to groan and Finley to laugh.

"Hanging up now," Desmond said. "I need to call Mom and fill her in on what my sister is up to."

"Don't you dare," Finley yelled, as the screen changed and Des disappeared. She rolled her eyes and put the phone down. "See what I mean?"

"He cares about you," Evan said. "It's nice. The friendship you all have is nice."

"Most days I want to throw him off a bridge," Finley said with a sigh. "But I guess I did get a better hand out of siblings than a lot of people."

"Where did you grow up?" Finley asked after a few minutes of silence.

"You really can't handle the quiet, can you?" he asked, with a teasing light in his eyes.

"You really don't like to answer questions about yourself, do you," she fired back, smirking at him.

"Touche," he said, laughing. "I grew up in a tiny little town in Georgia that I know you've never heard of."

"Why don't I hear a Southern accent?" she asked. "Also, maybe I have heard of it. I did a few years of travel nursing before deciding to settle down here. I've been to a lot of little towns."

"It's called Chisholm, and it's north of Savannah," he said.

"Hmm, it doesn't sound familiar. But I do love that area. I don't hear a southern accent," Finley said, confusion on her face.

"I spent the last thirteen years in Boston," he replied. "I think that can chase any accent out of a person."

"But you don't sound like that either," Finley said. "But maybe it's a combo. I'll have to pay attention now."

"Bless your heart," he said, causing her to laugh.

"Okay, point for you." She clicked a piece into the puzzle before looking back at him. "Tell me about your education."

"Really? Most people find that boring. Or think I'm bragging."

"Not me," she said, shaking her head. "I know it seems like I'm bothered by you mentioning Harvard, but I'm not."

"I never noticed you being bothered, other than that one time at the bar."

"Oh, I felt bad about that. But the rest of it was behind your back," she said, waving a hand in the air. "Water under the bridge."

He laughed, the sound warming the air. "Does that mean we get to put our past behavior behind us and start fresh?"

"We just spent the night together," Finley said dryly. "I think we've moved past fresh."

"If you say it like that, we'll definitely have people talking about us."

"I think your black eye will answer any questions," she said with a laugh. "Or have people thinking I gave it to you."

"That might be more fun than telling the truth."

"Alright, we'll revisit that idea," she said. "Does this mean my talking won't bother you as much anymore?"

"You took something I said at a staff meeting very personally," he said. "It wasn't specifically about you. All of the nurses spend a lot of time sitting at the desk talking. I'd say of all the staff, you do it the least. I don't mind you talking to the patients. You just thought that I was talking about that, and I wasn't able to explain."

"Why not?"

"I'm not sure if you've noticed," he said. "But I'm pretty shy. And you are so confident, and I just kept getting tongue tied. It was easier to let you dislike me."

"Then I apologize for the assumption," she said. "I've never been so happy to be wrong about something. Now, tell me about your years in Boston. And why you chose oncology. You must have done a fellowship?"

"Yes, at Dana Farber," he answered. She listened as he went through his years of school and training, fascinated by his dedication to studying cancer and medicine in general. She had always known he was smart but realized she had underestimated him. "It's a little like doing a puzzle, you know?"

"What do you mean?"

"I have a person in front of me with this complicated disease. Like seeing these thousand pieces all over the table, and I have to figure out what brings them together. They need to fit just so, and I can't force it," he said. "I get to do research and really get in there to figure it out. I just fell in love with it, with the feeling of being able to save someone."

"That's the good stuff. What did you think would be the hardest part? Or what was hardest to learn?" she asked when he concluded.

"Easy," he said. "It still is. When you realize all options have failed. Or there are none to try from the start."

She nodded, feeling the emotion he gave off. "I'm still sorry about that. I shouldn't have second guessed you. Especially in front of the patient."

"Water under the bridge, right?" He smiled at her, and she felt something flip over inside of her. "What about you? Why oncology?"

"I did travel nursing for a long time," she said. "I worked mainly in emergency rooms, or sometimes in post-surgical units. I saw people for a few minutes at a time, but never enough to connect. When I came here and interviewed, and saw how the nurses got to interact with the patients, I fell in love with it. And then you came along and suggested that we follow people all the way through their treatment, and it made it even better."

He smiled at her again, and she felt like she was being warmed from the inside. How could her feelings have changed so drastically in such a short amount of time? Before she could examine it too much, her phone rang again, now with JJ's name on the screen.

"Hey," he said when she answered. "How was your trip?"

"It was good, until the end," she replied. "You saw Evan this morning, so you heard."

"I'm glad you're okay, and that you were there to help him."

"Me too," she said, meeting Evan's eyes as she said it.

"I just wanted to let you know the tree has been cleared," JJ said. "For whenever you want to head home."

She felt a flash of disappointment, which she saw mirrored on Evan's face. After saying goodbye to her brother, she debated her options quickly. "I feel bad leaving this whole puzzle for you to do alone. And you probably should be monitored for at least a few more hours. If you are okay with the company."

"More than okay," he replied, his voice soft. "I don't even mind if you want to turn some music on."

She grinned at him and pulled up a playlist on her phone. Putting the volume on low, she set it down on the table and went back to the puzzle. Things were starting to come together, and it had nothing to do with the pieces on the table.

Chapter 13

"I heard you got mugged, but I didn't realize how bad it was." Mike had stopped Evan on the street outside the coffee shop. Evan had woken up with a headache, improved from the day before, but bad enough to require copious amounts of caffeine to get through the day.

"Yeah, they hit me pretty hard," Evan replied. "The cops think it was a brick. Or something solid like that."

"Oh, man," Mike said. "That's terrible."

"I've never wished I was your size until that day," Evan said with a grin. "They might have thought twice if it were you."

Mike shrugged. "You never know. If they thought they could get the jump on me, they probably would have done the same."

"Nice of you to say that."

"Not just saying it to be nice," Mike said. "Honestly, it could have happened to anyone. But if you want to come in, I can get you set up with a lifting routine."

"I don't have a lot of spare time," Evan answered. "I appreciate it though."

"Exercise is good for the brain and the mood," Mike said. "Keep it in mind."

Evan said goodbye as the other man headed into the coffee shop and turned to go to his car. He hated that he suddenly felt nervous walking down the street alone, even here in Windsor Peak. Hopefully, the feeling would go away over time. For today, staying away from alleys put his mind at ease.

He couldn't help but think of Finley as he started to drive. Their morning of puzzle building had turned into a lunch of grilled cheese sandwiches, Evan's specialty, and then a movie. Evan had fallen asleep almost instantly and woke at the end to find himself covered with a blanket and Finley sound asleep on the couch. Her rough night of sleep had finally caught up with her, so he had stayed still and dozed until she woke up. Although he had offered to order dinner, she had opted to head home to get ready for a busy week at work. Fortunately, she had remembered his car needed to be picked up and dropped him at the airport first. He blamed the brain injury for his forgetfulness, rather than acknowledging he was completely distracted by Finley's company.

As much as he hated to admit it, the house had seemed less alive without her. Even this morning, he had rushed to get ready, and he could only credit the knowledge that he would see her when he arrived at work with a sense of excitement on a Monday. His feelings seemed to have changed for her, and he couldn't quite place where they sat now. Was it friendship? Mutual respect? Something more?

"Morning, Dr. Lincoln." Dr. Collins was just inside the door when Evan walked in, and his eyes bulged at the sight of Evan's face. "What happened to you?"

"I was mugged," Evan said. "It looks worse than it feels now."

"Maybe you should take the day off?"

"I appreciate the concern, Neil," Evan said. "But I'll be alright. If it starts to hurt, I'll head out."

"Concussion?" Neil asked as they walked down the hallway, nodding at other staff members as they went.

"Yes, a mild one," Evan admitted. "The eye hurts worse than the head now. But improving each day. I slept through the night last night and felt much better this morning."

"I just don't want you to overdo it," Neil cautioned him. "The lights and computers here could set you back. I'd like you to do a half day, even if you go home and do work. It will be better than pushing yourself here."

"I can do that," he agreed, even though he felt disappointed. But the other doctor was right, a full shift in the lights and noise of the hospital could set him back.

"How was the conference?"

"It was good," Evan said. "Right up until I got hit in the face, at least. I met with several doctors who will come up for visits, there was a lot of interest when I said we were hiring."

"Excellent," Dr. Collins said, beaming at him. "I hope it was the same for the nurses. I knew we sent our two best representatives."

Evan dropped his bag in his office and went into the oncology suite to see what was on the agenda. Although he had told Dr. Collins that he was fine, he was going to ask other doctors to cover any new admissions. The patients needed to focus on their own health, not his bruised face. After reviewing the board, he was relieved to find that he only had one to pass off, and another doctor quickly agreed to take it.

Two nurses sat at the station, neither of them Finley, and Evan couldn't help but note the disappointment he felt. They both stared at him as he gathered charts to review but didn't ask about his injury. Relieved not to have to explain himself, he hurried to his office, only to run into Finley and Mrs. Lee as he did.

"Good morning, Edna," he said, watching as the older woman's eyes took in his face.

"Good morning, doctor," she said. "What in heaven's name happened to your face?"

"Don't worry about me, I had a little accident in Boston," he said. "How are you feeling?"

"Just fine," Edna said. "I'm about to hear all about your trip from Finley. Did you two get along?"

Evan felt himself blush under Edna's gaze as his eyes met Finley's. She was smiling, looking unfazed as she answered for both of them. "I think we finally understand each other."

He nodded and watched as they continued the walk to one of Finley's stalls. A volunteer was already sitting there, waiting to keep Edna company, since she always arrived alone to treatment. Finley chatted as she got them both settled in, and he had to force himself to walk away. Although he wasn't worried about her saying negative things about him anymore, a part of him secretly wanted to hear what she would say now.

***

He lasted until just before eleven, when his head started throbbing and he knew it was only a matter of time before he wouldn't feel safe driving. Rather than risk having to sleep in the doctor's lounge, he drove home slowly, grateful for his sunglasses. He fell asleep instantly once his head hit the pillow and woke two hours later feeling slightly better.

Once again, his phone was dead, so he plugged it in while making a fresh pot of coffee. The paperwork he had brought home was on the kitchen table and kept his attention for an hour, before his eye and brain demanded a rest. Just as he had the thought, his phone rang, and he answered without looking at the screen.

"Evan?" The voice that came through was as familiar as his own, but not one he wanted to hear.

"Zach," he said, his tone displaying the displeasure he felt.

"It's been a long time."

"Not long enough."

Zach's sharp breath came through the phone. "It's been a long time. I thought you might be happy to hear from me."

"Are you serious? You blew up my life. Almost cost me everything," Evan nearly shouted.

"It was a mistake," Zach replied. "I apologized."

"Did you? I don't seem to remember that."

"What do you want from me? There's not much more I can do or say," Zach said.

"There's a lot more," Evan said with a sigh. "But you choose not to. Why are you calling me?"

"I was thinking of coming for a visit," Zach replied. "See if we could talk things out. I saw that you're in Vermont now?"

"No, you cannot come for a visit," Evan snapped. "And lose my number."

It felt like his blood was on fire, and all Evan wanted was to slip on his running shoes and hit the road. But the lingering headache reminded him that it was a bad idea, so instead, he pulled on a sweatshirt to take a walk. The streets in his neighborhood were quiet, but as he got closer to town, there were more people about. He was starting to recognize people from town and was greeted with friendly smiles as he walked. It helped to calm him down, and within a short time, he realized his stomach was growling loud enough for other people to hear.

When the bell dinged over the bakery door, he heard his name called from the back corner. Desmond was at a small table, a laptop and sandwich in front of him. "Come join me when you get your food," he called out.

Piper was behind the counter and smiled as he approached. "Not typical to see you around this time of day," she said. "Especially on a Monday. How's the face feeling?"

"It's getting better every day," he said. "Just a lingering headache now. But at least my appetite has returned."

"Alright, let's get you some food," Piper said. He ordered a sandwich from the case, which she passed to him with a bag of chips and a bottle of water. "I'm throwing in a big cookie because it looks like you need it."

"Thanks," he said. He carried his plate over to Desmond's table and took the empty chair. "Hey."

"Hey yourself," Desmond replied. "You do look rough. I thought Fin was exaggerating."

"Looks worse than it feels," Evan said.

"I doubt that," Desmond said. His body language was relaxed, but his eyes showed that nothing got past him. "How are things between you and my twin?"

"She was very nice to take care of me," Evan said. "I appreciate it very much. And it gave us a chance to get to know each other. I think we're in a better place now than we were before."

"Bright side of getting attacked, I guess?" Des asked, his tone adding brevity to the comment.

"I guess so," Evan replied. "Although we were communicating better in Boston already. Maybe we just needed a change of scenery."

"She's been single for a long time," Desmond said, the sudden shift in topic making Evan's head hurt more than it already did.

"Oh, really?"

Desmond nodded. "The last guy she was with was a total jerk. Worked in finance and thought money was everything. He wasn't bad to her, or I would have stepped in, but he acted like she was beneath him. Just subtle enough that you couldn't catch him in it, but it was there."

"She's very accomplished, and incredibly smart. I'm surprised she put up with that."

"We all were," Desmond said. "It really got under Colin's skin something bad. And he's the one you don't want to be on the bad side of, I'll just tell you that now. You'd think it's JJ, since he carries a gun, but he's much more easygoing than Colin."

"He's been pretty quiet the few times I've hung out with him, so I haven't really gotten to know him," Evan said. "But I'll keep it in mind."

"No one knows him all that well," Desmond said with a laugh. "Are you planning to date Fin?"

"Oh." Words seemed stuck in his throat. Of course, he should be saying no, that the thought hadn't occurred to him. But hadn't it?

"I shouldn't put you on the spot like that, but I feel like we're becoming friends," Desmond said. "I'd hate to have to kill you if you hurt her."

"I thought you just said Colin was the one to watch out for?"

"At least I warned you," Desmond said with a laugh. "You'll never see him coming."

"I'll keep it in mind," Evan said. He took a minute to sip his coffee, the question still rattling around in his brain. "I am not sure what will happen with Finley. A week ago, I would have said you were crazy."

"I watch a lot of people when I'm working at the bar," Desmond said. "I wasn't much of an observer before, because I talk so much. But with this job, I'm forced to pay attention to subtle things like body language, and to read people. I'd say even a week ago, you and Fin had something going on between you. But you were both fighting it."

"Why would you say that?"

"When you were at the bar before your trip," Desmond said. "You may have been quiet, but you sat pretty close together. It seemed like you were taking comfort from the other person. I know Finley had said it was a terrible day, and you looked the same when you came in. But when you both left, you were more relaxed."

Evan thought back to that night and nodded. "I think you're right. I hadn't thought of that before, but I guess it did put me in a better mood."

"See? I'm smart," Desmond said, patting himself on the chest. "Will you please tell my family?"

"I will," Evan said, laughing.

"It helps that you're in the same field. You understand what she's seeing at work, and how emotional that is," Desmond said, serious again. "We can't relate to that. I try, but I can't be there for her the way she needs some days. I can feel it off her because of that twin thing, but I can't help."

"Technically, we probably can't even be more than friends," Evan said, the thought occurring to him. "Dating might be against the hospital policy."

Desmond snorted as he laughed. "You know how many doctors and nurses I see together? No chance it's a strict policy."

Evan checked his watch and stood up. "Speaking of policy, I should get home and do some paperwork."

"Me too," Desmond said, standing as well.

"What is it you do during the day?"

"Coding," Desmond replied.

"Above my pay grade," Evan said. He opened the door and gestured for Desmond to walk through first.

"Keep in mind what I said," Des said as he turned in the opposite direction of Evan's car. "I want to see my sister happy. If you're the guy to do that, I'm glad. If you aren't, preserve our friendship and leave it alone."

"I'll keep it in mind, I promise," Evan said. "We aren't anywhere near there now, and she may not even be interested."

Desmond grinned at him. "Half the fun is trying to figure out if they're interested. But we're talking about my sister, so I'll drop it. Will I see you tonight for poker?"

"I'll text you later," Evan promised. "If I feel up to it, I'd love to go."

As Evan started the short walk home, his friend's words were swirling around his head. Finley was attractive, no one could deny that. And he had been surprised to enjoy her company over the weekend, even as bad as he felt. Was it worth risking their professional relationship to explore more?

Chapter 14

Finley greeted the volunteer, who she knew from town, and got Mrs. Lee settled on the recliner for her treatment. As she reviewed the orders, she frowned. "They seem to have added an extra bag of fluid," she said. "I'm afraid this will have you using the bathroom more today."

"That's okay," Mrs. Lee said. "I'm sure it's because of my recent spell."

"What spell?" Finley's eyes scanned through the notes on the screen. "You were hospitalized? Why didn't I know this?"

"There was no need to bother you, dear," she said. "Dr. Lincoln was kind enough to come sit with me."

"He knew?" Finley battled with feelings of annoyance and relief. She was glad someone had been there for her patient, but she should have known as well.

"He did," Mrs. Lee answered. "Spent the whole night at my bedside. Second time in a month, I'll have you know. We might be starting some rumors if we keep it up."

The volunteer laughed as Finley ran through the last month in her head. "The medication error? He stayed with you then?"

"He did," she said, nodding. "Came right to the emergency room and then insisted I get moved to a private room. Said I couldn't be around all the other germs, but I think it was just to get me out of that chaos. I did enjoy listening in on the excitement down there, I have to admit. But it was much easier to sleep upstairs. Especially with my own private doctor."

"He spent the night then, too?" Finley asked, thinking back to those days. She had been so furious with him, she wouldn't have noticed if he looked tired the next day. Or if she had, she wouldn't have cared.

"He did," Mrs. Lee said. "Such a good man. Did you do that to his face?"

The sudden change in topic threw Finley off balance, and she laughed. "No, of course not."

"I had to ask," Mrs. Lee told the volunteer, who was also laughing. "I've been watching these two battle for weeks now. It reminds me of when Hank and I first met."

"How so?" Finley asked, hooking up the first IV bag as she did.

"His best friend was dating my friend," Mrs. Lee shared. "They couldn't be alone, because that would be improper, so they begged us to come along. We would fight like cats and dogs each time. Then one day, he shut me up with a kiss. It was so inappropriate, all I could do was slap him. And then kiss him myself."

Finley laughed, able to picture it. "And then you lived happily ever after."

"Well, I lost him young," Mrs. Lee said. "He was only sixty-one when he passed. Can you imagine? We had worked our whole lives, planning for retirement. Then he never got to enjoy it."

"I'm sorry," Finley said. "You had a happy marriage?"

"Very," she said. "We still fought like crazy, but it kept the fire alive. I think all those sparks that made us bicker were flames of passion. Kind of like you and Dr. Lincoln."

"Oh, no," Finley said quickly. "It's not like that. We might be able to be friends, but that's it."

"I see something more," Mrs. Lee said. "Don't rule it out. Sometimes what you're looking for is right in front of you, but you can't see it."

Finley nodded and ducked out of the room, her head spinning. Images of Evan, relaxed and laughing, flashed in her brain. She had enjoyed the day before so much, she had to force herself to leave. Admitting she was attracted to him seemed like a step toward disaster. It was better that she focus on a healthy work relationship and push these thoughts out of her head.

***

Her mother was waiting on the couch in Finley's apartment when she got home from work. Her brother was the only one to blame, but he had already gone down to work behind the bar, so she couldn't make him pay.

"How was your day?" Maggie asked, muting the TV she had been watching.

"Busy," Finley replied. "I'm ready to slip into some cozies and relax."

"You wear cozies to work every day," her mom said, laughing.

"Why do you think I chose nursing?" Finley said over her shoulder as she headed to her bedroom. "I'll be right back."

She changed quickly and brushed her hair back into a messy bun, then stuck her feet into slippers and headed back out.

"What's up?" she asked her mom as she plopped down on the couch.

"I need a reason to visit my only daughter?"

"No," Finley said. "But since you don't usually appear without notice, especially on a weeknight, it raises some questions."

"Your brothers are worried," Maggie said. "Which finds its way to my ears."

"Worried about me?"

Maggie nodded. "That's what they say."

"What exactly are they saying?"

"Des claims you've been moody for weeks," she said, ticking them off on her fingers as she spoke. "JJ said he thinks you're getting involved with someone too fast. And Colin says you're picking fights for no reason."

125

"Colin's one to talk," Finley said, fuming. "He barely speaks to anyone, but wants to talk about me? Why don't we talk about why he stays hidden away all the time and refuses to talk about his life?"

"We can," Maggie said, her tone mild.

"And Des, with his frat boy mentality," Finley continued. "He thinks he knows everything. Just because you're an accomplished flirt doesn't make you a know it all about life."

"Agreed." Her mom sipped from the glass she had on the coffee table before speaking again. "Want to criticize JJ now?"

Finley huffed out a breath. "He's not as bad as the other two. At least he has Zoe to balance him out."

"This is true," her mom said, laughing. "She's his better half for sure. But in their defense, they all have your best interest at heart."

"You think so? Because I think they're nosy and trying to keep the attention off themselves."

"Is there a reason the attention should be on them?"

"Other than what I just said? I guess not," Finley admitted. "But I feel like all three of us are in the same condition."

"And what is that?"

"We're all a mess," she admitted. "And need to get our lives together."

"Let's focus on you, since we're alone," Maggie said. "We can fix them another day. Tell me what's going on."

"You know about the doctor I work with?"

Maggie nodded. "The one you've been battling with for months, who you just went to Boston with. Des and JJ seem to think you spent the night with."

"I did, but not like that," Finley said, rolling her eyes. "He was mugged when we were in the city. Had a bad concussion, so he couldn't be left alone for the night. I stayed and woke him up every hour to make sure he was okay."

"That was good of you."

"Thanks," Finley said. "But anyone would have done it."

"Not true, but I'll let it go," Maggie said. "How was your visit to Boston before that happened?"

"It was good," she said, thinking back. "We left each other alone for the most part. It was weird to see him there, with his peers. He was different."

"How so?"

"I don't know how to explain it. Here, he's always very serious. Never wants to just talk to the other staff, or relax," Finley said. "But there, he was very social. Almost more than me."

"Interesting," her mom said. "Knowing you, that probably threw you off balance."

"A little," she admitted. "I was a little out of my element, and he was thriving. But even more important, he was being nice to me. And that's unusual."

"He's typically mean?"

"Not mean," Finley corrected. "Just standoffish. Aloof, you'd probably call it."

"Keeping his distance?"

"Yes."

"Could that be to maintain a professional relationship?" her mom asked. "Or maybe he's shy?"

"Maybe," Finley admitted. "But he's new here. And to make no effort to be friendly with any of us is a little weird."

"But he's your superior," her mom said. "And as you said, he's new. Some people like to get the lay of the land before they make friends. Not everyone jumps in with both feet before looking."

"I do no such thing," Finley objected.

Maggie stared at her until she laughed. "Okay, maybe I do. But what's wrong with that?"

"Nothing, if you feel confident that you'll be okay," Maggie said. "But if you had something in your life that made you feel like the jump wouldn't be safe, would you still do it? I'm not saying that's the case with him, but it is for some people. Not everyone has the same personality and history as you."

"True," she admitted. "He's just rubbed me the wrong way."

"It sounds like you did it to each other," Maggie said gently. "What happened when you came back here?"

"We actually got to talk," Finley said. "And I enjoyed his company. A lot."

"Are you admitting you were wrong about him?"

"That seems unlike me." Finley laughed when her mother stared at her again. "Okay, fine. I was wrong. But he was wrong about me too."

"And now?"

"I don't know," Finley said with a sigh. "Today confused me again. It turns out he knew my patient had been sick, and he didn't tell me. Just put orders in, and the patient had to tell me herself. I feel like he should have let me know."

"Would he have let another nurse know?"

"Probably not," Finley admitted. "But I don't know for sure. But he didn't spend days with the other nurses. He did with me."

"And hopefully you didn't spend all that time talking about work," Maggie said. "Want to know what I think?"

"No."

Maggie threw her head back and laughed. "Is that how you're going to be?"

"You're going to tell me anyway," Finley said. "At least when I don't like it, I can remind you that I didn't want to hear it."

"I think you knew you might like him when he started, so you made it as difficult as possible. I also think that this weekend broke down some walls you had erected, and now you're really scared." Her mother leaned forward and took her hand. "But not everyone is going to hurt you, Fin. It's okay to open your heart to someone new."

Finley found herself choking back emotions suddenly. She had kept them so tightly locked up for years, and now it all seemed too close to the surface. "I'm okay being alone."

"No, you aren't," Maggie said, squeezing her hand. "You have so much love to give. And you love being with people. You just need to trust yourself."

"How? When I was so wrong last time?"

"It's never wrong to love," Maggie said. "What he did was wrong. Not you. All you did was offer your heart, and that's never a bad thing."

Finley sighed and glanced around the room. "You could have at least brought wine if you were going to get me all emotional."

"I did," Maggie said, laughing. "And I asked Zoe to send dinner up, and a big portion of dessert. I covered all my bases."

"Now can we talk about what's wrong with the boys?"

"If that will help," her mom said. "And I'd like to hear your thoughts on when I can start asking JJ and Zoe for a grandchild. I think I've been more than patient."

"Deal," Finley said.

"Just don't forget what I said, okay?"

"I won't," Finley promised. "I honestly don't even know if that's the direction we're headed. He's hard to read."

"I think we skipped over the most important question," Maggie said. "Are you interested in him?"

Finley sighed and thought about it for a moment. "If you had asked me last week, the answer would have been a solid no. But now? I'm less sure. I did enjoy my day with him yesterday."

"And he's attractive?"

"That doesn't even begin to describe him," Finley said. "Although I had been reluctant to admit it before now. But he's shockingly handsome."

"Oh, I might need to stop in and say hello to you at work," Maggie said with a laugh. "I could use some shockingly handsome in my life."

"Don't let Dad hear you say that," Finley said. "Or your sons. They all think very highly of themselves in that department."

"Rightfully so," Maggie said. "They are all special in their own way."

Finley laughed as she stood up. "Where did you leave this wine?"

Maggie pointed to the kitchen, and Finley opened the bottle and poured two glasses just as someone knocked at the door. A busboy from the restaurant was at the door, holding a tray of food that he offered her. She thanked him and took the tray to the table, calling her mother over.

"It looks like Zoe sent enough food for the whole family," Finley said, uncovering plates.

"I told her to," Maggie said. "I'll make a little plate to bring home to your dad. And I made sure to give her enough to cover this. I don't want you guys to get kicked out for taking advantage of the food here."

"You don't want us back home?"

"Your dad and I are looking forward to getting back to an empty nest," Maggie said. "But don't tell Colin that. I don't want to hurt his feelings."

"Where is he moving to?"

Maggie shrugged. "He said he found a rental," she said. "I worry that he won't have any human contact once he moves there, but he's a grown up. I can't stop him."

"I'll try to talk to him," Finley said. "See if I can encourage him to get out more."

"Good luck," her mom said. "That would be like asking Desmond to stay in once in a while. He's off to play poker now?"

"Yes, he goes every week," Finley said. "It's rare that he's ever home at night. If he's not working, he finds something else to do."

"I heard he took your doctor friend last week," Maggie said.

"What? How did I not know this?"

Maggie laughed. "No idea. But he mentioned it to me and said they had a good time. Seems like he's settling into town finally."

"Desmond?"

"No, Dr. Lincoln," Maggie said. "Des told me that he's been in to the bar quite a few times and that he's been to poker with him. And JJ mentioned meeting him around town."

Finley nodded, her thoughts swirling. Was Evan socializing with Desmond and some of the other men from town? He hadn't mentioned anything, and even Des had been quiet about it. If he was getting out more, what else did that mean? Could he be dating? And why did the thought of that make her stomach spin?

Chapter 15

Evan had gotten back to his house close to midnight, much later than he had planned to be out. Unfortunately for him, he had kept winning at poker, extending his night. He hadn't joined the other men in the whiskey and beer offerings, which he credited the win to.

The concussion protocol he was following should have had him going to bed much earlier than he had, but it felt good to be making friends in town. He enjoyed their company, and it was the first time in his life he felt like he was fitting in.

He had slept later than usual, but without the ability to go for a run, he was still able to get to work on time. The morning passed uneventfully, and he probably would have worked through lunch if his stomach hadn't objected.

"Late lunch for you." The voice came from behind him, and he turned to find Finley in line to pay. Her tray held a simple salad and a bottle of water, the opposite of his burger, fries and coffee.

"It is," he said. "You too, I see."

"This was the best time for me to go," she said. "Busy morning."

"Everything going well?" he stepped forward in the line, then gestured for the cashier to include Finley's tray in his total.

"You don't have to do that," she objected.

"It's the least I can do considering how much you did for me over the weekend," he said. "As a matter of fact, I was hoping to run into you."

They carried their trays into the busy space, and Finley pointed to a table in the corner that was empty. He let her lead the way through the crowd and sat across from her.

"Why were you hoping to see me?"

"I was thinking that I'd like to do something to thank you," he said. "More than buying a salad. But I wasn't sure what you would like."

"You don't need to do anything," she said. "Honestly. I was glad to be there and to help."

"Your brothers were at poker last night," he said. He saw the question on her face and continued. "They had a lot of questions. Colin was sure you were the one to hit me, and Desmond thought I must have been hit hard enough to imagine you helping."

"Aren't they sweet?" She rolled her eyes as she asked.

"I mentioned it because I had thought I could get information out of them," he said. "But I think they were pulling my leg."

"Oh, no. What did they say?"

"Desmond told me that you collect dolls, the creepier the better," he said. "And Colin told me that you're a hardcore Brady Bunch fan. And that if I could get you a collectible lunch box, he was sure that would be perfect."

She leaned toward him, a glint in her eye. "If you really want to repay me, you'll make them disappear."

He laughed. "I had a feeling they were full of it."

"And then some," she said. "The doll would give me nightmares for weeks, and I haven't thought of the Brady Bunch for years. What would have even made Colin think of it?"

"Maybe he's the secret fan?"

"I think you just came up with the perfect Christmas gift idea," she said. "Maybe that will teach him."

"Okay, so those two ideas are off the table. Mike suggested I get you a gift card for a massage, which seemed too familiar."

"Were you planning to give me the massage yourself?"

He felt his cheeks blush at the thought and hoped she didn't notice. "Apparently, there is a spa at the mountain resort."

"I'm sure it's lovely, if Mike recommends it," she said. "That means that Natalie probably frequents it. And that it's too expensive a gift for me to accept."

"I'm not worried about the money, if you'd enjoy that," he said.

"No, that's okay. But thank you."

"That leads me back to square one," he said. "Where I have to just ask you how I can repay your kindness."

"Do you have plans this weekend?"

"None, other than resting," he said.

"If you're feeling better, maybe you could join me at the Harvest Festival?"

"That sounds nice," he said. "But how is that paying you back?"

"The first two hours, I'm volunteering at the First Aid tent," she said. "You can help me in there. And then we could walk around together?"

"That sounds perfect," he said.

"You say that now," she said, standing as she did. "But I'm officially putting you in charge of any vomit situations."

"Are there many?" He followed her to the trash can, holding on to his half-full coffee cup as he threw the rest away.

"I took the early shift on purpose," she said as they walked down the hall together. "Last year I had an afternoon one, and all I had were kids who had overdone it on the cotton candy and caramel apples. I'm hoping the morning will be quieter."

"Deal," he said. He held the door for her to enter their unit. "Should I pick you up?"

"I'll meet you here," she said. "A little before nine."

He watched as she walked away and couldn't help but feel a flash of excitement about the event. Whether it was being with Finley or being a part of a beloved local event, he wasn't sure. But it was something to look forward to either way.

Saturday morning, he was up earlier than usual. His headache was finally gone, and he felt better than he had in a week. He killed as much time as he could before he walked to town, over an hour early for when he would meet Finley. He grabbed a coffee and pastry to eat while he waited and chose a bench near the hustle on the town square. Watching all the vendors setting up for the day helped pass the time, since their excitement was palpable.

"Hey." He turned as he heard Finley's voice from behind him. She was dressed in jeans and a sweater with a down coat unzipped over it.

"Morning," he said. He held up the extra coffee he had. "This should still be hot. Or as hot as cream with a drop of coffee can be."

"Thanks," she said, smiling at him. "Nice of you to remember."

"I'll be honest, it's hard to forget," he said. "Let's not forget I went to medical school and should probably lecture you on the sugar intake in that drink alone."

"Let's forget it until after I have my caffeine," she suggested, winking at him. The smile it brought to his face was genuine, and he realized it did something else. That one little wink had his stomach flipping around, and he suddenly felt the need to reach for her hand. Which was highly inappropriate.

"Where are we set up?" he asked, pushing the other thoughts out of his head as he glanced around. The large tent was filled with everything from a dunk tank that would raise money for a local sports team, to vendors selling maple syrup and local wares, and food trucks along the outside.

"Over here," she said, pointing to a corner. "Last year we were too close to the rescue table, so they moved us a little."

"Too close to a rescue table? That doesn't make sense."

"Animal rescue," she explained. "Patrick Burrows sits there, and it causes quite a stir. I won't be surprised to find Liam and Natalie here as well, and that means all the vendors will do extremely well."

"Liam did mention something about the dunk tank at poker," Evan shared. "I didn't realize what he meant, but I think he's signed up to be a target."

"That will make the hockey team a lot of money if so," Finley said.

"That's what it is? Hockey?"

"Yes," Finley said. "Patrick's nephew plays on the team, so it doesn't surprise me that they would want to help out. Hockey is big up here, as I'm sure you can imagine."

"I'm sure," he murmured.

"Did you play?"

"Hockey?" At her nod, he laughed. "I don't even know how to ice skate. No, I never played. I really didn't play sports much. Ironically, when I did try soccer, I got a concussion. That's what turned me into a runner. I loved that part of the sport but not the headache. Plus, our parents didn't want to dedicate their weekends to taking us around, and running didn't require rides to practices."

"Us?" she asked, looking at him with interest. "Just you and one brother, right? You didn't say much about him the other day."

"Just the one," Evan said, keeping his tone light. "But we aren't like you guys."

"Now you're bragging," she said, laughing.

He laughed with her, surprised at the brevity she had brought. Maybe she sensed the tension that he felt when the subject came up. He helped her organize the bandages and quick-acting ice packs under the table, so they were all easy to reach. Once finished, he sat at the station alone when she said she would be right back. Within a few minutes, she returned holding a paper sack with steam coming out of the top.

"Here," she said, thrusting the bag at him. "You have to try this."

"What is it?"

"Hot apple cider donuts," she said. "I was able to get them before they officially opened for the day. They'll sell out by eleven, if not before."

He popped a small donut in his mouth and was surprised at the burst of flavor. Cinnamon and sugar mixed with apple, in a light and warm bite. "That's amazing."

"Isn't it?" she asked, pulling one out for herself. "They also sell full size by the dozen, but I would eat them all in one sitting. These bite-size ones are perfect."

"And gone too fast," he said, flipping the bag upside down.

"Should I run and get more?"

"No," he said. "Unless you want them. I'll save room for all the other delicious foods I can smell. I feel like I'll have to run a few miles tomorrow to make up for this."

An announcement overhead alerted vendors that the doors would be opening, and moments later, a sea of people entered the tent. Evan and Finley stayed busy for their two-hour slot, treating everything from blisters to a possible allergic reaction that they rushed out of the tent in an ambulance. Evan was surprised when the next two volunteers appeared, indicating their time was over.

"Want to walk around a bit?" Finley asked, tilting her head toward the booths.

"Sure," he agreed, happy to spend more time with her. They wandered the hallways, stopping so he could buy syrup, and she could purchase a knit scarf, before they found the crowd around the animal rescue table.

"Let's say hi to Emma," Finley said, pulling Evan around the crowd to meet the petite blond behind the table. He recognized her from Mike's living room and realized she was Patrick's girlfriend. Patrick was behind the table, signing autographs and holding puppies during pictures with fans.

"Hi," Emma said, hugging Finley before offering her hand to Evan. "I'm Emma. I know we've seen each other around, but I don't think we've been introduced."

"Nice to meet you," Evan said. Just as he let go of Emma's hand, the dog who had been lying at her feet stood and bumped his hand with his snout. He was midsize and looked like a mix of a black labrador retriever and something else, given the white spot he had on the crown of his head.

"Hey there, bud," Evan said, petting the dog's head.

"Sorry, he's struggling here," Emma said. "The crowds are freaking him out a little. He's been fostering with a local family because the shelter was too stressful, so we're really hoping to find him a home today."

"Want us to take him for a walk?" Finley asked, looking at Evan as she did.

"Sure, we can do that," he said, reaching for the leash. "If that's okay with you?"

"I'm sure he would be thrilled to get out of here for a while," Emma said with a grateful smile. "His name is Guinness."

"We'll be back," Finley said to Emma. She waved to Patrick, who had turned briefly to smile at them, before heading through the gap in the fence behind the table. She waved for Evan to follow her through. "If he's afraid of the crowd, this will be easier for him."

"Always looking to make your own way," he teased her as he ducked through.

"There's a time and place for rules," she said primly. "This isn't one of them. Look how much happier he is already."

True to her word, Guinness was looking better, sitting proudly on his leash as he took in the surroundings. They started walking away from the crowds, joining the slower traffic on the sidewalk to window shop. The stores and restaurants all had signs on the sidewalk indicating special offers for the weekend.

"This town really goes all out," Evan commented as they walked.

"They do," Finley agreed. "They do this a few times a year. It helps to bring in tourists and keeps the local businesses afloat. Before they started the festivals, people would maybe spend some money at the restaurants or a little at the stores, but most of it was spent at the ski resort. Or they would just drive through as they came to see the foliage. Now they spend the weekend and put a lot into our little economy."

"Brilliant," Evan said. The pet store had a fresh bowl of water outside, which Guinness was enjoying when the owner came out to say hello.

"Good morning, Finley," he said, offering his hand to Evan. "Ralph. I own the pet store here. I haven't seen you and this guy in. Is he new?"

"I'm Evan, and this is Guinness," he replied, shaking the other man's hand. "He's not mine. He was with the group at the shelter table and was having a hard time with the noise."

"Not yours yet, you mean," Ralph said with a laugh. "He looks like he claimed you."

Evan looked down to where the dog was leaning against his leg, looking up at him with what could only be described as a look of adoration. "I can't have a dog."

"You know how often I hear that?" Ralph asked with a laugh. "Every parent that comes in after a kid has convinced them."

"But I really can't," he said. "I'm a doctor. I am sometimes gone for twenty-four hours or more."

"Where do you live?" Ralph asked, nodding as Evan answered. "I know the street. My wife, Julie, is a realtor. She probably sold you the place. Lots of good families on that block, and some teenagers that I would trust to pet sit for me. I can give you a list."

"Des is home all day," Finley offered. "He could dog sit while he works."

"Maybe you should adopt him," Evan suggested, feeling the wheels come off even as he spoke.

"We live in an apartment," Finley said. "You have a fenced-in yard. He would be much happier there. And look how much he loves you already."

"Good luck," Ralph said, backing away. "And come in when you lose this battle, I'll get you set up with everything you need. We offer a discount to anyone who rescues an animal."

Evan stared at the dog, who was looking at him as if he was a wishbone. "I can't have a dog."

"Are you allergic?" Finley asked, starting to walk again.

"No."

"I don't see the problem," she said. "Ralph can get you linked up with people on the street for emergencies, and Des would happily take him during the day. It would be good for you to have the company."

His mind was spinning as they walked, Finley silent for once. Without allowing the thought to fully process, he stopped and spoke. "I'll do it if you'll have dinner with me."

Finley stopped a few steps ahead of him, and turned around. "Like a date?"

<h1 style="text-align:center">Chapter 16</h1>

Evan looked like a deer in the headlights but nodded. "Exactly. A date."

"You want to date me?" Finley was battling a wave of emotions. Excitement, uncertainty, and anticipation mixed with a healthy dose of self-doubt.

"Very much." He answered quietly, but with his eyes meeting hers in the steady way he had. "It surprises me as much as it does you. But the more time I spend with you, the more I want to. You're the first woman I've wanted to date in a long time, if I'm being honest."

"Me neither. I mean, I haven't wanted to date. Not that I wanted to date a woman. Not that there would be anything wrong with that. I'll stop talking now," she said, clapping a hand over her eyes, horrified at all she had said. She peeked out at him and saw him smiling. "Where would we go?"

"I'm going to have to ask my new friends for advice on that," he said, laughing. "I've only ever been to the Palace or picked up a pizza. But I'm sure there is somewhere that I can take you that's a little nicer. Maybe at the Inn?"

She shook her head quickly. "There is a small restaurant, but everyone would see us."

"Oh." He looked so disappointed in her words that she examined them quickly to see why.

"Oh, that's not what I meant," she said when it clicked. "I'm not embarrassed to be with you. I would just like a little privacy, maybe, before the entire town knows?"

"Finley, we're walking a dog around town together," he said. "I've already heard from twenty people this week about how nice it was that you took care of me last weekend. There's no keeping a secret here."

She laughed and nodded. "You're right. But let's still go somewhere else, at least so this first date can be just ours."

"Deal," he said. "When should we go?"

"Not tonight," she said. At the flash of disappointment on his face, she kept talking. "Kendra always hosts a small party after the festival. There is a garden behind the Palace, and it's pretty informal, but most of our friends will be there. I was going to tell you about it and ask if you wanted to go."

"Well, now I have a dog to think about," he said, glancing down at Guinness and then smiling at her.

"He can come," she said quickly. "It's all outside. And if he gets overwhelmed, you can put him up in my apartment."

"Sounds good," he said. "We have some time to kill between then and now."

"And lots of food to try," she said, leading him back toward the tent. "Let's see if Guinness can handle it now that he has a friend."

They stopped at the rescue table first, where a delighted Emma showed Evan the QR code to scan to begin the adoption process. "I'll vouch for you," she said. "That way you can take him right now. He wasn't doing great there, so we were really hoping to find him a home. If you hadn't come along, I would have made Patrick bring him home with us."

Patrick looked over, a pained expression on his face. "I can't thank you enough," he said. "I'm still dealing with rescue ducks. I can't have another animal right now."

"Ducks?" Finley asked, laughing as she looked at Emma.

"I'll explain later," Emma promised. "We'll see you tonight?"

"Yes," she said, nodding. "I'm hoping Patrick will be bringing a guitar?"

"He and Jake will be," Emma said. "It wouldn't be a festival weekend if we didn't get a private concert."

As they started walking away, Finley explained to Evan. "I don't know if you are aware, but Patrick is a fantastic singer. He has done Broadway, and his voice is amazing. And his brother Jake is just as good, if not better. They perform at the Palace a lot."

"I'm surprised they don't do more," Evan said. "Especially with Patrick's fame, it would be easy to put out an album."

Finley nodded. "I would think so too, and maybe they will one day. But Jake has only been back in town for a couple years now, after being in the military for a long time. He doesn't like crowds or loud noises, so it might be too much for him."

"PTSD?"

"Yes," Finley said. "He actually has a service dog now, so Guinness can make a friend tonight."

"Is that allowed? I thought they had to stay committed to the work?"

"They do," Finley said as they joined a line at a taco truck. "But Jake can tell the dog to play, as long as he knows the other dogs are friendly. He can't risk it getting hurt, but around animals he trusts, Rex can have fun when Jake isn't in distress."

"I've always wanted to know more," Evan said. "I see a lot of patients with emotional support animals, but not many with service dogs."

Finley ordered for both of them and tried to protest when Evan pulled out his wallet, but he was too quick. "I'll get the next one," she promised.

"You don't like people taking care of you," he commented. "It's interesting, considering what you do for a living."

"What do you mean?"

"Something that simple, letting me pay for the tacos, just threw you off."

"I just don't want you to feel like you have to," she explained. "I appreciate it that you do, but I do like being on an even playing field."

"We can do that," he said, his tone soft. "But I'd like to be able to treat you to things and not have it be an issue. Like when we go to dinner. Is that okay?"

Her brain flashed back to her last boyfriend, angrily shaking a receipt in her face. As she pushed it away, she looked into Evan's eyes and saw nothing but kindness. "Yes, that's fine. Thank you. But I'm still buying the caramel apples."

"Deal," he said. He fed a piece of beef from his taco to Guinness before taking a big bite.

They enjoyed several hours of eating their way around the food trucks before the dog started to look tired. "I'm thinking I should run to the pet store and let Ralph set me up with all the gear I need," he said. "And show this guy his new house. Do you want to come with me?"

"Why don't I meet you back at the Palace in a couple hours?" she suggested. "I'd love to take a shower and warm up for a bit. But I can come help you carry everything home first, if you want."

"No, that's fine," he said. "I'll just take the basics and see if he can get the rest delivered later. Worst case, I'll drive back when I am meeting you and can load up the car then."

"Okay," she said, hesitating where he would turn one way and her go the other. "I'll see you later?"

"I'll be there," he promised. And as hard as it was, she realized she believed him. Without even recognizing it, he had become someone whose word she trusted. That was worth puzzling over for the next few hours.

***

Finley made sure to arrive early at the party outside, where Des was working behind the bar. He grinned at her when she appeared. "What's up, sis?"

"How did you score this gig?" she asked, leaning on the bar.

"It helps to be the owners favorite," he said. "And I asked. I'd rather be out here having fun with my friends, even though inside will be busier with all the tourists."

"You'll make more money here, I would guess," Finley said.

"I don't even care about the money," he said. "This just gives me a chance to hang out. What can I get you?"

She glanced around the area, recognizing most of the faces, but not seeing Evan among them. "Nothing yet," she said to her brother.

"Who are you looking for?"

"Evan," she answered without thinking. When his face lit up with a grin, she realized her mistake and tried to backtrack. "It's not a big deal. Don't make it into something it's not."

"I like him," Desmond declared. "Far better than that last loser you stayed with for far too long."

"The greedy one?" Colin's voice came from behind her, and she spun around.

"He wasn't greedy," she said. "He was happy to spend money on me."

"And then hold it over your head," Des said. "The number of times I heard that creep tell me how much he had spent on you. He couldn't just buy you flowers, he had to tell me how much they were. As if that bought your undying loyalty. And mine."

"See? Not greedy," Finley said, smirking at her brothers. "Full of himself. Controlling. Not a great person. And a braggart. But not greedy."

They shrugged and started talking amongst themselves as she turned back to the garden. As she did, she saw Evan enter through the gate. He had Guinness at his side, and was glancing around, looking unsure of himself. He was normally so self-assured at work, it was unusual to see him off his game. JJ greeted him with a handshake, and she watched as Evan said hello to the other regular poker players. They gestured to an empty chair in their cluster, but he shook his head, glancing around until his eyes found hers.

The relief in his eyes was easy to spot, even from their distance apart. She picked up the two wine glasses that Desmond had poured and made her way to where he stood. The dog greeted her enthusiastically, making her laugh as she passed Evan a glass so she could pet Guinness.

"You would think we hadn't seen each other in months," she said to the dog.

"It feels that way," Evan responded softly, making her heart jump. The sudden shift in their relationship was making her dizzy, but now it was with anticipation, rather than nerves.

"How did you make out at the pet store?" She asked, needing to get back on regular footing before she did something she would regret.

"Not as well as Ralph, I'm afraid." At her confused look, he laughed. "I think I helped him meet his sales goals for the next three months. We have quite the setup going at home. And Guinness ignored it all and jumped right onto my couch, so we're going to have to work on that."

"Are you the type to get upset about pets on furniture?"

"I don't know," Evan said, his brow furrowed as he looked at the dog. "He's my first. But I know for sure that we will not be sharing a bed."

"No?" Was it getting hot in here? What was wrong with her?

He pushed his glasses up on his nose and met her gaze in his steady, serious way. "I'm not saying I prefer to sleep alone.

But I think the dog should stay on his bed. Or the crate that Ralph sold me."

"Gotcha," she said, taking a large sip of her wine. Her cheeks were flaming red, which he clearly noted based on his soft laugh. "Should we sit?"

At his nod, she led him to a small group of Adirondack chairs that were empty. Most of the crowd was clustered around where the three movie stars were sitting. Finley knew once the newcomers got their pictures with them, things would settle down, but it bought them some time and space from the crowd. At least it would have, if her brothers hadn't followed her and taken the empty seats.

"Hey," JJ said, grinning at her. "What's up?"

"Go away."

"I could probably arrest you for that," he warned her.

"What would the charge be?" Colin asked.

"Disorderly? Not obeying an officer?" JJ said, holding up fingers as he talked.

"Knock it off," Zoe's voice came from behind Finley as she came into the circle, taking a seat on JJ's lap and kissing him.

"You guys are gross," Colin said, rolling his eyes.

"I'll arrest you too," JJ threatened.

"You will not," Zoe laughed. "What's going on? The food will be out any minute."

"We were just going to get to the bottom of what's happening between Fin and the good doctor," JJ said. Zoe gasped and put her hand over his mouth before looking at Evan.

"I'm so sorry," she said. "He can't help himself. He's impulsive, and random words just come out without even thinking."

"That's how I got you to marry me," JJ reminded her. "And I'm not sorry. Better we all be on the same page, than to have people wondering for months if they're actually dating or not."

"He's talking about himself," Colin said to Evan. "Zoe made him work for it."

"She was worth it," JJ said, earning himself another kiss from his wife. "Now, back to you two."

Finley sighed. "We just barely started enjoying each other's company and not wanting to rip the other person's face off. Maybe you can let us figure it out."

"Face or clothes?" Colin asked, glancing between Finly and Evan.

"This is where I'll remind you that I'm your little sister," Finley said, scowling at him. "And you're being wildly inappropriate."

"I think it's better that we remind Evan that you're our little sister," Colin said, his tone light even though his expression was the opposite.

"You finally emerged from your self-imposed prison sentence just to torture me?" Finley snapped, causing JJ to laugh.

Waiters carrying trays of food came from the kitchen and began filling the buffet tables. Zoe stood and gestured for JJ to do the same. "Go, you two. You know you want first dibs on the food." She watched as JJ and Colin raced each other across the small patch of grass before turning back to Finley and Evan. "I'm so sorry. They have no manners. As the newest member of this family, Evan, I will warn you that it's always like this. But they are as fun and loving as they are intrusive and protective. Don't be afraid to tell them to butt out."

"Thank you," Evan said. Zoe stood again to join her husband, leaving Finley and Evan alone again.

"I'm so sorry," she said. "They are a nightmare."

"I think it's nice," Evan said. He reached for her hand, holding it lightly on the armrest of her chair. "They want to look out for you. And if it's not clear, my intention is to date you. Not just dinner one night as a thank you for all you did for me, I would like to see where this can go. I hope you feel the same."

"Shoot," Finley said with a sigh.

"It's not?" Evan asked, a concerned look on his face as he tried to pull his hand back.

She held tight, lacing her fingers with his, rather than let go. "I just hate that I have to admit my brother was right. It's nice to be upfront and clear on this."

He smiled at her, relief on his face, and she grinned back. She never would have thought that she would be hanging out with him, never mind looking forward to more time together, when they first met. All she had wanted was to be as far from him as possible, and now all she wanted was the exact opposite.

Chapter 17

A week after the Harvest Festival, Evan was finally prepping for his date with Finley. They had spent all week at work chatting over lunches in the cafeteria, flirting in the hallways, and even had dinner together at the bar one night. But both had agreed that it wasn't a date, since they had met up there in scrubs and with no forethought. Tonight would be different, and the thrum of anticipation all week was at its highest now.

He was in the process of changing his clothes for the third time when his cell phone rang. The screen showed a Vermont number that he didn't recognize, but worrying it was a patient or another doctor, he answered quickly. "Hello?"

"Hey." Zach's voice came through the phone. "Don't hang up."

"Why are you calling me? And how did you get it so that it looks like you're calling from Vermont?"

"Because I am," he said. "I rented an Airbnb. I wasn't sure how long it would take for you to talk to me, but I plan to stick around until you do."

"Zach," Evan sighed, sitting down in the chair in his bedroom. "Don't do this to me. We're both better off without contact."

"We aren't," Zach said. "I know I screwed up. I know I don't deserve your forgiveness. But I'm asking for a chance to prove that I've changed."

Evan's head dropped at his brother's words. He knew exactly what buttons to push to cut through Evan's armor and would undoubtedly make him regret any decision he made right now. "Let me think about it," he said finally. "I have to go."

"Okay, so not tonight," Zach said, sounding disappointed. "Tomorrow?"

"I said I'd think about it," Evan snapped. "You have no right to do this. Come to my town and push me, when I have told you how I felt."

"You did. But I haven't been able to tell you anything," Zach said, infuriatingly calm. "I know I'm pushing you, but there's a good reason. Meet me tomorrow."

"I'll text you when I decide." Evan hung up and threw the phone onto his bed, furious. He had been looking forward to his date with Finley all day, and now this dark cloud was overhead. As if sensing the tension, Guinness came into the room and pushed his head under Evan's hand.

Evan stared into space as he rubbed the dogs' ears, flashing back several years to when he had last seen his brother. It had started much like this, with Zach appearing and wanting to be in Evan's life. Evan had been foolish enough to welcome him in with open arms and had learned to regret the decision. This time, he would be more cautious, if he chose to talk to him at all.

Glancing at his watch, he saw he was going to be late if he didn't get moving. Realizing he was still only half dressed, he pulled a sweater out of the back of his closet and was finally satisfied with his outfit . Or so distracted with his brother that he could be walking out looking like the mess he felt like on the inside, but he pushed the thought aside and got Guinness set for an evening alone before racing to his car.

When he pulled into the small parking lot behind the Palace, where Finley had directed him, he could see how busy the restaurant was. As he climbed the stairs to her apartment, he was glad he had asked his new friends for recommendations and settled on a quieter spot just outside of town.

The door opened just after he knocked, and Finley stood there, taking his breath away. She was wearing a short black dress and heels, her hair curling around her bare shoulders. It was simple, and yet so different from how he usually saw her, it caught him off guard. "You look amazing," he said, kissing her on the cheek. "Not that you don't usually. But this is much different than scrubs."

"Thanks," she said with a laugh. "I spent hours getting ready, unlike the ten minutes I take before work. So, I appreciate the reaction. You look pretty fantastic yourself. I've never seen you without glasses before."

"Contacts," he said, gesturing to his face and feeling self-conscious. "I don't wear them often."

She studied his face and then smiled slowly. "Then I'm honored," she said. "Should we go?"

"Do you need a jacket?"

"Oh, yes," she said, laughing softly. "You have me flustered."

He helped her into a knee-length wool coat, which she cinched at the waist before grabbing a small purse from the kitchen chair. After opening the door for her, he found himself nearly pressed up against her on the small landing while she locked it behind them. Once she finished, he held her hand as she walked down the stairs gingerly.

"Sorry, I'm not used to heels," she said. "Zoe insisted on helping me get ready and said you were plenty tall enough, so I should wear them. I have learned not to ask questions when she has a certain tone."

"I can see that," he said, opening the car door for her. "She is a force."

"She has to be, to keep my brother in line," Finley said. He closed the door and hurried around to the driver's side, anxious to be next to her again. The feeling was so new and unexpected, it was almost overwhelming. He was trying to caution himself to proceed slowly so as not to freak her out or get too far ahead of himself. Unfortunately, his body was not listening to his brain when it came to Finley.

"Where are we going?" She asked, turning to face him in the seat.

"Patrick recommended a restaurant in Stowe," he replied. "He said it's small and quiet, and when I called for a reservation, they were so happy to hear I was his friend they promised a great table. I hope I'm not a disappointment when we arrive."

"I'm sure you won't be," she said. "I'm excited. I haven't explored Vermont as much as I should."

"How long have you been here?"

"A little over a year," she said. "Des and I decided to come when our parents moved up. I had recently stopped travel nursing and was looking to settle into one place but couldn't quite find the right fit. We came to visit one weekend, and both loved it. I took a travel position for six weeks so I could make the move without fully committing. But once I saw the job posting for oncology, that was it. I already loved the hospital and knew that was the job I wanted. It was lonely being the only ones in Massachusetts, we both decided we wanted to be closer to everyone."

"Where was Colin?"

"Who knows," Finley said, shrugging. "We rarely know. And it's not like he is the type to check on us regularly or want us to stop in on him. We are close with our parents and JJ, and it made sense to come."

"You're happy with the decision?"

"Very much," she said. "I never knew a town like this existed. I'm so lucky that I was able to find a job I love, and to settle in so easily. Everyone has been so nice."

Evan pulled into a hidden parking lot behind a building exactly like Patrick had described. If he hadn't been looking for it, he would have missed the restaurant entirely. It looked like a small house, but the smells coming from it were enough to know his friend hadn't steered him wrong.

"This is so cute," Finley whispered as he opened the door to the building for her.

"Good evening." A well-dressed woman was right inside the doorway, as if she was waiting for them. "You must be Dr. Lincoln?"

"Yes," he said, glancing over at Finley and seeing that she was as surprised as he was that the hostess could identify him immediately.

"Come this way," the woman said, leading them to a small table by a window. There were four other tables in the same room, but they were spaced out and walls of plants and flowers separated each. Quiet, romantic music played overhead, making it impossible to hear any other conversations around them and setting the mood. Evan helped Finley remove her jacket, which the hostess offered to hang for them before disappearing.

"Wow," Evan said. "Patrick didn't tell me all of this."

A short, stocky man appeared suddenly, offering his hand to Evan. "Wyatt," he said simply as they shook. "Thanks for coming in."

"We're already impressed with what you've done here," Evan said. The white jacket Wyatt wore indicated he was the chef, and Evan had been told that he was also the owner of the establishment.

"It's so beautiful," Finley said, smiling at Wyatt.

"Thank you," Wyatt said, starting to back away from their table. "I'll leave you to it. If you need anything from me, don't hesitate to ask them to get me."

"I guess it helps to have well-known friends," Evan said quietly to Finley, leaning across the table to say it as softly as possible.

"I have a feeling he genuinely cares about everyone who dines here," Finley said, equally quiet. "He couldn't make a place this small and out of the way work if he didn't."

"True," Evan said, leaning back when the waitress appeared.

After ordering a bottle of wine to share, they perused the menu. It was small and clearly thoughtfully planned out with fresh ingredients each day, and they debated their options before telling the waitress their choices. Once she was gone again, Evan took Finley's hand on top of the table. "I'm glad we finally got here."

"To the restaurant or this point in time?"

"Time," he said, smiling at her. "Although the food sounds worth it too."

"I agree," she said. "On both. If you had told me a month ago that I would be nervous about a date with you, I would have said you were insane."

"You were nervous?"

"You weren't?"

"True," he said, laughing. "I wish we hadn't gotten off to such a bad start."

"I don't know," she said. "In some ways, I'm glad."

He waited while the wine was poured, and a basket of warm artisan bread was put on the table before continuing the conversation. "Why?"

"It forced me to get to know you as a professional, and then as a person, and not just on your looks," she said.

"I'm glad for that," he said. "You never would have gone out with someone like me just based on looks."

"Are you nuts?" she asked, laughing. "Have you seen yourself?"

"I'm skinny and have always been a nerd," he said. "I fail to see how that impresses."

"Evan." He looked up when she didn't continue, seeing the serious expression on her face. "I shouldn't tell you this, because you might decide to drop me and run off with someone else. But you are gorgeous. There is nothing wrong with how you look."

He stared at her in shock, unused to getting such a compliment. "Thanks."

"No, really," she persisted. "Why would you think anything else?"

"Growing up, I was a nerd," he said. "Certifiable, unequivocally, nerd. I was valedictorian. I was always the teacher's favorite. My clothes never matched or fit half the time, but I didn't care because I was too busy solving an equation. Plus, I was so socially awkward, it was easier to hide in plain sight and not think about how I looked. My hair is always too long or too short, and I have no idea what is fashionable. I'm still unsure of myself, if I'm being honest. I worry all the time that I'm saying or doing the wrong thing."

She laughed and squeezed his hand. "What I hear is that you're incredibly smart, and not full of yourself. You care about the people around you, but you shouldn't worry about what they think. Especially not about superficial things. Not being full of yourself is a good thing, in my book."

"Huh," he said, leaning back in his chair and smiling at her. "Who would have thought that?"

"Don't let it get to your head," she cautioned him. "As a matter of fact, forget I said anything. I don't need you to go out exploring this new discovery."

"Are you kidding? When I've finally got you to have dinner with me?" he asked, leaning forward again. "I have to tell you, I was intimidated by you. You're so beautiful, and so confident. When I first started at the hospital, I was afraid to even talk to you."

"And then you told me to stop talking," she said, her tone teasing.

"Not like that," he said. "You clearly misunderstood me."

"Would you care to explain now?"

The waitress reappeared with their first course, and he took the moment to get his brain on track. This wasn't about his thoughts of himself, or his poor communication with her at work. He wanted to use this time to see if they actually had common ground they could build on.

"Actually, no," he said. "I'd rather not talk about that. Or work. I really do want to get to know you better."

"With anyone else, I would think that was a line," she said. "But I believe you."

"I know your brothers," he said. "Based on all of you, I assume your parents are happy and well-adjusted people."

She laughed. "Yes, that's one way to describe them. They've been married for a lot of years, and they either want to kill each other or they are madly in love. There's no in between with them."

"That sounds like a roller coaster."

"A little bit," she said, her face pensive. "But it's all passion, you know? Even when they're fighting, they're not mean. It's because they love each other and they get frustrated when the other person doesn't agree or follow what they're saying. But it's always fiery, and we never worried about them breaking up. It sounds like yours are different. Are they still alive?"

"They are," he said, nodding. "My mother lives in San Francisco, where she runs an art gallery, so she spends all her time schmoozing with big names. My father founded an investment company that he still runs today, although he has a full team to delegate to. But I think he likes the control and being busy. They divorced after we graduated. It's like they just looked over one day, realized they were alone, and they could finally go in their own directions. My father is living the bachelor life in Arizona. Both still working like crazy and prioritizing that over anything or anyone else."

"I'm sorry," she said softly. "I can't imagine feeling that way."

He shrugged. "We got used to it."

"You've said we a few times," she said. "And yet you don't have a relationship with your brother at all?"

"No," he said, battling the feelings he had about Zach. "Not for a few years now. Before that, we were either best friends or not speaking at all. It was a constant roller coaster, but for a long time, he was all I had, so I stayed on. I tried to leave it behind when I moved to Boston, but he showed up one day. Said he really wanted to be a part of my life, so I let my guard down, and he was just there to make a fool of me."

"Do you want to talk about it?"

"No," he said, shaking his head. "Not tonight. I want to talk about you, and us. Tell me your favorite movie or book. What was your favorite subject in school?"

She answered, carrying the conversation while he battled with his feelings. When he forced his thoughts back on her, she smiled at him kindly. "I'm sorry. I feel like I upset you asking about your brother."

"No, I'm the one who's sorry," he said. "I'm in my head. I don't know how to shake this."

"I love this song. Will you dance with me?" She stood as she asked and held out a hand. She was so beautiful, and the excuse to hold her close to him had him jumping to his feet where he would normally have blamed his two left feet.

When she came into his arms and rested her head on his shoulder, something inside of him settled. It was like a piece put into place exactly where it should be, making him feel more of something he had never felt before. As they danced slowly to the soft music overhead, amid the flowers and soft lights of the restaurant, he realized how far he had fallen in such a short time.

Chapter 18

The drive home from the restaurant was quieter than the dinner had been, or the ride to the neighboring town. Finley could feel a thrill of excitement running through her, like a current of electricity. The brief touches that she had shared with Evan over the last week had her more than ready for something more, but she also knew she shouldn't rush things. For now, the heat of his hand, heavy in hers on the console, was thrilling. The idea of more was making her feel hot and slightly nervous, and she couldn't put her finger on where the nerves were coming from.

He parked behind the bar, which was still hopping with a crowd, and walked around to open her door. After offering her a hand, he walked toward the stairs with her, moving his hand to the small of her back as they climbed the stairs. She could feel the pressure, light but burning, as she walked and debated what to do.

"Thank you for tonight," he said, his voice husky, as they got to the top of the stairs.

"I should be thanking you," she said. Her keys were in her hand as she turned, finding him close behind her. "Dinner was amazing. Everything was amazing."

He stared at her, his eyes warm. They dropped to her lips before meeting her eyes again, and she realized he was nervous. She stepped closer, tilting her chin up toward him. With the heels she was wearing, they were closer in height, and she could feel his breath on her forehead. As she looked up at him, he slowly lowered his lips to hers.

Her breath left her body, and her knees felt weak. She leaned into him more, feeling his arms slip around her as the kiss deepened. Her own hands found their way around his waist, and she could feel his strength through the thin sweater he wore.

Just as she was about to invite him in, he stepped back, throwing her off balance. "Oh, I'm sorry," he said, helping her steady herself. "I should go. I don't want to, but I need to."

"Why?" She couldn't help the petulant tone that came with the question. Kissing him had been like being offered a bite of a candy bar, and then having the rest snatched away.

He brushed a piece of hair off her face and tucked it behind her ear before gently kissing her on the forehead. Her eyes drifted closed as he did, allowing her to savor the moment. Then he pulled away, leaning down to pick up the keys that must have slipped from her hand when they started. He found the right key for the door and unlocked it, opening it slightly for her.

"I'll call you tomorrow," he promised.

She stretched up on her toes to steal one last kiss, wishing she could convince him for more, but knowing he was right. "Thank you for the best night I've had in a long time."

"Right back at you," he said, winking at her as he started to pull the door closed.

She stood in the kitchen, hugging herself, for so long she would have been embarrassed if anyone had seen her. Going into the date, she had expected to have fun, get to know him better, and maybe be excited for a second. She had not anticipated this.

He had been sweet, funny, and vulnerable even. And had actually listened when she talked, which was so rare, she was shocked by it. Most guys seemed to get glassy-eyed when she shared her favorite books, but Evan had asked questions and even added one to his Amazon cart to order. She felt like she had made a new best friend, only this was also someone she was physically attracted to. Almost to the point of distraction, she realized, glad again that he had shown restraint where she was lacking.

As she slipped off the high heels to walk into her bedroom, she smiled again. If this was what JJ had felt for Zoe, no wonder he had rushed off to Vegas to marry her. Finley was shocked to find herself thinking far down the road with Evan, something she rarely let herself do after just one date. But there was no harm in hoping for sweet dreams, right?

***

"How was your night?" Finley was seated at the island in her brother's new house, watching as Zoe cooked dinner when her sister-in-law asked the question. Their Sunday evening get-togethers had become regular lately, allowing the whole family to spend time together. Zoe hosted more often than not, so everyone got to enjoy her cooking. No one had wanted to tell Maggie Monahan that they preferred the food at JJ and Zoe's, but she had given up the hosting gig without a fight.

Zoe was dressed casually in yoga pants and a long sweater, her hair pulled into a bun as she stirred a sauce on the stove. She had dark circles under her eyes and looked paler than usual, causing Finley concern when she had first arrived. She had waited until they were alone to bring it up, not wanting to worry JJ. "First, are you okay? You look exhausted."

"I'm fine," Zoe said. "Just a little tired. The pollen always gets me this time of year."

"Are you sure? When was the last time you saw a doctor?"

"Two weeks ago," Zoe said. "Stop worrying. I'm fine. Now tell me about your date."

"As long as you promise to tell me if you aren't feeling better in a few days," Finley said. At Zoe's nod, she continued. "It was amazing. The best first date I've ever been on."

"Really? Tell me more."

165

"He was romantic and sweet, funny and kind. And he listened like I was the smartest person he's ever met," Finley shared. "And he went to Harvard, so we know that's not true."

"People can be smart in different ways," Zoe replied. "Don't put yourself down."

"True, sorry," Finley said. "But, Zo? I'm crazy about him. And now what do I do?"

Zoe grinned at her. "Oh, I like this. What do you mean, what do you do? You fall in love. You find out more about each other, and you fall deeper."

"That seems like a big jump," Finley said.

"Is it, though? That's the goal, if you want to be married and have a family," Zoe said. "Obviously, it's fine if that's not what you want. But if you want a partner, you want someone who you're crazy for."

"Like you are JJ."

"Yes," Zoe said. She put the spoon down on the rest next to the stove and moved to lean on the counter across from Finley. "I denied it for a long time, but I fell for him fast. It didn't feel real to me, because I had known nothing like it before. Luckily, he believed in us enough for us both. He just kept pushing me oh so gently in the right direction."

"I don't even need to be pushed," Finley said. "I practically dragged him into my bedroom and locked him up to keep."

"Did you now?" Zoe raised an eyebrow and looked at her until Finley laughed.

"Trust me when I say I wanted to," Finley said. "But he didn't want to rush things. And he was right. If we fell into bed together on night one, and then things fell apart, it would make it hard at work."

"And how will it go, working together? Have you thought about that?"

"No," Finley admitted. "I should, though. We do work closely together, and it could get messy. I'll have to give it some thought."

"I'm happy for you," Zoe said. "I know you haven't wanted to admit it, but I felt like you were lonely."

Finley considered the words as she sipped her wine. Had she been? She had never considered the possibility before, but now that Zoe had said it, she had to admit it was true. "I guess I was. I haven't dated since I came here. My last relationship was a mess, and the boys all hated him. And then when I came here, I was starting all over with everything. New job, new friends, and not a lot of dating prospects."

"You weren't ready," Zoe said. "There are plenty of options, but you weren't looking."

"I guess that's true," Finely said. "And living with Des is fun, but he's never there. So, I guess you can say that I have been alone a lot."

"You can be alone and not lonely," Zoe said. "And the opposite as well. It's nice to see you coming into your own."

Finley said hello to Colin as he wandered through the kitchen, following the sounds of JJ and Desmond watching football. Zoe shook her head as he left the room. "What?" Finley asked.

"He's the perfect example," she said.

"Of what?" Finley looked at the door that Colin had vanished through while she waited for Zoe to answer.

"He's both lonely and alone," Zoe said. "We need to snap him out of it. That's why I told JJ to start these family nights. Force him to be out and socialize with people."

"I wish I knew why he was so miserable," Finley said.

"It's always a woman," Zoe said. "Someone broke his heart, and he's not ready to tell anyone."

"He'll never tell us," Finley predicted. "He's always been a closed book."

"Let's go back to talking about you," Zoe said. She moved back to the stove after checking the contents of the double oven.

"Or about Evan," Finley said, feeling the butterflies start up again at the thought of him.

"How did you guys leave it?"

"We talked this morning," Finley shared. "He called me early to say he was thinking about me. I debated inviting him to dinner but thought it might be too soon."

"For this crew, yes," Zoe said with a laugh. "Maybe give him a little time before you plunge him into the deep end."

"Everyone has met him, other than my parents," Finley pointed out. "And you know they'll be nice."

"I'm not worried about your parents," Zoe said. "I'm worried about the inquisition that will take place when you put him in a room with your three brothers."

"I think he's capable of holding his own," Finley said. "But we'll wait until we get through at least two dates before I do that."

"Sounds good," Zoe said. "And reasonable. Nice to see that someone in this family understands how to take things slow."

"I heard that," JJ said as he came into the kitchen. He circled the island to embrace his wife, making her laugh when he nipped at her neck. "You loved me from the first moment. You couldn't imagine living without me."

"Thankfully, you have only made me think about that possibility once," Zoe said. "Never do that again."

"I'll try my best," JJ quipped. "The boys have sent me in for sustenance."

Zoe pulled a charcuterie board already loaded with meats, cheese, crackers and nuts from the refrigerator and passed it to

JJ, patting him on the bottom as he left the room with it. "I'll return that later," JJ promised, winking at his wife.

"Do you guys have to be so gloriously happy all the time?" Finley asked, laughing. "Now all I can think about is running as fast as I can to Evan's house."

"No, slow and steady is better," Zoe advised her. "Enjoy this. The first few months, when everything is magical and new, can never be repeated."

"You don't think so?" Finley asked, just as her mother entered the room.

"Think what?" her mom asked. Maggie kissed Finley on the cheek and then Zoe. Her dad, Tim, followed suit before disappearing to watch the game with the boys.

"That the first days of falling in love can never be felt again, so they should be savored," Zoe said.

"Oh, I don't know about that," Maggie said. "I think you have different phases of life, and you have chances to have those feelings during each other them."

"What do you mean?" Zoe asked, looking perplexed.

"The first time I saw your father hold JJ," Maggie explained. "I fell even more deeply in love. It was unlike anything I had ever experienced before. Seeing him hold the baby we had created together, a product of our love, was beyond my imagination. And then it happened again and again, as the rest of you came along. Then we had different phases where it happens again, even now."

"Let's spare us the details," Finley said with a laugh. "But that's nice to hear."

"And I'm glad to hear that you're experiencing some firsts yourself," Maggie said. "I take it the date went well?"

Finley gave her mother the shortened version of the night before, leaving out many of the details she had shared with Zoe.

Her mom beamed at her, looking as though she was on the verge of tears. "Mom, why are you crying?"

"I'm not," Maggie sniffled. "I'm just so happy."

"It was just one date," Finley cautioned her mom.

"Hey Mom," Desmond said as he came into the room. "Dad sent me to get him a drink."

"Your father is capable of walking in here on his own," Maggie said with a laugh.

"Yes, but the game is about to go into overtime, and he said you made him late," Des shared. "Don't shoot the messenger."

"We'll come join you," Zoe said, taking off her apron.

Her dad and brothers were all on the edge of their seats, watching the Patriots game on the TV. Zoe was pulled onto JJ's lap, leaving the middle seat on the couch and a club chair open. Finley hustled to the chair, letting her mom sit between her brothers.

"This is nice," she said, stretching her arms around Desmond and Colin. "What's new with you two?"

"You live with me," Colin said.

"Not much longer," Maggie said. "And then what will I do?"

"You're moving?" JJ asked Colin.

He nodded and then put an almond in his mouth, indicating the end of the subject. Desmond laughed, causing Colin to scowl. "Don't share the details, whatever you do."

"I'm renting a place," Colin said. "What more do you need to know?"

"What if I need to find you in the middle of the night? And I don't have your address?"

"Why would you need to?" Colin shot back.

"I don't know," Desmond said, rolling his eyes. "Maybe our brother, the cop, gets shot."

"Don't even put that out in the universe," Zoe said. "Once is enough."

"Agreed," Tim said.

"What if I meet gorgeous twins who will only go out with handsome brothers?"

"I'm not dating," Colin said.

"Well, that settles it," JJ said. "Colin can go live in his cave alone."

"Go easy on your brother," Maggie said. Colin stuck out his tongue at JJ, earning him a light slap on the back of his head from his mother.

"Let's go eat," Zoe said. The ref on the screen blew the whistle, and everyone looked happy, so Finley assumed the game was over. As much as she loved the time with her family, she was anxious to go to sleep. The faster she did, the sooner she would see Evan at work.

Chapter 19

It was amazing how quickly seeing Finley had become a priority, as much as air to breathe and water to drink. He had missed her on Sunday when she spent time with her family, and he had resisted the urge to cancel his poker night to see her on Monday. He knew he had to hold himself back a little and still focus on the new friendships he was making in town. Fortunately, she seemed equally eager to spend time with him, and they were on their second night in a row of spending time together. The night before, he had taken her to the small restaurant at the Inn, and they had just enjoyed a quiet dinner at his house. He wasn't much of a cook, so he had picked up heat-and-serve meals from Palace Plates. If Finley had noticed her sister-in-law's touch on the meal, she had refrained from saying anything.

They settled on his couch after the meal, Finley scrolling through a streaming service to find a movie they could agree on. Her feet were on his lap, and he knew he was far gone when he realized how much he appreciated massaging them. If touching her feet was this exciting, he had a lot to look forward to.

He was hiding a smile when Finley looked at him. "What?"

"I was just thinking how much I'm enjoying your feet," Evan said. "And how it bodes well for the future."

She laughed. "And if how much I'm enjoying this foot rub is an indication, I'm excited about that future."

Evan's phone rang, and he silenced it quickly. His brother had been calling and texting incessantly, and he knew he would have to deal with it soon. Just not tonight.

"Who was that?" Finley asked, watching him in the way that made him feel like she could see right through him.

"No one," he said quickly, hoping she would let it go.

"It can't be nothing," she said. "Your expression tells me that it's something upsetting."

"It's a little scary that you can read me so well already," Evan said softly.

She pulled her feet away and kneeled on the sofa between them, kissing him softly. With one smooth move, she pulled him back with her, so his head rested in her lap. With one hand on his chest and the other playing with his hair, relaxing him more than he would have ever thought possible, she sat in silence for a moment. "Please tell me," she said, her voice so soft he barely heard her.

Sensing that secrets were a problem for her, even when the subject didn't affect her, he decided to spill. She would find out eventually anyway, knowing Zach. "It was my brother."

"And you don't want to talk to him?"

"No," he admitted. "I really, really don't."

"Why not?"

"I wish I could explain it in a way that doesn't make me sound like a petulant brat," he said. "But unfortunately, that's not possible. If I simplify and say that he did me very wrong, and I'm not ready to forgive him, would that be enough?"

"You don't have to tell me any details," she said. "I just don't want to have secrets or withheld information getting between us. Obviously, we're still in the early phases, and if you'd rather wait to tell me, I won't be insulted. But if you want to talk about it, I'm here."

"Thank you," he said. His eyes were closed so he could enjoy the sensation of her hand in his hair, but he opened them to look at her. "He's here."

"Here, as in the house?" She glanced around, startled.

"No, in Vermont. In Windsor Peak, I think," he said. "He called me last weekend and said he was staying until I talked to him."

"Oh." She bit her lip, looking deep in thought. "I suppose that makes things a bit more challenging. You know what my mom told me once?"

"What?"

"If you dread something, do it quickly. It's like ripping off a Band-Aid, the more you think about it, the more you fear it. Sometimes you just have to force yourself to do the opposite of what you want to do," she said. "And as terrible as it feels at the time, you end up feeling better when it's done. It's usually not nearly as bad as you thought."

"Oh, this will be," he said.

"Bite the bullet," she said. "If you get hurt in the process, I'll be there to kiss it and make it all better."

"Promise?" he asked, smiling up at her.

"Do you need a preview?"

"I'm afraid I do," he said. "I'm the type that works best with examples."

***

Early on Saturday morning, Evan clipped a leash on Guinness and headed to town. He had texted his brother the location and time to meet and had barely slept the night before in anticipation. Finley had tried to ease his nerves over dinner at the Palace the night before, but he had left her early, too anxious to enjoy the night together. He had promised her he would get this over with so they could enjoy the day together, and that was what kept his feet moving.

Zach was already sitting at the table outside the coffee shop, two mugs on the table. He stood when Evan approached and then took a step back at the sight of Guinness. "Is that your guard dog?"

"Do I need one?" Evan said, his tone snippy. He told himself to calm down as he sat, Guinness lying at his feet.

"No, I just never thought you would have a dog," Zach said. "I'm surprised."

"Glad I could surprise you for once," Evan said. "Let's get this over with."

"Ev," Zach said with a sigh. "I know you've heard it all before. I know you have no reason to believe me when I say I'm sorry, but I am. I truly am."

Zach was thinner than when Evan had last seen him, and his dark hair was neatly trimmed for a change. He had scruff on his face, but it looked like he maintained it. The clarity in his eyes was what caused Evan to consider his brother's words. It gave him pause, seeing him like this. "What's different?"

Zach took a deep breath and crossed his arms on the table, as if protecting himself. "I'm sober."

"For how long?" Evan saw the hurt in his brother's eyes but had to ask. He had to know.

"A year," Zach said. He reached into his pocket and pulled out a chip, placing it on the table.

"So, this is when you make amends?"

"I'm not doing it because a program told me to," Zach said. "I'm doing it because I need to. Because I hurt the only person who ever really cared about me. Whoever looked out for me. And it's killing me."

"What do you think it did to me?" Evan snapped. "And I didn't have any excuses to hide behind. I was left with my life in ruins, and you long gone."

"I know." Zach hung his head, and when he raised his eyes, Evan could see true remorse there. "I hit rock bottom a few months later. I swear, that was the lowest I could go. What I did to you was unforgiveable, and it just drove me into a darker place. I didn't see any way out, especially without you in my life."

"What changed?"

"Believe it or not, Dad," he said. "I was in Southern California, and I called him one night in desperation. It was either I get help or die. And I can tell you, Ev, that I didn't care which way it went. I thought it would be easier for myself and everyone else if I died."

"That's not true," Evan said. "Maybe for you, but not for Mom and Dad. Or me."

"You would have mourned me?" Zach looked hopeful, but Evan could only shrug.

"I don't know, Zach. You were dead to me already. What you did, how you did it, it destroyed me. Cutting you out of my life, my thoughts, my heart, it had to be done," Evan said. "I don't know how I would have felt if I had found out you were dead. But at least now, I can say I'm glad you aren't."

"Thanks," Zach said. "Anyway, I called Dad. He was as surprised to hear from me as I was to call him. But he came. Right away. Picked me up, took me right to a rehab. He didn't even stop so I could shower and change but brought me right there. And he stayed. He came to visit me when I was allowed to see people. He was there to pick me up when I got out. And he took me back to Arizona with him so I could have a fresh start."

"Dad did all that?" Evan was shocked. His father had always been a remote, hands-off man. It had been surprising when he had shown up at graduations, never mind anything else. He had missed birthdays and holidays and was far from the person who Evan would think to call in a crisis.

"He did," Zach confirmed with a nod. "Mom even came to see me. She invited me to come stay with her when I got out, but I could see she would be easier on me. Old Zach would have gone there. But I wanted to change, so I stuck with Dad. And he never let up, making sure I went to a meeting every day, sometimes more than one. He pushed me to get better, and to fix things with you."

"I don't know if that's possible," Evan said. "I appreciate you coming, and I'm glad you're sober and healthy. But the damage might be too much."

"I'm not asking for forgiveness right now," Zach said. "I'm asking for a chance to prove myself to you. Let me be the brother I never was."

"What does that even mean?"

"We should be friends," Zach said. "Not enemies. You aren't my competition, and I always saw you as that. And you set a pretty high bar, that made me angry. It's not your fault, but it just drove me crazy that I could never be as good as you."

"The only thing I was good at," Evan said. "Was school. You were the one with a social life, who had girlfriends. I was studying and goal oriented. It had nothing to do with you."

"I know that now," Zach said. "But teenage Zach? He was a failure in his own eyes. His parents didn't care what he was doing, his brother was the best at everything. Every teacher I had would get this look of disappointment when they realized I wasn't like you."

"It sounds like you're blaming me for your actions, just like when we were kids," Evan said, unable to keep the hurt inside.

Zach sat quietly for a minute, looking thoughtful. "You're right," he finally said. "I'm sorry. My feelings are my own, and no one else's responsibility. I am a work in progress."

"Aren't we all," Evan said softly.

"Can I stay here for a while?" Zach asked after they had sat in silence for a minute.

"With me?" Evan sat back in his chair, horrified at the thought. He was relieved when his brother shook his head.

"No, I have the rental," Zach said. "I'd like to stay in town, if you don't mind. See you, prove that I've changed. And I like it here."

"I can't have you ruin what I've built here," Evan said. "If I'm being honest, I don't think I like the idea of you staying."

Zach nodded. "I get that. I do. But could you think about it? I'll take your cues and do what you ask. If you really want me to leave, I will. I know you've already given me more chances than I deserve, and asking for one more isn't fair. But if you can find another tiny shred of belief in me, I'd like to try."

"Let me think on it?" Evan asked. Guinness stood, as if sensing the meeting was almost over.

"Of course," Zach said. "Any answer other than a flat-out no is a good one. Thank you."

"You'll stay away from my work, and my house," Evan warned him. "That's the fastest way to me asking you to leave."

"I'll follow your lead," Zach said. "Just let me know when I can talk to you again, okay? I know we have to work through things, and the only way to do it is to confront it."

"You sound like someone else I know," Evan said, smiling at the thought of Finley.

"Oh?" Zach looked at him with questions in his eyes, but Evan knew better.

"I'll be in touch," he said, rather than addressing his own comment. "Enjoy your weekend."

Evan walked away, Guinness happily trotting at his side. They walked through the still-sleepy streets of town, no destination in mind. At the town square, Evan circled the area four times before sitting on a bench to process what his brother had told him. Was it something he could believe? He looked sincere, but Zach was a master manipulator. Or had been, Evan corrected himself. Everyone deserved a second chance in life. But with Zach, this would be yet another second chance. And Evan didn't know if he had it within him to allow that.

He stood, starting the walk home as the thoughts continued to swirl. Zach had played him for a fool so many times, this could be more of the same. As he walked, his phone rang, this time showing his father's name on the screen. Bob Lincoln was not one to make the time to call, and Evan couldn't remember the last time it had happened.

"Hey, Dad," he said. "This is early for you."

"I'm in Chicago, so not as early as you think," Bob replied. "Zach told me he saw you this morning."

"That was fast," Evan replied.

"I've been keeping tabs on him, making sure he's staying on track."

"Wow. Parenting a little late, aren't you?" Evan hated himself even as the words came out but couldn't stop them. "I'm sorry. That was rude."

"It was, but it's also not untrue. I wasn't there for either of you. We weren't. Your mother and I have been talking about it quite a bit since Zach first called me," Bob said. "We both owe you an apology. But I'll do that in person one day soon."

Evan didn't know what to say to that. He stopped in his own driveway, looking at Guinness as if he could provide answers. "Does that mean you're also coming here?"

"I'd like to be invited, but I will if I feel like I'm needed," Bob said. "And I mean by either of you. I know it seems like I've been there for Zach all this time and not for you, but I was trying to protect you. If he failed at his attempt at sobriety, you would get dragged back into it. I wanted to make sure he was ready. And that you had a chance to say no if you aren't."

"I don't know what I am," Evan admitted.

"That's fine too," Bob said. "This is all sudden for you. Take some time, think on it. That's all we can ask."

Evan hung up, more confused than ever. It was like his world was flipped over, and everyone was acting the exact opposite of how he had known them. All he wanted to do was focus on the happiness he was finding in this little town, and with Finley, and now he had to revisit old feelings.

Chapter 20

"Let's take our food to go," Finley said. She and Evan were at a small table at the Palace, which was packed with locals and tourists. They had spent the afternoon together, exploring a farmer's market in a neighboring town, before dropping Guinness off and coming to the restaurant. Now she could see that whatever had been distracting him all day was still with them.

"What? No, I'm sorry," he said. "We don't need to do that."

"I feel like your mind is somewhere else," she told him. "I don't want to keep you here if you would rather be home, or wherever your thoughts are."

"I saw my brother this morning," he said. She could tell there was more to the story, based on his body language, but didn't want to push in the busy restaurant.

"Let's go back to your place and eat," she said. "And you can tell me about it. You'll feel better if you get it off your chest."

"I wish I had your optimism," he said, a small smile on his face.

The waitress returned minutes later with a bag containing their meals, wishing them a good night. "I'm just going to run upstairs quickly," Finley said. "I'll meet you out front, okay? We're walking, right?"

"I walked into town," he said. "But would you rather we drive? I don't mind either way."

"No, walking is good. I just wanted to make sure I met you in the right place. Just wait for me on the front porch."

She raced up the stairs that were just off the kitchen, grabbing her larger purse from the closet where she had stashed it. Switching her wallet, keys and cell phone to the larger bag, she darted down the back stairs and around to where Evan was waiting on the porch.

"Ready?" he asked, offering his hand.

"Yes," she said, smiling over at him.

They talked about their week as they walked, and within minutes they were being greeted by an ecstatic Guinness. Evan placed the bag of food on the table and went to let the dog out into the fenced-in yard. While he was gone, Finley started pulling out plates and silverware, having grown comfortable in his house. They had hung out there for several evenings in a row, choosing his place over her apartment for the dog's sake. Plus, it was nice to have privacy and the quiet the house offered. Living above a busy restaurant wasn't peaceful, and although she didn't mind the noise, when she was with Evan, she would rather focus on him.

Once they were settled at the table with plates of food and glasses of wine in front of them, Finley squeezed his hand. "Tell me what happened."

"This is why you're a good nurse," he said instead. "You have a way of making people feel comfortable enough to tell you anything."

"I hope that's true for you," she replied. "I'd like us to be able to always be open and honest with each other."

He fiddled with his wineglass for a moment before taking a sip and meeting her eyes. "My brother is two years younger than me," he said. "We were close but not, if that makes sense. We were so different, but also all we had, because our parents weren't around much. As young kids, we were always together, and best friends. As we got older, we would team up together when needed but rarely confided in each other. I was the nerd in school, and he was popular, so that really set us at odds. It seemed the more I did right, the further apart we grew."

"He didn't follow in your footsteps academically?"

"The opposite, in fact," Evan said. "He struggled and would get mad anytime I offered him help. Part of me thinks he might be dyslexic, but he refused any testing. He got by on charm and good looks, and I think the school was just happy to have him out, so they graduated him. But he didn't get a good education."

"There are different types of smart," Finley commented. "JJ is street smart but couldn't write a paper to save his life."

"That's true," Evan said. "And generous of you to assume that Zach has other talents. I suppose he does, but it was hard to see them then. And now."

"What happened between you that made it so bad?"

"I got a lot of grants and scholarships to attend Harvard, and my parents paid the rest," he said. "But medical school, they said I was on my own. I applied for every grant there was, and got a fair amount of money that way, but I had to take out loans and work nonstop to pay for the rest. I would work overnight sometimes and go to class in the morning on no sleep. It was all worth it, in my mind, to become a doctor."

"A great doctor," she added in, smiling at him.

"Thanks. Anyway, I saved up a lot of money. Zach had been working odd jobs for years, and wanted to live with me," Evan said. "I found a cheap two-bedroom apartment not far from campus, and we moved in there. It was more affordable for me than living on campus, and I figured I was helping him."

"That makes sense," Finley murmured. Seeing that he was getting more stressed, she pushed back her plate. "Should we move into the family room for the second half of this? Maybe bring the wine?"

He nodded and grabbed the bottle off the counter, following her to the couch. She nestled close to him but partly turned so she could see his face. He nodded, almost to himself, before continuing. "We lived there for a little over a year. I had a girlfriend at the time, only the second I'd ever had. We met off campus where I worked, and I think she was more impressed with the degree I was getting than she was with me."

"That can't be true," Finley said. "Objectively, you're nice to look at, and she had to have noticed."

He smiled at her. "Maybe she did. But she loved to introduce me as her boyfriend, the doctor. I was happy. I was broke and exhausted, but I thought I had everything going for me. Money in the bank to pay for the next semester, a girlfriend who said she loved me, and a good relationship with my brother."

"And then what happened?" Finley prodded when he stopped talking.

"One day, I got home after school and work, almost eighteen hours total," he said. "And Zach was gone. Not only was all of his stuff gone, but anything of mine that had any value. My TV, a gaming system, a computer, a watch my dad had given me for graduation, all gone," he said.

"Oh, no," Finley whispered.

"And so was Celeste."

"What? The girlfriend?"

He nodded, a pained look on his face. "She left me a note. Said she had been in love with Zach for months, and she was sorry. Apparently, she was spending her days with him and her nights with me."

"I'll never understand cheating," Finley said, fuming. "If she wanted to be with him, she could have just broken up with you. She would still look trashy, but at least she wouldn't be total scum."

"I haven't even told you the worst part yet," Evan said. "I honestly didn't care that Celeste was gone, or the TV, when it came down to it."

"Was it that your brother did that to you?"

"No," he said, shaking his head. "He also cleaned out my bank account. Took every penny that I had saved, so I had no tuition for the next semester. Which was due the following week, but the idiot that I was, I opted to leave it in my savings to earn a few extra cents in interest before I paid it on the due date. I didn't even have money for rent, never mind my tuition."

"Oh, Evan," Finley gasped, talking through the hand she had clasped over her mouth. "What a nightmare. How could he do that to you?"

"That's a good question," Evan said. "It turns out, he had some substance abuse issues. I think Celeste did as well, and they burned through all their money. When he saw what he could cash out from me, he didn't think, he just did."

"All that hard work, and he used it for drugs?" Finley was outraged on Evan's behalf. "I know it's a disease, and I have sympathy for anyone struggling with addiction. But how could he do that to you?"

"That's the thing," Evan said, running a hand through his hair. "It's like it wasn't him, if that makes sense? The Zach that I talked to this morning, that was my brother. A better version of who I knew as a kid, almost. The guy who stole from me and almost ruined me? I don't know that guy."

"That's what addiction will do," Finley said. "It's terrible. But it does change people."

"He says he's sober now, and has been for a year," Evan said. "Another shock to the system was finding out that my dad helped him get there."

"Really?"

"That's what he told me," Evan said. "And then my dad called right after I met up with Zach. Offering him backup, I guess."

"At your expense?" Finley held up a hand at Evan's look. "I'm sorry. I know they're your family, but why doesn't your dad have your back? You didn't do anything wrong here."

"I know," Evan said. "But I can't be mad at him. He saw Zach at his lowest and stepped in. He apologized to me and said he would like to make things right. I just don't know if I have the headspace to make things right with him and Zach."

"Heart space," Finley said. At Evan's questioning look, she continued. "You're a logical person. Your head isn't the issue, it's if your heart can handle it."

"And what if it can't?" Evan's voice was so quiet, so broken, that Finley couldn't help herself. She climbed onto his lap and held him, trying to let him absorb some of her faith in him.

"You don't have to," she told him. "You can just go on living your life as it is. But could you live with yourself if you did that? That's what you need to ask yourself. If you say no, and send Zach away and refuse your dad, will you be happy with that decision in a year? Or when you get married?"

He choked out a laugh. "Was that a hint?"

She laughed and squeezed him tighter. "No, I would never be that subtle."

"I'll have to really think about it," Evan said.

She pulled back to look at him. "What did you end up doing about your tuition? How did you stay in school?"

"I was ready to withdraw," he said. "I went to the bursar's office, and they called the dean. They helped me apply for loans, and every other funding available. They even let me resume classes while some of it was pending, and I found out later that the dean had purchased my books for me. The bookstore told me they were included in the loan, but apparently, they weren't."

"Wow," Finley said. "You must have been a prize student for them to do all that."

"Top of the class," Evan said, smiling at her. "How could you forget? And he said it would be a loss to the medical community if I left, and he couldn't allow that to happen."

"What about your apartment?"

"I went to my landlord and explained," he said. "Told her I couldn't stay, and that I would have to pay her back for the months left. But she could rent it to someone else immediately, so at least she wouldn't be out the money. She offered me a small studio in exchange for some help taking care of her father. He had some medical issues and couldn't be left alone, so she was struggling."

"That's amazing," Finley said.

"It was," he agreed. "I was able to work a little less, without the rent to worry about. And I studied while he slept, so I got even further ahead in my schoolwork. It all ended up being okay. But I'll never be able to forget that Zach did that to me."

"Nor should you," Finley said. "But there's a difference between forgiving and forgetting. You can forgive him and also make sure you're never in that position again."

"But if he's really changed, is that fair? To keep him at arm's length?"

"It wasn't fair what he did to you," she pointed out. "I think making sure you have time to see that he's changed is smart."

"What if he asks me to move in here?"

"You think he would?" She looked at him to see his slight nod. "You say no, especially right now. You have the right to protect yourself, Evan. And to have an expectation that your brother, who is a grown-up, can support himself. He's not your responsibility. It's nice if you can have a relationship with him, but he doesn't get to become your burden."

"Why are you so smart?" he asked, toying with a piece of her hair. "Brains and beauty, it's not fair."

"Like you're one to talk," she teased, sensing he needed a change in subject. "I've seen you without your shirt, I can't believe you keep those abs hidden under scrubs."

"I think the patients would object to me walking around with no top on," he said, laughing.

"You'd be surprised," Finley said. "Mrs. Lee in particular thinks you're something else. She tells me regularly that I need to, and I quote, get on that."

"No, she doesn't," he sputtered.

"Oh, but she does," she said, laughing. "Said if she were twenty years younger, she'd be making a play for you herself."

"She's eighty-two," he said.

"Not in her mind," Finley said. "In her mind, she's fifty. She told me that she had decided never to acknowledge another year after that one."

"She's quite the lady," he said.

"Should I be jealous?"

"Never," he said, looking very serious. "I'm a one-woman man, and you're that woman. You never have to worry about anything else."

"Does that mean we're official? Because I know there is no one else I'd rather be with than you," she said, feeling shy suddenly.

He kissed her soundly before responding. "I'd like it to be," he said. "I asked human resources, and there is no issue with us dating. They would prefer we didn't work so closely together, but they said if they enforced that, half the hospital would need to change departments."

"Well, I asked Dr. Howard if I could switch with Audrey, so she would have your patients," Finley confessed. "I thought we could start a slow transition, so I'll work closer with Dr. Howard and Audrey with you."

"You're okay with that?" he asked, looking touched.

"Of course," she said. "I don't want to change departments, and Audrey and I figured we could do a slow transition. I'll take Dr. Howard's new patients as they come in, and Audrey will take yours. That way, we can see our existing patients through their treatment without a change, and as they finish, we'll transition to being with the other doctor."

"I'm glad you did that," he said, his voice soft. "I didn't want to be presumptuous about where we were. But I am falling for you, Finley. Hard. And the idea that you might feel the same makes me happy."

"I very much feel the same," Finley said. "As a matter of fact, I haven't felt like this about anyone, ever. It's a little scary for me, but you make me feel safe. In every way."

"As long as there isn't a mugger around the corner with a brick," Evan said, winking at her.

"I think I owe that mugger a thanks," Finley said.

"Why?"

"If that hadn't happened, we wouldn't have been thrown together," she pointed out. "We would have come back and probably started sniping at each other again, and this wouldn't have happened."

"I think it would have. It had already started between us before either of us were willing to acknowledge it," Evan responded. "I am not strong enough to have resisted you forever."

"Speaking of," Finley said, kissing him softly. "I happened to bring an overnight bag with me. If that's okay."

His eyes darkened as he nodded slowly. "More than okay."

Chapter 21

"Are you sure I should be here?" Evan put his car in park before looking at Finley.

She nodded confidently. "You're my boyfriend now," she said. "That means you come to family dinners. Besides, my parents will love you. And you already know my brothers and Zoe."

"I feel like I'm intruding," he said. "Did you let them know I was coming?"

"Zoe cooks enough for twelve people every weekend," she said. "We all get sent home with leftovers. Trust me, one extra person won't be a problem. And I'll make sure my brothers are nice."

She opened her door and jumped out of the car, prompting him to climb out as well. She had told him earlier in the day about her regular family dinners and asked him to join her. He had agreed, not realizing it was that night. Without the time to properly freak out over the social interactions that were about to happen, he felt utterly unprepared. Normally, he would have thought through some topics he could discuss with her family that wouldn't make him stand out. He would have spent a fair amount of time agonizing over what he should or shouldn't bring to the dinner.

Instead, he was arriving with just a bottle of wine that Finley declared perfect, and what he hoped was a working knowledge of how to interact with other people. He had been so happy in his little bubble with Finley all day, and now he was jumping into what felt like a shark tank. Although he was being unfair, he realized. They were all nice people, and he was the problem. Or rather, the crippling social anxiety that he'd felt most of his life was the problem. Unless he was in a setting where he could feel confident, like when he was at work or at a conference, he struggled. Even at work, he struggled unless it was a conversation about a patient. He couldn't just make small talk, because he would rehash the conversation for hours after to see if he had made any missteps. The simple socializing that Finley did with her coworkers was foreign to him, although he was hoping it would start to rub off on him, eventually.

"Wait," he said, stopping Finley before she could open the front door.

"What's wrong?"

"Desmond is going to know you didn't come home last night," he said. "What if he tells everyone?"

As Finley opened her mouth to answer, JJ's voice came out of nowhere. "Video doorbell, dude. Now we all know. Come on in."

"Oh no," Evan whispered to Finley. "He's going to shoot me."

"He won't shoot you," she whispered back. She directed her next words to the doorbell camera, which Evan could now clearly see. "No one will be commenting on it."

Evan followed Finley through the door and then into the kitchen, where Zoe was stirring something on the stove. And trying not to laugh, Evan noted. "Hi," Finley said cheerily to her sister-in-law. "Can I help with anything?"

"I'm good," Zoe replied. "Hi, Evan. Nice to see you."

"We're official now," Finley announced. "I thought trial by fire would be easier. Get to know everyone at once."

"Not a great way to put it," Zoe commented.

"Are you okay? You still look so tired," Finley said. "You should let one of us host one of these days."

"Your brother has been on nights, and it takes its toll on both of us," Zoe said. "Nothing to worry about. And it's easier for me to cook in my own kitchen than yours or your mom's."

Finley laughed. "So, you're saying we're bad cooks?"

Zoe just looked at Finley, causing all of them to laugh. JJ appeared in the doorway, glancing among them. "What's so funny?"

"Finley thinking she could cook," Zoe said. JJ slipped an arm around his wife's waist and kissed her quickly.

"That is funny," JJ said. "Evan. How are you? Sleep well?"

"Hey, JJ," Evan said. He sounded like an idiot, but he couldn't stop his voice from sounding as insecure as he felt.

"You like football?" JJ asked, releasing his wife to open the refrigerator.

"Sure," Evan said.

"Alright, come in here," JJ said, gesturing with the two beers he held. "You can get a good seat before everyone else gets here."

Evan allowed himself a brief moment of relief that no one else had heard him over the doorbell before realizing he would be alone with Finley's oldest brother. The one who was a cop.

Finley gave him an encouraging look and a shooing motion with her hand. "I'll be in soon. I just want to keep Zoe company."

He nodded and went into the room, where a football game was already streaming on a large TV over a fireplace. JJ was taking a seat in a large chair, putting his feet on an ottoman, but held a beer out to Evan. "For you."

"Thanks," he said, opting to sit in a chair rather than on the couch. Realizing he might be taking someone's favorite spot, he stopped before he sat all the way. "Does anyone sit here?"

"What do you mean?" JJ asked.

"I don't know if your brothers or Dad have places where they like to sit."

"If they were that particular, they should have gotten here first," JJ said. "Sit."

Evan nodded and settled into the chair, taking a healthy sip from the beer bottle before putting it on the table next to him.

"So." JJ let the weight of the word sit in the air for several minutes, making Evan sweat in places he wasn't comfortable sweating, before gesturing to the TV. "Are you a Pats fan?"

"I suppose I've become one," Evan answered. "I grew up in Georgia, but I've been in Patriots territory for so long, it's natural."

"Did you play?"

"Me? No," Evan said.

"I'm surprised," JJ answered. "You're built like a tight end."

"I'm not sure if that's a compliment or an insult," Evan said with a laugh. "Although I enjoy watching games, I'm new to it."

"The tall guys who look fast," JJ said, gesturing to the TV. "I bet your high school coach was hoping you would play."

"I doubt he knew I was alive," Evan replied with a laugh.

They watched in silence for a few minutes, until Evan heard the front door open and close, then the voices of Finley's other two brothers talking to the women as they came in. JJ leaned forward just then, so he could barely be heard over the noise. "Should I remind you she's my baby sister? My only sister?"

Evan swallowed hard at the intense expression on JJ's face, which was conveying way more than his words. The message was clear: if he hurt Finley, he would have to deal with JJ. And likely the other two, who were as big and intimidating as JJ. At least, Colin was intimidating.

"Got it," he said finally, nodding just as Des and Colin came into the room.

"What's up, doc?" Desmond said, reaching over to fist bump Evan as he sat on the couch. "You kept my sister out last night, huh?"

"What's this?" Colin asked, glancing between them.

"Nothing," Finley yelled from the kitchen. "Move on."

Colin shrugged and put his feet up on the coffee table, which JJ promptly kicked off. The brothers started bickering and yelling at the TV, and Evan allowed himself to relax. He managed to stay that way for ten minutes until the front door opened again.

"Uh-oh," Desmond stage whispered to Evan. "The parents have arrived."

"Finley is going to kill you," Colin told his brother.

Evan stood, unsure of what to do. The other three men looked at him, surprised. He shrugged. "I should probably go meet them," he said finally.

"Good luck, my friend," Desmond said, saluting him with a beer.

He heard the volume on the TV go lower as he left the room, as if JJ wanted to hear the conversation. Finley was standing by the island, hugging her mother, and her dad was with Zoe.

"Evan," Finley said, grinning at him. "This is my mom, Maggie. And my dad, Tim."

"Nice to meet you," he said, offering to shake Maggie's hand. She brushed it aside and hugged him instead.

"Anyone who makes my little girl so happy deserves a hug," she said. "It's so nice to meet you."

Tim accepted the handshake with a firm one in return. "Good to meet you. Are her brothers behaving?"

"Yes, sir," Evan replied. He saw the twinkle in Tim's eye and relaxed. Tim and Maggie were exactly as Finley had described them. Good-natured, down to earth, and they loved their kids. Nothing to be afraid of.

"Evan, would you mind getting something off a shelf for me?" Zoe asked, pointing above the microwave. He got the tray she was indicating and turned to hand it to her, seeing her swaying slightly and her eyes looking unfocused.

"Zoe?" He caught her with his empty hand, dropping the tray on the counter so he could use both to lower her to the floor. "Can you hear me?"

Finley rushed to his side, looking frantic. "What's wrong?"

"Can you go get my bag? It's in my trunk," he said, his tone confident now. He could be here as a doctor and be sure of himself in a way he struggled socially. Finley grabbed his keys and raced out the door just as JJ came into the kitchen.

"What happened?" JJ asked, rushing to his wife's side.

"She passed out," Evan said. "I want to check her vitals and see what's going on. Anything you can tell me?"

JJ glanced over at his parents, who were hovering a few feet away. "Can I carry her into the bedroom? She's okay to be moved, right?"

"Yes, she didn't hit her head," Evan said. JJ stood, holding his wife in his arms, and rushed down the hall to the bedroom on the first floor. Evan followed, hoping Finley would be back soon with his medical bag.

As soon as the door closed behind him, JJ looked up from where he had just put Zoe on the bed. "She's pregnant," he blurted out. "But she doesn't want anyone to know yet. Please don't say anything, unless you need to. Just make sure she's okay."

"No problem," Evan said. "How far along?"

"Eight weeks," JJ replied. "She wanted to wait until twelve to tell everyone. She has a whole plan for it."

Evan resumed taking her pulse, happy with the strength of it, and was glad when Finley raced in carrying his bag. He pulled out a stethoscope and blood pressure cuff, checking her over as best he could without moving her. Happy with her blood pressure and lung sounds, he pulled out a glucometer and checked her blood sugar. Just as he pricked her finger, her eyes fluttered open. She looked around the room in confusion before seeing him.

"What happened?"

"You fainted," Evan said. "I'm just checking you over as best I can right now."

"You're okay, honey," JJ said, relief on his face. "Everything is okay."

Evan glanced over to where Finley stood at his side. "Can you go let your family know she's alright? I just want to talk to her alone."

"Sure," Finley said, looking slightly put off. She disappeared behind the door before Evan looked at Zoe again.

"JJ told me your news," he said. "I'm going to ask questions quickly before anyone comes in here. Any bleeding? Cramping?"

"No," she said, shaking her head. She looked terrified. "Do you think I'm miscarrying? I had one a few months ago; that's why we're waiting to tell everyone. I don't know if I can handle that again."

"I don't have the tools to know for sure," Evan said. "Your vitals are good, and you aren't bleeding. That's good. I can do a quick blood test here, or I can order labs and an ultrasound, and you can go to the hospital right now. That would confirm that things are okay."

Zoe glanced at JJ before nodding at Evan. "If you can do bloodwork here, that would be great. I'd still like to do the ultrasound either way, but if I could go tomorrow that might be better."

"Not a problem." Evan pulled a machine out of his bag, explaining that he needed to prick her finger again before doing so and dropping blood onto the test strip.

"What is that?" JJ asked.

"Since we're a rural hospital, they equipped us with what is effectively a mobile lab," Evan said. "These little machines can do bloodwork in minutes. We all have them, because there are times when we have to go to patients and we need to be able to do total care."

"That makes sense," JJ said. "I didn't know you did house calls."

"Not always," Evan said. "But if weather is an issue, I'd rather go see someone than add to their trouble. And some patients are just too fragile to be in the hospital."

The machine beeped, and Evan read the results quickly before smiling at the couple. "Everything looks good. You're dehydrated, but hormone levels are right where they should be."

"Oh, thank you," Zoe cried, hugging JJ. "You have no idea how happy I am to hear that."

"I'd like to start an IV for you," Evan said, once they had wiped their tears away. "That should help you feel better."

"Whatever you want," Zoe said. "Thank you."

"Thanks, Doc," JJ repeated, smiling at him. "I guess I do need to go easy on you."

"Why don't you go tell everyone I'm going to live?" Zoe suggested to her husband. "Let me get myself composed and then I'll be out."

JJ kissed her lightly before leaving, clapping Evan on the back as he passed by. Evan set up the IV kit and wiped Zoe's arm with alcohol to prep for the needle to go in.

"I hope we aren't putting you in an awkward position with Finley," Zoe said as he worked. "Asking you to keep our secret."

"No," he replied. "It's okay. She understands doctor-patient confidentiality."

"But we're her family," Zoe said. "I think she's going to have questions. If you have to tell her, I understand."

"It's your news to tell," Evan said. "Please don't worry. It will be fine."

"Okay, but don't forget what I said," Zoe replied. "Four weeks is a long time to hold a secret."

He nodded and finished the IV placement. "I can get you set up in the living room with everyone else," he offered. "If you feel okay walking out there."

"Are you sure?"

"Not a problem," he assured her. Once she was on her feet, he took her elbow to support her and tucked the bag of fluids under his arm. JJ helped her the rest of the way, placing her in the chair he had been in earlier, and insisting she put her feet up. Evan quickly hung the bag from the curtain rod behind her, connected the tubes and started the drip.

"You'll feel better after this," he assured her. Once confident everything was running smoothly, he moved to Finley's side.

"What's going on?" she whispered to him, pulling him into the hallway.

"She's dehydrated," he answered. "She'll see her doctor tomorrow to make sure, but I think she's fine."

"Why did you make me leave?"

"First, I needed my bag," he said. "And then it seemed like she was embarrassed. I didn't want to add to it."

"But I could have helped," she said, crossing her arms.

"And if I had needed you, I absolutely would have asked you to stay. Or come in. But I can manage vitals and start an IV."

"That's all it was? You're sure she's okay?"

"Yes," he said, pulling her into his arms. After a brief resistance, he felt her arms go around his waist. "She's going to be fine."

Better than fine, but he couldn't say that. If Finley was mad when Zoe and JJ shared their news, he was sure she would eventually understand. It wasn't his secret to share.

Chapter 22

"It's weird, right?" Finley asked, sitting on the bench in the women's locker room at the hospital. Audrey was pulling off her scrub top, which she threw in the direction of the dirty laundry bin with a sigh.

"I need to start working out," she said. "That was way too tight."

"It didn't look it," Finley said. "Don't be hard on yourself."

"I'm in a funk," Audrey said, sitting next to her. "I'm chronically single, and the first attractive man I have met is keeping me at arm's length. And you're upset that your perfect boyfriend helped your sister-in-law because he's kind and caring. Do I have that right?"

"But he asked me to leave the room," Finley said. "Why? I'm a nurse; what if he needed me?"

"I assume he didn't ask you to leave the planet," Audrey said with an impressive eye roll. "He was offering her some privacy. He probably wanted to ask her questions and didn't think she needed an audience. It happens all the time."

"What doctor have you worked with that does that? They always want us there to take notes and smooth things over."

"I don't know," Audrey said. "The kind who sits at his sick patient's bedside all night long? Or takes the time to visit a dying patient at home? Or even to go to funerals or follow up with families after the fact?"

"Does he really do all that?"

"How do I know this, and I'm not getting the benefits of it?" Audrey threw her hands up in a sign of frustration. "I should have a smoking hot doctor in my bed, and yet I don't."

Finley nudged her friend with her shoulder. "You should see him without a shirt."

"You're cruel, and I have no reason to be friends with you," Audrey said, her tone light. "You need to make it up to me by having a drink at the bar. I need to flirt with your brother to make myself feel better."

"You can do better than Des," Finley said. "I'll ask Evan if he has any friends to fix you up with."

"I can do a drink," she said, pushing thoughts of Evan and Zach out of her head. "Evan is going to play poker tonight, so I'm free."

"Oh, how nice," Audrey said with sarcasm so thick Finley could feel it. "I'm glad you can squeeze me in."

Finley hugged her friend quickly before grabbing her purse. "I promise I won't be one of those girls who forget their friends. It's just so new, that's all."

"It's fine," Audrey said. "I plan to do the same to you one day."

***

"My favorite nurse," Desmond said, placing a napkin down in front of Audrey. "You just made my day."

"I'm right here, Des," Finley said, rolling her eyes.

"Do you have one of those white nurse dresses?" he continued, ignoring his sister as he leaned toward Audrey.

"Like the Halloween costumes?"

"Exactly like that," he said. "I had a dream—"

"Do not continue that sentence," Finley ordered her twin. "I'm literally right here."

"Should we talk about your love life instead?" He slapped a napkin down forcefully in front of her as he asked. "Since you're so determined to ruin mine."

"Talking about your nurse fantasy is not exactly ruining things?" she said.

"That depends on what Audrey thinks," he said, winking at her friend.

Audrey laughed. "You're terrible."

"But in a good way, right?" Des asked. "What are you doing later? Want me to stop by?"

"No, I do not," Audrey said.

"You kill me," Des said, an exaggerated pout on his face. "You know I'm head over heels for you."

"Until you get me into bed," Audrey shot back. "Then you'd be a ghost."

He staggered backward, covering his chest. "You wound me, my love."

"Enough," Finley said. "Is Zoe here?"

"No," he said. "She called in sick, I guess. Linda was the manager on duty, and she didn't tell me much."

"I hope she's really okay," Finley said, frowning. She reached for her phone to text Zoe when Desmond replied.

"I talked to JJ. I called him right when I found out she wasn't here. He said she's fine, feeling much better," he said. "But she wanted to rest some more and just follow up with her own doctor."

"You don't think something is wrong, do you?"

"No," Desmond said, shaking his head. "JJ is too happy for that."

Des walked away to get their drinks, and Finley looked at Audrey. "I wonder if she's pregnant."

"That would make sense," Audrey said. "And explain why Evan asked you to leave."

"But if he knows, and I don't? And he doesn't tell me?"

"Why would he?" Audrey challenged. "If he saw someone in your family as a doctor, he can't share that with you."

"But this was at her house," Finley argued. "I was right there."

"It doesn't matter. You know that."

"This is frustrating," Finley muttered, thanking Desmond when he brought their drinks. He vanished again, leaning over to talk to two women at the other end of the bar. "See? He flirts with everyone."

"Trust me, I know how he works," Audrey said with a laugh. "I wasn't born yesterday. I just needed the confidence boost."

"As long as you know what you're dealing with," Finley said.

"Oh, who is that?" Audrey whispered after a sharp breath in.

Finley turned to look and saw a new face in the doorway. Tall, dark hair covered by a baseball hat, dark scruff on his cheeks. He was wearing a thermal shirt and jeans, looking like a townie, although he wasn't familiar to her.

"Must be visiting," Finley said. "I've never seen him before."

"Oh, he's coming this way," Audrey gasped. "Do I look okay?"

"You look great, but he's probably here to meet someone," Finley cautioned her friend. "Don't fall in love just yet."

The stranger slid onto the barstool one away from Audrey, and Finley could feel her friend's desperation to talk to him. He was looking around the room as if he had never been there before and turned when Desmond approached.

"Hey there," Des said, putting a napkin down. "What can I get you?"

"Just a Coke, please," the other man replied. "And a menu?"

"Absolutely," Desmond said, pulling one from under the bar. He passed the man a cup of soda and then went to do a refill down the bar.

"Any recommendations?" the man asked, turning his head to Audrey when she didn't respond.

Audrey flushed a bright red color and simply stared at him until Finley elbowed her in the side. "Oh. The pot pie is good on a cold night. Or the salmon, if you like seafood."

"Thanks," he said, smiling at her. "You from around here?"

"I am," Audrey said with a gulp. "I grew up here. I don't recognize you."

"Excuse me," Finley said under her breath, standing up to go use the restroom. Better to let her friend sink or swim on her own. After taking her time using the bathroom and washing her hands, she found her way back to the bar, where Audrey's new friend had moved closer.

"Hey, Fin," she said. "This is Cary. Cary, this is Finley."

"Nice to meet you," he said, offering a hand to shake. "My lucky night to find two beautiful women to have dinner with."

"I should go," Finley said, hesitating. She didn't want to leave Audrey with a stranger but also didn't love the idea of her quiet night turning into something more.

"Stay and eat," Audrey urged her. "I won't make you stay out later, I promise."

She nodded, and they put their orders in when Desmond returned. As Audrey and Cary talked, she checked her phone, disappointed to find no messages from Evan. Even as she was lecturing herself about making too big a deal of it, she got a text message from him. He apologized for not seeing her at the end of her shift and told her to have fun with Audrey before reminding her he was going to play poker. A second text seconds later said that he would catch up with her before bedtime, since he was sure he would be out of the game early enough.

She smiled at her phone; glad he had thought to check in with her. Quickly responding that his plan sounded good, she kept herself from offering to wait for him at his house. Too much, too fast, she told herself. They didn't need to be together every night, even though it was still so new and exciting.

Chapter 23

Evan waited almost a week before reaching out to his brother again. During that time, he had gotten multiple calls and messages from both of his parents, encouraging him to give Zach a chance. His parents seemed concerned about his brother's sobriety if Evan turned him away, which was an extra weight to carry. If Zach was still in a fragile state, why would he have come now?

He got to the coffee shop first, surprised at how cold it felt early in the morning. They were meeting before Evan went to work on Friday morning. That would avoid him having to give up precious free time with Finley, something he had been looking forward to all week. Other than the poker night, they had hung out each night, but the weekend would allow them more than just those few hours of time.

It was both scary and encouraging how quickly they had fallen into a routine together. They played cards and watched movies, took walks with the dog, and talked endlessly about everything. Evan had considered himself a quiet, private person until now. Suddenly, all he wanted to do was share every thought and feeling he had, and she seemed to be the same. He worried they were moving fast, but her reassurance that her feelings matched his kept him from holding back. It had been a long time since he had felt like he could depend on someone, and he had forgotten how good it felt.

Zach appeared just after Evan had taken a seat. He had ordered two cups of coffee, asking for to-go cups rather than the mugs they provided for patrons who stayed longer. Even if his brother wanted to linger, Evan wanted to make it clear that he had a time limit on this visit.

"Hey," Zach said as he pulled out the chair across from Evan. "I can't believe how cold it is here."

"Yeah, it's Vermont," Evan said. At his brother's wounded look, he softened a bit. "I thought the same thing when I went outside."

"Do you live far from here?" Zach asked. "I've been doing some exploring. It's a nice town."

"A few blocks," Evan said vaguely. He wasn't ready for his brother to know his address, and that made him feel terrible.

"I'm glad you found a place that you like," Zach said. "I wouldn't have pictured this as a place you would choose."

"Why not?"

"It's small," Zach replied. "Smaller than where we grew up. After all those years in Boston, I thought you would have just stayed there. No offense, but you aren't big on change."

"No, I'm not," Evan admitted. "I thought I would just come for a year and then move on, but I'm rethinking that now. I like it here."

"I can see why." Zach sipped his coffee and leaned back in his chair. "Should I apologize again?"

"No," Evan said, weary suddenly. The anger towards his brother had been running through his veins for so long, it was exhausting. But letting go of it seemed impossible. "Words don't mean much."

Zach nodded. "I get that. Any chance we could hang out this weekend? Maybe I can prove that I've changed."

"It's not going to be like that, Zach."

"What do you mean?"

"You can't just come into town and expect me to be your friend," Evan explained. "I don't trust you. I don't know how to fix that."

"I would think the only way is to spend time together, so I can show you," Zach argued.

"Of course, you think that," Evan said. "But from my perspective, that would be a mistake. I gave you a chance in Boston and almost lost everything."

"What does that mean? How do I make it better?"

"I don't know," Evan said with a sigh. "I guess time. I can't make any promises."

Zach blew out a breath and looked around, then back at Evan. "I was working with a realtor this week to find a place to rent. Something more permanent than the Airbnb that I'm in. That's going to get too expensive once the ski season kicks in."

"You aren't moving in with me."

"I know that," Zach said, a hint of his temper behind the words. "But I also don't want to sign a lease if my presence in this town is painful for you. As much as I want to fix things, and I want to stay to show you that I've changed, I won't do it if you're totally against it."

Evan's emotions raged as his brother waited for his answer. He wanted to say no. Make Zach leave town and never come back. But would that solve anything? He'd be left on the outside of his family, dysfunctional as it was. And despite all the years of thinking he was okay on his own, the possibility of having his parents in his life had been exciting. Could he throw that away over pride?

"I'm in a really crappy position here," he said finally. "If I say that I want you to leave, I'm the bad guy. But if I say you can stay, you have expectations I'm not sure I can live up to."

"I promise there are no expectations," Zach said. "Hope, maybe. But I know how wrong I was, and the damage I caused. I just want a chance to prove that I've changed and to make up for it. I don't know how, but I'd really like to try."

"Fine," Evan said with a sigh. "But you're going to have to be patient."

"I will," Zach said, smiling at him. "I won't even ask you if you have plans for Thanksgiving."

"I haven't thought much about it," Evan said. "Other than signing up for the Turkey Trot race. And letting the hospital know they could put me on if they needed me."

"I thought your department would be closed?"

"It will be," Evan said. "But there are plenty that aren't. And a lot of doctors want to travel or spend the day with family. I figured I could help if needed."

"Always looking out for others," Zach said. Evan examined him carefully but didn't detect any sarcasm behind the words.

"I should get to work," Evan said.

"About the Turkey Trot," Zach said, standing at the same time. "Would you be upset if I signed up? I was talking to the owner of the bakery about it, seems like a lot of fun."

"Yeah, go ahead," Evan said. There would be a lot of people running in the race, they likely wouldn't even see each other. And for all he knew, he'd end up working in the emergency room and skipping the race.

"Great, thanks," Zach said. He grinned, and it brought Evan back to another time, when they had been young and innocent. The memory cut him deep, so he pushed it away. Going that far back in the past meant skipping over the betrayal, not to mention the years of hurt before that, which would be a mistake. He needed to keep his guard up and make sure Zach's charm didn't make him overlook something again.

Evan opened the door and stepped onto the sidewalk, shivering again as the wind blew down Main Street. "I'll catch up with you," he said to Zach. As his brother started walking away, he shook his head. "Are you walking far? Do you need a ride?"

Zach shook his head. "I'm okay, thanks. I'm going to meet the real estate agent now. I told her I would either be by to tell her I was leaving town or to sign a lease."

"Okay. Good luck," Evan said. Once his brother had started down the street again, he hurried to his car. The brief visit had given him a lot to think about, but not a lot of time to do so. He was surprised that his instinct had been to allow Zach to stay in town and hoped that he wouldn't regret it.

***

"Dr. Lincoln?" A young man wearing a heavy parka and a ski cap knocked on Evan's open office door.

"Yes?"

"I have a delivery for you," he said. He held out a clipboard, and after Evan signed, pulled a package from the messenger bag he wore. Thankful that he had stuck his change from coffee in his pocket, he passed the man a tip as he accepted the box.

He waited until the driver had disappeared before opening the long package. It was neatly wrapped, and he didn't recognize the handwriting on the envelope. When he pulled it open, he realized it was from Zoe. The note thanked him for what he had done the weekend before and shared that she had been cleared by her doctor. She had included a nice bottle of wine and a gift card to Palace Plates, encouraging him to come choose his own meal for the weekend. He tucked the card and gift card into his pocket and stuck the wine into his backpack just before Finley appeared in the doorway.

"Did you have lunch yet?" she asked, coming around his desk to kiss him quickly before going back to the doorway.

"No," he said. "I've been out straight. You going now?"

"Yes," she said. "I was waiting and waiting for my boyfriend to come get me, but my stomach couldn't take it anymore. Also, I don't have anyone coming in for half an hour, so it's the only time I can sneak away."

They walked to the cafeteria, chatting about their day, and chose their meals. Soup and a sandwich for Evan, a salad and cookie for Finley. As they approached the cash register, he pulled out his wallet, and the card from Zoe fell out of his pocket.

"What's that?" Finley asked as he picked it up and shoved it back where it came from.

"A card," he said.

"I can see that," she said, rolling her eyes. "From who?"

"Zoe," he said. At her raised eyebrow, he continued. "Thanking me for Sunday and saying she feels better. She sent me wine and a gift card to go into Palace Plates to pick up a meal. I thought we could grab one for dinner tonight."

"That's a good plan," she said. They went to the table, and then Finley held her hand out to him. "Can I read it?"

"What? No," he said. "I mean, I'm sorry. But it's private."

"Private? Between you and my sister-in-law?"

"I wouldn't want her to be passing notes I sent her to someone else," he said, hearing how lame the excuse was even as he said it. But Zoe had specified the name of the obstetrician she had seen, and he knew Finley would piece together the truth if she saw that.

Finley frowned, stabbing at her salad as if it had offended her. "This is weird."

"I'm sorry," he said. "I really am. But I also don't want to betray Zoe's confidence."

"But why is there a secret? You said she was dehydrated," Finley argued. "Is there something wrong?"

"No, she's absolutely fine," he said. "She just told me about her visit to her regular doctor, and I feel bad sharing that. I'm sure she'll tell you herself, if she hasn't already."

"Fine," she said with a sigh. "But let's not make it a habit to have secrets, okay?"

"Deal," he said, feeling relief. He knew Zoe would be okay with him sharing the truth with Finley, but he still hated the idea of spoiling the news.

"How did it go with your brother this morning?"

"Good," he said. "I'm sorry it meant we had to bring two cars here. I'd gotten so used to dropping Guinness off, I was all mixed up this morning."

"You still dropped him, right? I think Des loves him more than me."

"I did, before I saw my brother. I didn't want to leave it to you when I was going to be right in the area. I have to agree about Des and Guinness," Evan said with a laugh. "They seem like best friends. And shockingly, Desmond didn't make any comments today about you not going home last night."

"Will wonders never cease?" she said. "He was probably half asleep, I'll hear about it later. Or maybe not, since I brought enough to last me the weekend."

"Oh, did you now?" he asked, reaching under the table to squeeze her thigh. "I like having a girlfriend who plans ahead."

"Speaking of," she said. "My mom asked me if you were coming for Thanksgiving. I said yes. Is that okay?"

"Of course," he said. "Zach and I were just talking about it this morning. I had offered to work, but they don't need me. I'm planning to run the Turkey Trot in the morning, and then I'm free all day."

"I'll come cheer you on," she said. "We can go over a little later. JJ has to work until the race and the high school football game are over, so we have time."

"Good, because I'll need to be warmed up after a run," he said. "If you remember that from nursing school, they encourage skin to skin contact."

She laughed, and the sound warmed him even more than the soup did. They finished their lunch quickly and enjoyed several minutes of privacy in his office before she slipped out to get back to work. The benefits of working with his girlfriend kept him in good spirits until he came to a set of labs on his desk that brought him crashing back down. He sighed and turned to his computer, hoping to find a miracle, but afraid of what he would find.

Chapter 24

Finley pulled a caramel apple pie out of the oven and placed it on a cooling rack before accepting a glass of wine that Evan had poured for her. "You aren't having one?" She asked, noting his water.

"No, I have to get up early and run," he said.

"Oh, I want to go watch you," she said. "I'll just have this one. I don't want to oversleep tomorrow."

"How much more baking do you need to do?" he asked. He was sitting at the kitchen table reading while she worked. They had worked together to slice the apples, which they had picked the weekend before. Finley had chopped with wild abandon while Evan had carefully sliced, so their two bowls looked as different as possible but worked once together in the crust.

"I'm going to make some pecan tartlets," she said. "And cookie bars. And then I'm done."

"What are cookie bars?"

"Like chocolate chip cookies with walnuts, but cooked like brownies," she explained. "They come out thicker than cookies and oh-so delicious."

"Sounds good," he said, smiling at her. "Is anyone going tomorrow other than your family?"

"Emma and Patrick will be there for a bit, but I don't know if they'll eat with us," Finley answered. Emma was Zoe's sister, but Patrick had his own big family in town, so they had to divide their time. "I think that's it."

"Mike mentioned that he and Nat were going to his family in New Hampshire," Evan said. "It sounded like he was excited to show her around."

"So, just us," she said, grinning at him. "I'm glad you already got to have a couple of Sunday dinners with them. Hopefully, this will be fun and not intimidating."

"It will be," he said. "After that first night, JJ has been great. He was the scariest in your family."

"Because he carries a gun?"

"That, and he's imposing," Evan said. "Which I guess is good in his position. Colin doesn't say much but also doesn't seem unhappy that I'm there. And I really like Des. He had already started to become a friend, before us. And of course, your parents couldn't be nicer."

"They like you too," she said, beaming at him. "Des even said he wanted to run tomorrow, but he'll be up too late tonight. It's an unofficial reunion at the Palace, I guess, for all the people who come home for the holiday."

"Oh, that will be a late night," Evan replied. "I'm not keeping you from that, am I?"

She shook her head. "No, I didn't grow up here. And I'd rather have a quiet night with you than be in a crowded bar."

"Same," he said. "I'm really happy."

"Me too." She walked over to kiss him, careful to keep her hands with flour on them away from his dark shirt. "Who would have thought?"

"Not me," he admitted as she walked back to the counter. "But I was transfixed from the start."

"That's an interesting way of putting it," she said with a laugh.

"More than you were, I'm sure," he said. "You were distracting to me. Still are."

"Oh, yeah? Are you trying to get me to abandon my baking with these sweet words?"

He laughed, the sound rich in the quiet room. "No, you work. We have all night."

"Not quite," she said. "You have an early bedtime, after all."

"I accounted for the time," he answered, flipping a page. "Don't worry about that. And it's not like I've never been tired before. I survived medical school; I can make it through a Turkey Trot on a little less sleep."

***

Evan was gone when Finley woke up, but she still had plenty of time to shower before clipping a leash on Guinness and walking to town with him. The race would start and end just in front of the Palace, and she had been invited to participate in the morning festivities.

Zoe had set out a continental breakfast buffet and was fussing over it when Finley came down from her apartment. She had left Guinness there with a sleeping Desmond until it was time to go back outside, not wanting the dog in the restaurant.

"Happy Thanksgiving," she said, giving Zoe a brief hug. "This looks great."

"Doesn't it?" Kendra Burrows, Zoe's partner in Palace Plates and the owner of the Palace, appeared from the kitchen. Her daughter Calle was at her side, and a baby was in a carrier on her chest. "Tell her to stop worrying that it's not enough."

"Maybe just some scrambled eggs?" Zoe said. "I feel bad not having more."

"We have plenty," Kendra assured her. "This is just for our family and friends. And it wasn't worth you waking up at four this morning to cook, when I know you're hosting today. Relax. It's fine."

Zoe sighed but took a seat. Finley filled a plate and then joined her, noticing that she looked better. "How are you feeling?"

"Fine," Zoe said, looking at her with a weird expression on her face. "Why do you ask?"

219

"Oh, I don't know," Finley said with an eye roll. "Maybe because you passed out a few weeks ago? But you look better."

"Glad to hear I looked terrible," Zoe said, grinning at her so Finley knew she was teasing.

"Sorry," Finley said. "Truth hurts."

Zoe laughed. "Evan is running?"

Finley nodded. "Yes. He is big into it but hasn't motivated me to get out there yet."

"But things are good with you guys?"

"So good," Finley said, hearing her giddy tone. "I never thought I would be this happy. We're so compatible, even though we're different. He's amazing."

"He's good for you," Zoe said. "Makes you slow down a little. I like him a lot."

"He's kind and thoughtful, and so smart," Finley said. "If you had told me I'd be looking forward to a night of playing Scrabble or doing a puzzle, I would have said you were crazy. But he is easy to talk to and teaches me things."

Zoe smiled at her. "You sound like you're in love."

"I can't be," Finley said. "It's too soon. Right?"

"I can't tell you that," Zoe said. "Your brother claims he fell in love with me at first sight. And if I were to admit the truth, it happened fast for me too, but I wasn't willing to admit it. There's no right or wrong length of time."

"For what?" Kendra asked as she joined them.

"Falling in love," Zoe answered.

"Interesting," Kendra said, smiling as she met Finley's eyes. "Things are good with the hot doctor?"

"They are," Finley said.

"We all have different experiences," Kendra said. "Falling in love is not a one size fits all situation. There are so many things that factor in, but trust your instincts and don't question whether or not it's too soon."

Zoe nodded. "There's no right or wrong way. It's what your heart tells you, not one of us."

"You don't think it's too soon?"

"I got married before I admitted I was in love," Zoe answered. "You think I'm the right person to ask?"

Kendra laughed. "It's not. There's no such thing as long as you're being open and honest with each other. Don't question it, just enjoy."

Stella and Ben, Kendra's mother- and father-in-law, came in, and Finley stood to hug them both. Finley was happy to see that she looked healthy and was back to her full strength after her treatment. Her hair was growing back, short and spiky around her face, and it suited her.

"You look great, Stella," Finley said.

"Thank you, honey," Stella said. "You do as well. I heard a rumor about you and Dr. Lincoln. Is it true?"

"Yes," she said, blushing. "Evan and I are in a relationship now."

"I knew it," Stella said, smiling at her. "Benji, did you hear that? I was right about those two."

"You always are, my darling," he said, kissing her on the cheek as he walked to sit with his grandchildren.

"I'm so happy for you," Stella said. "Stop by and visit us one day, will you?"

"Absolutely," Finley promised. After hugging the other woman again and agreeing to give her best wishes to Evan, she ran upstairs to get the dog. She didn't want to miss seeing Evan before he started his run and would have plenty of time to socialize when the race was going.

She grabbed her thick down coat and the dog's leash before running back down the outside stairs. The racers were congregated on the street, which had been blocked off from traffic for the event. Finley stood on the porch of the Palace, scanning the crowd for Evan. Thankfully, his height helped, and she was able to make her way to him at the starting line.

"Morning," she said, standing on her toes to kiss him. "You ready?"

"More than," he said. "It's cold. I'm looking forward to warming up. Can you take my coat when we're about to line up? I had planned to leave it inside, but I would have frozen by the time they let us go."

"Of course," she said. "This is a lot of people."

"I know," Evan said. "JJ told me that people come from neighboring towns. It's for charity, and it's a lot of fun, so that draws people. And of course, people want to catch a glimpse of our local celebrities, which helps raise more money."

"Plus, think of all the pie you can eat and not feel guilty," she said. "I probably should have done it with you."

"This would be a big jump," he said. "From not running to a race. But if you want to start, we can run together."

"No, I'd just slow you down," she said. "And I like watching."

He laughed and looked over at where the mayor was climbing onto a stage at the starting line. "I think we're about to start. You should get back onto the porch, so you don't get trampled."

She took his coat and walked with Guinness back to the safety of the Palace porch. The Burrows family and their friends were making their way outside to watch the start, but there was still plenty of room for Finley. She waved as Evan ran across the starting line and then caught sight of Audrey on the sidewalk. Her friend saw her and made her way through the crowd to join her.

"Hey," Audrey said. "I was looking for you. Evan is running, right?"

"He is," Finley said. "But I wasn't expecting to see you here. I thought you would be out late last night with the informal high school reunion."

"I was," Audrey admitted. "I have a nap in my future. But I was hoping to catch a glimpse of Cary before they start."

"Oh, is that a thing?"

"I wish," Audrey said. "I ran into him once more, at the coffee shop, and we talked. That's when he mentioned he was running today. He seems like a good guy. And he's hot. But I'm not sure he's into me."

"He'd be crazy not to be," Finley said loyally. "Just make sure you don't fall for another guy only based on looks."

"I should have learned my lesson a long time ago," Audrey said, sighing. "But I can't help it. Tall, dark and handsome will get me every time."

"If this doesn't work out, we're going to find you a short, pale, ordinary guy to go out with," Finley said.

Audrey rolled her eyes. "Because that's what you did."

"I got lucky," Finley said. "I almost overlooked Evan. And that would have been a mistake. That's all I'm saying, be open to someone who might not strike you right away as your type."

Audrey looked annoyed, crossing her arms across her chest. "I guess you're an expert now, huh?"

"I'm sorry," Finley said. "I don't mean to upset you. Or gloat."

Audrey looked away, glancing down the street. "I think I'll head down to the finish line," she said. "See if any of my friends are that way."

She walked off, her message clear. Finley had just upset her, and Audrey was angry. As much as she wanted to chase her and apologize again, she stayed where she was. This was her first Thanksgiving with a boyfriend, and she wasn't going to act like she wasn't excited about that.

There was nothing she could do about Audrey right now, so she pushed it out of her head. She could apologize again when they went back to work, or text her over the weekend. Her words had been meant sincerely, and she hadn't realized Audrey would get upset. But if she were the single one and felt like her friend was bragging, she would have probably reacted the same way.

Shaking her head to clear her thoughts, she turned to catch sight of Evan coming down the street toward the finish line. She cheered loudly, the Burrows joining her when they saw him, and he was among the first to finish. Finley rushed down to meet him as he approached the Palace, hugging him as Guinness jumped on both of them.

"Congratulations," she said. "You were so fast!"

"I had a good reason," he said. He put his arm around her as they walked into the Palace, leaving Guinness on the porch with Kendra's daughter.

"You did?" She watched him walk slowly up and down the length of the bar, letting his breath come back to normal and his body cool down. While it was cold outside, he had worked up a sweat, and she was glad it was warm inside the restaurant for his sake.

"I did," he said, finally stopping right in front of her. He gave her a salty kiss before continuing. "You were at the end. That made me a little faster."

"Plus, the turkey," she teased him.

"Are you calling my dog a turkey?"

She laughed and hugged him, feeling the sweat soak through her sweater. "Uh oh. I might need another shower now."

"Funny thing," he said. "I do too. Should we head out?"

"Sure," she said. "If you're ready? I don't want you to freeze on the walk home."

"I'll be alright," he said, pulling on his coat. "And I have something at the next finish line to really warm me up."

She smiled at him, taking his hand as they walked out to say goodbye to everyone. Thoughts of Audrey and their spat were gone now; only happy thoughts of the day ahead ran through her brain. This was all she had ever wanted, and she almost wanted to pinch herself to see if it was real. Maybe Zoe was right, and she was in love. The idea didn't scare her, she realized. Instead, it felt exciting and true. Now she just had to hope he felt the same and, for once, stop herself from speaking before she wanted the words out in the universe.

Chapter 25

Finley insisted on bringing Guinness with them to Thanksgiving dinner, not willing to leave a member of the family home alone. That left Evan driving with the dog in the front seat, Finley in the back protecting the baked goods.

"Your family is going to see us and think I'm insane," he said as he pulled down the street.

"No, they'll think I'm being a princess," she said. "Making you drive me like this."

"If Guinness had any manners, we wouldn't have this problem," he said, shooting a look at the dog. Guinness, happy as could be with his head out the window, didn't seem concerned.

"Any word from your family today?" Finley asked. The question was soft, and he knew she was treading carefully, as he hadn't been willing to spend much time talking about his situation. The sudden need his parents felt to be involved in his life was difficult to handle, and having his brother in town didn't help.

"They called yesterday," he answered. "All of them. But I was busy at work and never got back to them. I got a few messages this morning too, from my mom and dad, but I'll call them later."

"They probably just wanted to wish you a Happy Thanksgiving," she said. Ever the optimist, Evan knew Finley couldn't begin to understand the drama that had happened in his family over the years. And he'd rather not get into it, especially on a day that had started out great. Better to leave out the fact that all three had called again this morning, or she would probably insist on him returning the calls.

"I'm sure that's it," he said finally. "I'll worry about that tomorrow. Today, I want to eat and enjoy time with you and your family."

"And watch football," Finley said. "They all expect you to be in there with them, but I'll be helping Zoe and my mom. I'll check on you a lot though."

"I could help too," he offered.

"No, better that you bond with the men," she said. "If you're in the kitchen, they'll accuse you of being a suck-up. Trust me, it's better this way. And we will be out there a lot; there isn't much to do until the turkey is ready."

"I should probably learn more about sports," he said as he parked. "It seems like your dad and brothers know everything."

"It just sounds like that because they are all know-it-alls," Finley said. "And they played a lot when they were younger. But it's fine; they already like you. Don't pretend to like something you don't."

"For you, I would," he said, opening the door and helping Guinness out before getting a pie from the backseat.

Finley picked up the other two containers and led the way to the door, which already had a Christmas wreath on it. Evan was shocked to think that the next holiday was only a few weeks away, and he might spend it here as well. Obviously, he and Finley hadn't discussed it yet, but it was nice to know that he had the promise of something to do when the day came.

Over the years in Boston, he had made sure to be working on all the holidays. He had picked up shifts in the emergency department, or anywhere else they could fit him. If they didn't have a need, he had found a project to occupy his time during those days. Better to be busy than to think of his abject loneliness as people around the world celebrated with their families. And this year, for the first time, he didn't have to do that.

"Hello," Finley called as she opened the door. "Happy Thanksgiving!"

Voices called back wishing them the same, although they had seen almost everyone at the race that morning. Finley greeted her parents with hugs and poked a sleepy Desmond, who was wearing flannel pajama pants and an ugly Christmas sweater. "What are you wearing?"

"I'm a little behind on laundry," he said. "And I knew Zoe was going to be all decorated for Christmas."

"Drop off your laundry with me," Maggie offered. "You're working so hard. I can do that for you."

"Mom, he's a grown adult," JJ said, rolling his eyes. "And he works from home all day. He can do it himself."

"Hey! Don't deny our wonderful mother the chance to take care of one of her babies," Desmond cried. He put his arm around his mother as if protecting her from JJ. "You're going to upset her."

"I won't be upset if I can't do your chores, Des," Maggie said with a laugh. "But I don't mind. Or maybe you can throw yours in with Fin's."

Desmond's eyes lit up as he met his twins. "That would be amazing, Mom, but she's a little busy. As a matter of fact, I haven't--"

Colin elbowed his brother hard enough to stop him from talking. Maggie glanced between them. "What am I missing?"

"Nothing," Finley said quickly.

"You kids," Maggie said. She pulled a bottle of water out of the refrigerator and went out onto the deck where Tim was watching the dog in the backyard.

"Des, you are the worst," Finley moaned. "She's going to be all over me to tell her what you were trying to say."

"You don't want your mom to know that you abandoned your twin brother?" Desmond put his hand over his heart, a shocked look on his face. "How was I to know that? It's not like you've seen me in days."

"I'm sorry, Des," Finley said. "I didn't mean to abandon you."

Colin rolled his eyes. "He's playing you. Having the apartment to himself means his late-night antics can happen right there, so he doesn't have to go anywhere."

Finley's eyes narrowed at her brother. "You better not be having random women upstairs."

"You say random, I say new friends," Desmond said, shrugging.

"You're unbelievable," Finley said.

"Me? You moved out without telling me," Desmond said.

"No, I didn't," she all but yelled at him.

Zoe stepped between them, holding both hands up. "Stop," she said quietly. "Neither of you are mad at the other. Des, don't rain on her parade. She has a right to be happy, and she's not obligated to tell you everything. Finley, he can have guests anytime he wants. If he was being courteous before so he wouldn't wake you, I think that's nice. Don't worry about what happens when you aren't there."

Evan was watching all of this from the doorway between the family room and kitchen, not sure if he should step in. In his family, any drama or fights resulted in days or weeks of silence. But in all honestly, they didn't care enough to fight about much. Finley and her siblings were tight, and seemed to share almost everything, and emotions ran high.

When Finley's shoulders sagged slightly, and Desmond stepped over to hug her, the room seemed to let out a sigh of relief. Everyone went back to their own activities, with Colin and JJ heading to the TV, gesturing for Evan to follow.

"They'll be fine," JJ said conspiratorially. "They have always been like this. It's like they share a brain."

"Scary thought," Colin said from where he had settled on the couch.

"Stay quiet, or they'll take aim at you," JJ cautioned his brother.

Colin mimed zipping his lips shut and then turned his gaze to Evan. "Things with you guys are good?"

"Yeah," he said, swallowing his nerves. "Finley is great, and we're having a lot of fun."

Colin nodded and turned to the TV, apparently satisfied with the answer. Within a few minutes, Desmond had joined Colin on the couch, and Tim eventually returned with Guinness.

When Evan's phone rang a short time later, he almost ignored it. But one glance at the screen told him the hospital was calling, so he excused himself to step onto the porch. "Dr. Lincoln," he said after clicking answer.

"Doctor, I'm sorry to bother you on a holiday," the other voice said. "This is Dr. Coveney in the emergency room."

"Is everything okay? Is it my brother?" Evan felt panic at the thought, having no idea why this doctor would be calling unless it was about Zach.

"Your brother? No, I'm sorry," Dr. Coveney said. "We have a patient of yours here. According to the notes I've been reading, you've been diligent in following her in two recent admissions, so I wanted you to know what was happening."

"Is it Edna Lee?"

The other doctor confirmed and then ran through what was going on. "It doesn't appear she has much family," Dr. Coveney concluded.

"No, she doesn't," Evan said. "I'll be there as soon as I can. We're about to have dinner here."

"No rush," Dr. Coveney said. "She's comfortable and safe. I just wanted you to know since it's a long weekend."

"I appreciate it," Evan said. "I owe you a coffee in the cafeteria one day."

The other doctor laughed and wished him a happy holiday, and Evan slipped the phone back in his pocket. Through the window, he could see JJ carving the turkey, and the whole family gathered in the kitchen. He could put the situation with Mrs. Lee out of his mind for a few hours to enjoy Thanksgiving and then get to the hospital before it was too late.

***

After the family had stuffed themselves with all the delicious food that Zoe had made, JJ stood at the head of the table. "Zoe and I have a little gift for mom and Dad," he said. Zoe produced two boxes from the buffet behind her, and JJ passed them to his parents. "Before you open them, we also have something for my siblings. Evan, I'm sorry to leave you out of this."

Evan nodded his understanding, suspecting what the gifts were about. JJ handed boxes to everyone at the table and then indicated they should start opening, which turned into a flurry of paper and tape flying everywhere. Suddenly, Maggie could be heard crying out as she rushed at her daughter-in-law, hugging her tight.

"What's going on?" Desmond groused as he fought with the tape on his box. Before he got it open, Tim stood, hugging his son and beaming a smile.

Finley got her box open next to Evan and pulled out a t-shirt with Best Aunt written in big letters across the front. "Oh, Zoe!" she cried, pushing her chair back to join in the hugging. Colin and Desmond soon opened their uncle shirts, Desmond pulling his on over the sweater before hugging Zoe.

"It's a little early," Zoe said, once everyone had taken their seats again. "I won't be out of the first trimester for another ten

232

days. But my doctor assured me that everything is going well, and I should be okay. And we wanted to tell you all today."

"Is this what happened a few weeks ago?" Finley asked, her glance going between her brother and Evan.

"Yes," JJ said, nodding. "I told Evan as soon as we got her into the room. I'm sorry we asked him to keep quiet. We didn't want everyone to be upset if something went wrong again."

"But we would be no matter what," Finley said. "We love you guys. Of course, we would want to support you again if something went wrong."

"I'm sorry, Fin," Zoe said. "I wasn't thinking clearly. I hope you won't be mad."

"Mad? I'm one of the world's best aunts, according to my new shirt," Finley said, smiling back at her. "I can't be mad when there's a baby Finley on the way."

"That settles it," Maggie said to Tim. "We are not going to Florida for the winter. I'm going to be here doing my grandmotherly duty."

"Don't be silly," JJ said. "We don't expect you to do that. We figured Des could babysit, like he does Guinness."

Both Desmond and Guinness's heads snapped up, one looking happier than the other. "I don't change diapers," Desmond said. "This will not work. Mom has to stay."

"I'll babysit anytime," Finley promised.

"But you work," Maggie said. "Dad and I have all day to watch the baby while JJ and Zoe are busy."

"Zoe will be off for a few months," JJ said. "And we both have some flexibility in our schedules."

"Good," Tim said with a smile. "That means you can make us a second one in record time."

"I have three siblings," JJ said, pointing around the table. "Maybe one of them could produce grandchild number two."

"Not it," Colin and Desmond called out, as if they were being asked to do the dishes. They dissolved into a fit of laughter, and Maggie huddled with Zoe to discuss the pregnancy.

"You aren't mad, are you?" Evan asked Finley, leaning close to her. "I didn't want to take this moment away from them. If I had thought something was wrong, I would have told you right away."

"No, I trust you," she said. "I understand now why you were acting so weird that night. But I'm glad you were here to help her."

"I had her come in the next morning for an ultrasound with obstetrics," he told her. "They made sure all was fine. She was really just dehydrated."

"I promise I'm not mad," she said. "No more secrets though, okay?"

"Deal," he said. He wanted to kiss her, but doing so in a room with her entire family watching was one step more than he was comfortable with. Instead, he squeezed her hand under the table.

"Did you get a peek at the gender?" Finley asked, her eyes sparkling. "Now that we have an all-honesty pledge, I have to ask."

"I didn't go to the ultrasound," he said with a laugh. "And I think it's too soon."

"Darn," she said. "Keep me posted if you stumble across it."

Everyone helped clear the table and pull the desserts out, the family still buzzing over the news. A few hours later, so full he felt he could burst, Evan was driving home. Finley was sleepy, yawning every few seconds next to him. Guinness, also exhausted from a busy day, was sound asleep on her lap.

When they walked into his house, he helped Finley out of her coat but kept his on. "I have to run to the hospital," he told her. "I'll be back as soon as I can, but don't wait up."

"What? Why?"

"A doctor from the emergency room called earlier," he said. "Edna Lee was brought in by ambulance. She's not doing well, but she has no one. I just want to go check on her, make sure she knows she's not alone."

"I can come," Finley said, fighting off a yawn.

"No," he said, kissing her. "We'll go together in the morning. You're exhausted."

"Will you call me if you need me?" she asked.

"Of course," he promised. "I'll text you no matter what, in case you're awake and want an update. But I'll be back as soon as I can."

He raced back out to his car after kissing her one last time, hoping he would find Edna awake. It was bad enough she had been alone on Thanksgiving; he didn't want her to be alone and scared in the hospital as well. Even if he knew what the tests showed, he wasn't willing to accept that his patient was slipping away.

A knock at the kitchen door early on Friday morning interrupted Finley's online shopping and got Guinness barking. She shushed the dog and hurried to open the door, not wanting Evan to be woken up. She had fallen asleep quickly the night before and noticed that the sun was rising as he came in but didn't see the exact time. She had gone back to sleep and been awake an hour later, figuring she could get a jumpstart on her holiday shopping. The unexpected visitor was preventing her from spending money on baby toys that wouldn't be needed for at least two years, so she should be grateful.

An older couple stood on the porch, unfamiliar to Finley. "Good morning," she said. "Can I help you?"

"Oh, I'm sorry," the woman said. "We must have the wrong house."

"Who are you looking for?" Finley asked, holding Guinness by the collar so he didn't jump on them. They were both well dressed, and a muddy dog print likely wouldn't be welcome.

"Dr. Evan Lincoln," the man said.

"This is his home," Finley said. "But I'm afraid he's asleep. He had a late night at the hospital."

"We can come back," the woman replied. "We have been trying to call him, and he wasn't answering, so we wanted to make sure everything was okay."

"Do you want me to leave a message for him?" Finley asked, perplexed. Were these patients? Family members of patients? Salespeople bold enough to track a doctor to his home?

"No, that's fine," the man said, taking the woman's elbow to steer her away. "We'll try calling again later."

Finley shrugged and closed the door, unsettled somehow by the encounter. The woman had been examining her in a way that felt uncomfortable, but she couldn't put her finger on why. Whoever they were, they had left, and Evan had slept through the encounter, so she should be happy about that and let the rest go.

Guinness followed her loyally back to the couch, where she found her cell phone and laptop. Before she could give it any more thought, she hit the button to call JJ.

"Hey," he said, answering on the first ring. "What's up?"

"Are you working?" she asked, hearing noise in the background.

"Yes," he said. "Little early-morning excitement at the toy store. Apparently, they only had three of some hot toy that everyone needed, and people were fighting."

"Like, physically fighting?" Finley couldn't imagine being that intent on a toy for a child. Then again, she had already spent hundreds on a baby that she hadn't met yet, so she just might.

"Some shoving," JJ said. "We settled it peacefully. A couple of the ones causing trouble don't even have kids; they were trying to get the toy to resell it for more. Once we figured that out, we got them into the right hands."

Finley heard the door of a car open and then close, and then it was quieter on JJ's end. "I'm at Evan's," she said. "And two people just came to the door. It felt weird, so I wanted to call you."

"Weird, how? Were they threatening?" JJ asked, all business. "Want me to come right there?"

"No, it's okay," she said. "They left. And they were older, so not threatening. But Evan doesn't really know many people around here other than patients and people at the hospital. Why would someone come to his house?"

"Could it be another doctor?"

"No, I would have recognized them," Finley said. "It's such a small hospital, we all know each other. And I know most of his patients too, and their families. Although I'm switching to work with another doctor, I guess it's possible these two came in and dealt with Audrey."

"Charity folks?" JJ suggested. "Or door-to-door salespeople?"

"They didn't have any pamphlets or anything with them," Finley replied, thinking back to the couple.

"Then probably not trying to sell him something," JJ said. "Are you sure he doesn't have any family that could be popping by for a visit?"

"No," she said. "His parents don't live nearby, and it doesn't sound like they have a relationship like that. I'll ask him when he wakes up."

"Late sleeper, huh?" JJ asked, a teasing note in his voice.

"He went to the hospital last night," Finley told him. "Apparently he got a call that a patient had been admitted, and he didn't want her to be alone."

"Wow. Would other doctors do that?"

"No," Finley said. "He's pretty special."

"And you're happy?" JJ asked, ever the protective older brother.

"Happier than I've ever been," Finley said. "I'm waiting for the other shoe to drop."

"Don't say that," JJ said. "When it's right, you don't have to think like that."

"I know you're right," she admitted. "But it's hard. I've had so many bad boyfriends, how do I know this one isn't the same?"

"Well, he spent the night sitting with a lonely, sick patient," JJ said. "After being with your family all day. I'd say he's showing you in all the right ways. I know you were upset a few weeks ago when Zoe passed out, but Evan was amazing. He put our minds at ease and followed up with Zoe the next day. No one you've ever dated before would have done that."

"I've never dated a doctor before," Finley reminded him. "I always thought it would be too complicated."

"Even without any previous experience regarding your boyfriends," JJ argued. "He cared. He was kind to us when we were both terrified. He didn't dismiss Zoe's fears, and he found a way to put us at ease without having to go sit in the emergency room for hours. I think it says a lot about the kind of person he is."

"You're right," Finley said. "He really is remarkable."

"Don't screw it up with your insecurities," JJ cautioned her. "You're pretty awesome yourself. I don't know how to say it without sounding sappy or like I'm just saying it because I'm your brother. But all those guys who made you feel bad? They weren't worthy of your time. Trust the good one, not the bad ones."

"Thanks, JJ," Finely said, feeling emotional. "You're going to be a great dad."

"I'm just hoping I get a boy," he said with a laugh. "I can't imagine having to do this every day."

"Stop," she said. "You'd be a great girl dad."

"I already love this baby so much," he said, his voice quieter. "Nothing matters. They can be or do anything, and I'll still love them."

"You're going to make me cry," Finley said. "Go back to work."

"Call me if the strangers appear again, or if anything else weird happens," he said. "I'd rather be cautious than have something bad happen. As a matter of fact, I'm heading past Evan's street, so I'll do a drive-by just to make sure no one is lingering outside."

"Do you need his address?" Finley asked.

"You think my baby sister has been spending nights at a house and I don't already have it?"

She laughed, then sobered. "I hope that's all you looked up. You didn't do a background check on him, did you?"

"No," JJ said. After a moment of silence, he cleared his throat. "I did make sure that the hospital would have run one before he started."

"JJ!" Finley punched the pillow next to her, startling Guinness.

"Gotta go," he said. "If I see anything weird, I'll let you know. Call me back if you need me."

***

Evan came downstairs shortly after ten, yawning as he came over to hug her. "Morning," he said, burying his face in her hair. "You smell good."

"Thanks," she said. "It's probably a mix of coffee and pine needles from getting dragged through a tree by Guinness. He was determined to catch a squirrel and didn't mind the branches we had to go through in the process."

"I assume he failed?" Evan looked over at the dog, who appeared to be smiling at the sight of his favorite person.

"Miserably," Finley reported. "The squirrel seemed to taunt him from a branch just out of reach."

"Tough break," Evan said, rubbing the dog's head. "What are you up to?"

"I did some online shopping," Finley said. "Who knew having a niece would be so expensive? And now I'm reading."

"You don't know if it's a niece or nephew," Evan pointed out as he walked toward the kitchen. "I hope you aren't buying a lot of things that need to be returned."

"No," Finley said. "I thought of that. I've stuck with neutral colors. And giraffes and elephants. You can't imagine how cute some of the little clothes are. But the second I find out, it's on."

"I'm a little frightened about our future suddenly. If you're this excited about a niece or nephew, what will happen when it's

241

our turn?" He left the room briefly, leaving her head and heart swirling with the possibilities he had introduced before he reappeared with a steaming cup of coffee. "I need to update you on Mrs. Lee," he said. "She's your patient too, and she said it was okay for me to share."

"How is she?" Finley leaned toward him on the sofa, feeling like he might need the comfort as he spoke as much as she would when hearing them.

"Not good," he said. "I got her latest bloodwork the other day. It showed that what we are doing might be working, but it's also damaging other organs in the process. A lot of it is what we're giving her for the side effects, but the overall effect is bad for her. Her heart is showing signs of failure, among others. She called for help yesterday when she was having chest pains, and it confirmed what I suspected when I saw the lab results."

"That's terrible," Finley said. "Poor Edna."

"I know," he said, running a hand through his hair. "We talked a lot last night, when she was awake. She's going to stop treatment. I explained hospice to her, and she was going to think about it. She asked me to have the chaplain come visit her today, so I'll make sure that happens. She thanked me, and you."

"We were just doing our jobs," Finley said.

"No, we were going above that," Evan said. "Don't diminish what you do. You make a difference in your patient's lives. You could just hang medications and move on, but you don't. You sit and talk to them, make sure they have a companion if they come alone, and keep their spirits light."

"Thank you," she said, moved at all he had noticed.

"I left a message with the volunteer coordinator, and she texted me this morning that they had a long list of people who were willing to sit with Edna," Evan shared. "She's popular among them. So, she won't be left alone."

"Good," Finley said. "You are remarkable, Dr. Lincoln. Not many doctors would have done the same."

"Sure, they would have," he said. "We aren't in a profession where we can leave it behind, either of us. If I can do something to make her final days happy and comfortable, I'm going to."

Finley nodded, surprised at the emotion she felt at losing Edna. They lost a good number of patients over the years, and it always hurt. But this one seemed especially poignant. Edna had become a friend, and Finley would miss her.

"I'd like to see her," she said. "If we can."

"Absolutely," Evan replied. "I told her we would be by this weekend, either at the hospital or at home. I'm hoping they'll be able to get her set up to go home today."

"Good," Finley said, slapping her hands on her thighs. "You must be starving. Why don't I make you something to eat?"

"Should we go to lunch instead?" Evan suggested. "We could walk around town after and see what the Black Friday sales look like. Maybe you can help me with some ideas, because I'm going to be very stumped when it comes time to shop for you."

"I don't need anything," she said. "But did you just say I was a bad cook?"

"Did I?" Evan stood, pulling her into his arms to kiss. "I don't think so. I just meant that scrambled eggs are challenging to everyone."

She laughed but hugged him back. "I don't believe you. But I can hear your stomach, so let's go get ready."

"Maybe I could get you cooking lessons for Christmas," he suggested as they walked up the stairs. "Or a gift card to Palace Plates."

"You're going to regret that," she vowed, chasing him up the stairs.

He ran into the bathroom, peeking out when she got to the landing. "Do you need to shower? I can wash your hair."

"No," she said. "I've been up since seven, so I'm just going to change. And you need some alone time to think about what you just said."

She could hear his laughter, and then his voice as he sang in the shower. Despite the difficult night he had, he still woke up with optimism and was ready to face the world. She couldn't believe how much she had misjudged him for months and almost wished they could start all over again. That way, she wouldn't have wasted all that time disliking him and could have just fallen straight away. Because no matter what her head tried to say, she was crazy in love with him, and if his comments about their future were any indication, she had a lot to look forward to.

Chapter 27

"I realized something when I was showering," Evan said. Finley was across from him in the small booth, set in the back half of the local diner. The restaurant only served breakfast and lunch daily, and was busier than usual with locals and tourists.

"What's that?" Finely asked, setting her menu down.

The waitress came by and offered them both coffee, so he waited until she finished before he continued. "Yesterday was my first nice holiday in a long time, if not forever. I think it was my favorite so far."

"Really?" she smiled at him, then frowned. "I'm really glad that you're enjoying my family. But that's also really sad."

He shrugged. "I worked most years, before this," he said. "And when I was a kid, it just seemed normal."

"What was it like? Didn't you have aunts and uncles? Cousins or grandparents?"

"No," he said, shaking his head. "My parents were both only children. We had grandparents when we were little, but I only have vague memories of them. I think I know where my parents get their parenting style from."

"That's sad, for all of you," she said. "I'm glad you avoided that gene."

"Me too," he said. He stirred his coffee and took a sip before asking her the question that had been on his mind. "Do you want kids?"

"Yes," she said, looking surprised. "I thought you would have picked up on that by now."

"I just wanted to make sure," he said. "We haven't had a lot of those conversations, about what the future would look like. I'm really hoping that it is us together. With a family of our own."

"Here in Windsor Peak, right?"

"Where did that come from?"

"I don't know," she said, shrugging slightly. "A lot of doctors come in for a few years when they're young and then move to bigger hospitals. All I've heard since I started was that most young doctors come and go quickly, moving on to better positions. I guess I always thought you would do the same."

"No," he said, shaking his head. Then he stopped himself from answering quickly, thinking back a few months. "I don't deny that I originally thought that way. I had been offered a position at Dana Farber right before I came up here, but I had already accepted the spot and didn't want to leave them in a bind. I thought I would stay for a year and then could take them up on it. But I've fallen in love with this town, and the hospital. I never got to spend the time with patients in Boston like I do here, and I enjoy that. And there's one more thing."

"What's that?" She looked so beautiful, sitting across from him. Her eyes were shining with happiness, and everything about her made him feel better.

He reached for her hand, which she willingly gave him, squeezing lightly as they linked. "I've also fallen in love," he said slowly, suddenly unsure of himself. The doubt made the final words came out as a whisper. "With you."

She smiled so brightly it could have powered the whole diner, or maybe the town. "Good," she said. "Because I happen to be crazy in love with you."

"This is kind of the worst possible setting for an announcement like this, isn't it?"

She looked around, then back at him. "I don't know," she said. "I think it's kind of perfect. We're surrounded by life and joy. All these familiar faces enjoying time with their loved ones, and the tourists who came to see our perfect little town. I think this is just the right spot."

"And that's a big part of why I love you," he said.

"What?"

"You see the sun in places other people would find darkness," he said.

"I think that's just about the nicest thing anyone has ever said to me," she said. "I'm glad I already told you how I feel, because otherwise, I would have said it first."

"Well, never forget that I did," he teased her. "I know how competitive you are."

***

They were full and happy as they set out down Main Street to see what the local stores were offering for sales. Although Finley had done some damage on her credit card earlier, she insisted she had more to buy and wanted to support the local stores. He was happy to tag along, hoping to find the perfect gift for her.

"I'll also need you to help me pick things out for your parents," he said. "And probably your siblings? Do you guys still exchange gifts?"

"We do, but I'm sure that will change once the baby comes," Finley said. "Eventually, we will all just want to buy for the kids, but since she's not here yet, we'll still exchange this year."

"Okay, so I have a lot of shopping to do," he said. "I should make a list."

She squeezed his hand. "Relax," she said. "We can get most of them together. JJ and Zoe give gifts from both of them, no reason we can't do the same."

"We have to spoil Guinness," Evan said as they walked by the pet store. "We can stop there later; it looks busy."

Finley glanced in the window as they passed and laughed. "It looks like Patrick Burrows is in there. That's why there's a crowd; the tourists must have all followed him in."

247

"Should we let JJ know?" Evan asked, looking back at where his new friend was trapped by fans.

"No, I'm sure the store will if it gets bad," Finley said. Then she gasped and put her hand over her mouth. "Oh, I can't believe I forgot."

"Forgot what?"

"It happened so early this morning, and I got distracted by the shopping and the love confessions, it slipped my mind," she said.

"What did?"

"Early this morning, when you were sleeping," she said. "A couple came and knocked on the door. I didn't recognize them, and when I told them you were sleeping, they said they would come back. I offered to take a message, but they said no. That they had called you a few times and wanted to make sure you were okay?"

She was looking at him with a question on her face, and he knew he had to answer. But first, he had to take a minute to compose himself and his thoughts. After a deep breath, he responded, looking away from Finley's open and honest face as he did. "I think it was probably my parents," he said.

"Your parents? Here? Why do you say that?" She tugged on his arm and pulled him toward a bench in the town square, which was busy but not as crowded as the street. "Tell me everything."

It felt as if parts of him were shutting down on the inside. The happiness he had been feeling all morning, the sense of belonging her family had offered him the day before. All clicking off at the thought that his family was invading this private life he was creating. Before he could drift too far, Finley pulled his face so their eyes met.

"I love you," she said. "Nothing will change that. I'm on your side. Don't shut me out."

"I won't," he said, his voice sounding hoarse suddenly. "I'm just overwhelmed."

"Why are they here?"

"Because Zach is," he said with a rough laugh. "They are showing up for him. They want me to give him a chance, to let him back in my life. I can't believe they showed up this way, for him. They have never done it once for me. Did you know they didn't even attend my graduation from medical school?"

She shook her head silently, gripping his hand tightly, as if she was afraid he would run off. "No, that's terrible."

"They had work obligations, they said," Evan continued. "But then I find out that my father dropped everything to help my brother. Can you imagine? Too busy to see me graduate with honors from Harvard, but ready to rescue Zach."

"Helping him how? Hadn't he already destroyed your relationship by then?"

"Yes," Evan said, nodding. "But after he blew through what he stole from me, he was hopelessly addicted to drugs and had nowhere to go. Zach called our dad as a last resort, never thinking that he would actually show up. My dad was living in Arizona, and he went straight over to get Zach. Brought him to rehab and visited him any time he was allowed. Then when he got out, they lived together."

"Wow," Finley said. "I can't imagine what a betrayal that feels like. Especially when you felt like your dad didn't care about you all this time."

"Both of them," he said. "Or all three, however you want to put it. No one told me what was going on. Neither of my parents stepped up when Zach did what he did. I was all alone in the world and had to fight for everything. And Zach, who screwed up in the worst way possible, gets their love and attention?"

"I think you need to say this to them," Finley said gently. "Let them know how much they have hurt you. You're entitled to ask them to leave, to continue your life without them. But if I could give you one piece of advice?"

He nodded. "Of course."

"Listen to them," she said. "With all the families that come and go from our unit at work, I've seen people heal from worse. I know it feels like the worst right now for you, but it's not impossible to fix this. If you send them away now, you might never have a chance again."

"Does that mean Zach too? Now that he's sober and claiming to be a good person, do I need to forgive him too?"

"I can't answer that," Finley said. "I can see that you're hurt by your parents, and that you might never be fully okay if you let this continue. Even if you just say what you just told me, and get it off your chest. You owe it to yourself, and your future kids, to be heard. To feel seen by them."

"I thought I could outrun it," he said, his voice quiet. "If I just built my own life here, and pushed all of them out of my mind, it would just go away."

"That's not healthy, and you know it," she said. "I know my family is different, but we have fights and then go back to normal all the time. With the right attitude, and some good communication, hopefully you can get to a better place with all of them. A place you can be happy with. You don't have to let them into your life any more than you want to, but I think you need this."

"Will you go with me?" he asked. "To sit down with my parents?"

"Of course," she said. "Do you want to do it now?"

"No," he said, shaking his head. "I'm running on four hours of sleep. I've already experienced all the emotional highs and lows that I can for today. I'll set it up for tomorrow, unless you have something else going on?"

"Tomorrow is perfect," she said. "That gives you time to think and get a good night's sleep."

"And do some more shopping," he said, standing up. "It's supposed to be therapeutic, right?"

"We can go home," she offered. "Or I can go up to my place, if you'd rather be alone."

"That's the last thing I want," he said. "You give me something to hold on to. If it weren't for you, I'd probably be packed and halfway out of town by now."

"Well, I'm glad that's not happening," she said. "If you decide quiet would be better, just say the word and we'll get out of here."

He nodded, and they started walking towards the crowded street. His mind was swirling, but her hand in his felt solid and sure, and that was enough for now.

***

After a full day of shopping, Evan was ready to sit with his feet up. Finley had been running her purchases up to the apartment over the Palace all day, so they didn't have to carry bags with them from store to store. He wasn't entirely sure, but it was possible that she had purchased one of everything for sale as they made their way through town.

"Want to grab a pizza and salad from Slice Girls on the way home?" he asked when she returned from bringing the latest bags up to her apartment.

"That sounds perfect," she said. "The bar is packed. I was going to say we should eat there, but it's too full. Audrey is in there with her new friend."

"Oh?" Evan took her hand again as they started walking toward the pizza palace. "I didn't know she had one."

"You really need to get better with your hospital gossip," Finley said. "She's been seeing a guy for a few weeks. It doesn't seem to be going anywhere, but she's trying her hardest."

"I will never be paying attention to the nurses' love lives," he said with a laugh. "Other than yours, of course."

"It's like a little soap opera," she said. "And we have a front-row seat. How can you not want to know who's dating who?"

"Give me one, and we'll see if I care."

"Gabe, the X-ray tech? He's with Hannah from the emergency room," Finley immediately rattled off. "But she had been dating Oscar from ortho before that, so it's quite the scandal."

"Huh," he said. "Turns out, I don't care at all. Who would have known?"

She punched him lightly in the arm as she laughed. "All you big-brain doctors," she teased him. "But if I told you what doctor from Cardiology was dating another doctor from Obstetrics, I bet you would want to know."

"Only if it impacts my use of the doctor's lounge or sleep quarters," he said. "But maybe I should know, just to be safe."

Her laughter rang out as they sat to wait for their food to be ready. He knew that he would have some dark thoughts later, when he finally responded to his parents, but for now, she had chased them out. Just being next to her made him feel more settled and positive, and he felt better about the next day, just knowing she would be at his side.

Chapter 28

Finley sat next to Evan at the table in the Palace. He had opted to have the meeting with his parents there rather than at his house, figuring it would help everyone control their emotions to be in public. The Saturday afternoon crowd was heavier than usual, with all the tourists looking to escape the biting cold outside for a warm lunch. Evan looked as though he would far prefer to be out in the cold than to be where he was.

"Are you okay?" she asked him, putting a hand on his arm. "I feel like I made you do this. If you want to cancel, we can run out the back door."

"No, you were right," he said. "I need to do this. I would never be able to live with myself if something happened to one of them and I didn't have this conversation. And we both know, better than most people, how fast life can be flipped upside down."

"I'm right here," she said. "Do you want to have a safe word? If you say it, I'll make an excuse for us to leave immediately."

"Like what?" he asked, glancing at the door nervously when it opened, and then relaxing when it wasn't his parents.

"Pickle," she said. "If you say pickle, I'll get us out of here. Deal?"

"I hate pickles," he said with a laugh.

"Okay, let's go," she made to stand up, making him really smile.

"Got it. Pickle if I need saving," he said.

"I think that will be our way to stop a fight in the future," she said. "Just because we haven't had one since we became a couple doesn't mean we won't. We're both stubborn and can be ridiculous."

"Speak for yourself," he said.

She jabbed him with a finger. "I was referring to you," she said. "But from now on, when we want to call a truce, we just say pickle."

The door opened, and Evan took in a sharp breath when his mother stepped in, followed by his father. The mysterious brother was nowhere in sight, but Evan had told her earlier that his parents knew it was to be just them. His issues with his brother were separate from those with his parents, and he didn't want to be ganged up on.

"You can do this," Finley said as they stood up.

He squeezed her hand before letting go as the older couple came to the table. They all stood awkwardly before Evan gestured at the chairs. "Please, sit," he said. "This is my girlfriend, Finley Monahan. Finley, this is my mother, Vicki, and my father, Bob."

Finley reached across the table to shake their hands. "Nice to meet you. Formally."

They nodded before turning their attention back to Evan. "Thank you for meeting with us," Bob said. "We know we don't have any right to ask that of you. Or anything of you, for that matter."

The waitress came by and took their drink orders before disappearing again, giving Finley a chance to really study Evan's parents. His mother had a distinguished look, with a neat bob haircut and careful makeup. She was dressed formally for the setting, in a knee-length dress, cinched with a belt, and a sweater over it. Bob was also overdressed, wearing a button-down shirt and dress pants, looking as though he had probably pulled off the tie just before walking in. He was bald and wore glasses similar to Evans. Together, they looked like the powerful, successful couple that Evan had described.

"We know you're angry," Vicki said. "And we understand that. We didn't know what Zach had done to you until he came here. Before that, he had just told us you had a falling out, and that he was at fault. He said he would fix it."

"Why didn't you call one of us?" Bob asked. The question sounded defensive to Finley's ear, despite the soft tone it was asked in.

"What would you have done?" Evan quietly snapped. "You had made it clear that if I wanted to go to medical school, I would do it on my own."

"If we had known he stole from you, we would have helped," Bob said. "I admit, medical school wasn't my first choice for you. With your brains, you could have taken over my company and made it even more successful. I was selfish in trying to force your hand there."

"And I would have had your back," Vicki said. "It wasn't until we were apart for years that I realized all I had missed."

"Apart from me? Or Dad?" Evan's shrewd gaze was moving between them, and Finley shared his question. For a divorced couple, they seemed awfully friendly.

"You," Vicki said. "And Dad. I should have been more present. We both should have been. Our dedication to success and providing for you boys was at the detriment of our relationship with you."

"Did you get that from a counselor?" Evan asked. "Or a self-help book. Because what we needed couldn't be bought, and you both know that."

"Now, son," Bob said, but stopped when Vicki held her hand up.

"I deserve that," she said. "We both do. But all we can do is admit we were wrong and try to make it better. Would it make you feel better if we went through a list of all the ways we know we screwed up?"

Evan ran a hand through his hair and hissed out a breath before standing suddenly. "Would you excuse me for a minute?"

Finley watched him walk away before turning back to his parents. "You're doing this all wrong," she said. "I don't know if your intention is to make up with him or justify why you let it get this bad?"

"To make up with him, of course," Vicki said, looking shocked. "We came all this way."

"Yes, you did," Finley said. "You showed up on his doorstep uninvited, and now you want credit for that. If you have any interest in making things better, why haven't you asked him about his life? Said you're happy to see him looking healthy and happy? Even acknowledged me?"

Bob looked stunned to be spoken to so harshly, but Vicki nodded. "You're one hundred percent right."

The waitress returned with drinks, and Finley put in an order for some appetizers that she knew Evan liked. If his parents didn't, even better. Once that was done, she leaned forward toward the other couple. "Apologize to him. Mean it. Then show that you care about who he is now and be proud of what he did all on his own. And whatever you do, don't try to champion for his brother. That's Zach's mess to fix, and if you so much as indicate that you think Evan is wrong in any way, I'll get him out of here so fast your head will spin."

They both nodded mutely as Evan reappeared, taking his seat. He looked stressed and pale, and Finley could almost feel him shrinking back to who he was. The man who hadn't wanted to make friends or let anyone into his life when he came to Windsor Peak, who was now a loved member of the community. She would not let him go back under any circumstances.

"Evan," Bob started, then glanced at Vicki before continuing. "We are sorry. Terribly sorry. There are no words to describe how awful we feel for the parents we were and continued to be right until Finley here set us in our place."

Evan glanced at her, so she patted his thigh in a sign of solidarity. She didn't want to speak, so his parents would be forced to step up for him.

"We would really like to hear about your work," Vicki said. "And your life in this wonderful town. If you're willing to share. And we'd like to get to know Finley."

"What happened while I was gone?" Evan murmured to Finley, leaning close.

"I'll tell you later," she whispered. She directed her next comments to his parents. "Evan is one of the best doctors we have at the hospital. He saves patients that other oncologists might give up on. He works endlessly to make sure they have the best care and goes above and beyond. He's amazing."

His parents exchanged stunned looks. "We knew you were going to work in oncology," his mother said. "But I guess I didn't know what that meant. Not really. I thought you would be doing research?"

"I did, for a bit, in Boston," he said. "Then I decided I wanted to be more patient-focused, and I accepted the position here."

"And you like it in Vermont?" Bob asked.

"I do," Evan said. "It's cold outside, but the people who live here are the warmest people I've ever met."

"I'm happy for you," Vicki said. After a glance at Bob, she amended her response. "We are."

"Are you two back together?" Evan asked, his eyes darting between his parents. "Because I haven't seen you in the same room without a battle happening in a long time. If ever."

"We are," Bob said.

"It happened when your father and I were thrown together," Vicki said. "We didn't expect it, obviously. But we had to do some hard self-examination. And with that, some difficult conversations. Once we finished, we realized we had more in common than not."

"Because of Zach," Evan said, his voice expressing his displeasure.

"Somewhat," Vicki said. "But also, you. When we were faced with what we had done, how we had failed you, it pushed us together. Who else could understand how we were feeling?"

"And yes," Bob said. "Because of what we were going through with him. But we know you don't want to talk about it."

"I don't want to hear you take his side," Evan said.

"We wouldn't," Vicki said. "We don't. Everyone knows he was wrong."

"But you want me to talk to him?"

"Not if you don't want to," Bob said. "If you tell us to leave and take him with us, we will."

"He said he was renting an apartment, or something," Evan said.

"We can deal with that," Vicki said. "Your dad can make some calls."

"This is Vermont," Evan said with a harsh laugh. "Dad can't bend the rules here."

"Well, we could pay the lease and still take him out of here," Bob said.

"We want you to be happy," Vicki said. "And it appears you are. We don't want to ruin that."

The conversation paused when the appetizers were delivered. Evan smiled at Finley when he saw the selections before piling some buffalo wings and celery on his plate, along with some tempura cauliflower. He handed her the sauce after he poured it on his plate, knowing she would want it.

He handed her the sauce after he poured it on his plate, knowing she would want it.

"Finley, did you grow up here?" Vicki asked after watching the exchange between her and Evan.

"No," Finley said. "But I moved here about a year before Evan. We work together."

"Are you also a doctor?" Bob asked.

"No, I'm a nurse," she answered. "We worked closely together until we started dating. Now I work for another doctor in the unit. I'm biased, but I think Evan is the best."

"And you're the best nurse," Evan said to her, smiling as he responded.

"And do you have family here?" The question sounded stiff, coming from Bob, but Finley appreciated the effort.

"My whole family does. My parents live about five minutes outside of town, so I see them often. I have three brothers, including my twin," she replied. "Desmond and I share an apartment just upstairs from here. My oldest brother is the town sheriff, and his wife is the head chef here. She also owns the business next door. And my other brother just moved up here as well, so we're all here now."

"You're close, then?" Vicki asked, with a wistful look in her eyes.

"Very," Finley answered. "And we're happy to have Evan among our ranks now."

"They had me for Thanksgiving," Evan shared. "And every Sunday, her family has dinner together. It's really nice."

"Oh, that sounds lovely," Vicki replied.

The sad look on Vicki and Bob's faces had Finley opening her mouth wide enough to stick her whole foot in as she spoke. "You should join us. Tomorrow."

"Oh, we couldn't impose," Vicki said.

Finley kicked Evan under the table when he didn't say anything. He sighed but nodded. "You should. It's an open-door policy; I don't think her family even notices when there's extra people there."

"If you're sure it won't be an imposition," Bob said. "We would love to get to know Finley better, and her family."

"When are you going home?" Evan asked. The question seemed to set his parents back on their heels, but Finley didn't detect malice in his tone. Just curiosity, and a healthy dose of self-preservation.

"We left our plans open," Bob answered. "We didn't want to leave without talking to you, and we weren't sure how long that would take."

Evan nodded and devoted his attention to his plate of food. Finley turned back to his parents, wanting to keep the conversation going. "Where are you living now?"

"We're back in Georgia," Vicki answered. "It's quite a bit warmer there. I hadn't expected this kind of cold so early in the winter."

"We have a longer winter than most," Finley said. "Even fall gets cold fast. But it's so beautiful, it's hard to get upset. Plus, all the people who come to ski keep the economy here healthy."

"Do you ski?" Vicki asked Finley.

"A little," she said. "Not anything like what the people who grew up here could do. I feel like I'm on the mountain with Olympians when I'm with them, and they insist they aren't that good."

"It can be dangerous," Vicki said, looking worried. "I hope you're careful."

Finley nodded. "I am."

"And the dog?" Bob asked, looking between them. "Who does that belong to?"

"He belongs to me," Evan replied.

"I'm surprised," Bob said. "I never took you for the type to want a pet."

"I would be insulted if that weren't true," Evan said with a soft laugh. "He kind of adopted me, rather than the other way around."

"That sounds about right," Vicki said. "You've always had a kind heart, but it was hard to get you to take chances on others."

"Life has taught me to be careful," Evan said quietly.

"And luckily, we're fixing that now," Finley said, leaning into him. "Between Guinness and I."

They finished the lunch with his parents, with only a few brief silent pauses that felt awkward. His parents had shown interest in Evan's life and asked more questions of Finley. By the time they were leaving the restaurant, Evan seemed more relaxed. They said goodbye to his parents so they could take their short walk to the Inn, and Finley and Evan started theirs in the opposite direction to Evan's house.

"How do you feel?" Finley asked, linking her arm with Evan's.

"I don't know," he said. "We kept it pretty surface level. I guess it was nice to see them, and to have a normal conversation."

"You can't expect to dig into your troubles on day one," Finley said. "All that would have done is shut you down. Let them get to know you, and you do the same to them. Obviously, they've been going through some changes of their own."

"They seem different," Evan said. "Do I want to know what you said to them when I went to the bathroom?"

"I reminded them why they came," Finley said. "They needed to be refocused."

He laughed and opened the door to his house, letting Finley go first. "I believe that. I felt like I was on trial for a while there."

"I felt like they were unsure of themselves," Finley said. "They are business people and needed to change their way of thinking. You're their son, not a business contact."

"Do you mind if I take Guinness for a walk?" Evan asked. "It's nothing against you, I just need a little time alone to process."

"I can go to my apartment? If you want me to," Finley offered.

"No, I want to end my day with you," he said. "And we said we were going to start watching Christmas movies tonight."

"If you're sure," Finley said. "I don't mind if you want to be alone. I know that was a lot."

"The best thing for me," he said, pulling her closer. "Is to spend the night next to you. I just need to shake this off."

"I'll be here when you get back," Finley promised.

She watched him go with the dog and felt a pang of sadness that she pushed off. The insecure part of her brain whispered that this was the end. Evan would end up leaving Windsor Peak to escape the ghosts his family had brought with them. As much as she loved him, she didn't want to leave her family and follow him somewhere else. She had to find a way to help him repair his broken relationship with his family so he could move forward with her. That was the only way she could see them having a future together, without any ghosts between them.

Chapter 29

Evan was up early after a fitful night of sleep. Thoughts of his parents, Zach, and his childhood had chased out all other dreams, or the possibility of deep sleep. He had attended his required therapy sessions for years for the hospital, talking out any trauma witnessed in his workdays, or grief over lost patients. His first appointment with the Windsor Peak Hospital therapist had started with her asking about his family.

"I don't have one," he replied.

"Everyone has a start somewhere," she said. "Tell me about that. Do you know who your parents are?"

"Yes," he had said, sighing heavily. "I do. They raised me. But we don't have a relationship."

"Why not?"

"Do we really need to do this?"

"No," she said. "But I think it's important. A lot of times we can't see how our past impacts our daily lives. Facing something head-on is the best way to chase away whatever negative thoughts or decision-making comes with those feelings."

"It's not like that," he had said. "I don't think about them. They weren't really present in my life; they didn't care. They still don't."

"Do you think that's why you care so deeply about the people you treat?"

That question, and the rest of their session, had run through his mind all night. Was his connection to someone like Edna Lee because he wished he had grown up with someone like her in his corner? A person who would have offered smiles and hugs and provided nonstop love and support? When he sat with families to go over treatment plans, did he pay more attention to how they treated each other than what he was saying?

He laced up his sneakers just as the sun started creeping over the mountain. It would be cold for a run, but he needed the physical release it would offer. And maybe it would stop his brain. The repetition and monotony of running had soothed him many times over, and he needed that now.

Finley was still asleep as he slipped out of the kitchen door, leaving Guinness undisturbed in his crate. He had learned early on that the dog was not built for distance runs, and he felt the need to put a lot of miles between himself and the day before.

As he started toward town, the thoughts were even louder than before. His brain was insistent that he couldn't leave this unsolved, he needed to find a treatment plan. Letting his clinical side take over, he evaluated the situation. His parents would be at dinner this evening, and he could find a way to make peace with them. Without making any promises regarding his brother.

With Zach, he couldn't see a path to forgiveness. Or could he? His heart was making a case for his brother, and even his brain couldn't shut it down. If Zach was sober now, and determined to stay that way, wasn't he a new person? And wouldn't that entitle him to some kind of reprieve? Maybe he couldn't forget what had happened, and would always be on guard, but offering him a fresh start was the kinder thing to do.

As he ran through town, footsteps matching his pace came from behind him. Still cautious after his attack in Boston, he glanced over his shoulder to see who it was. Zach was a few steps behind him, running at the same pace but giving Evan the option to invite him to his side.

The parallel between where Evan's thoughts had been and the literal situation in front of him made him laugh suddenly, and he had to stop running to bend over and get it out. He had his hands on his knees, laughing and feeling close to a breakdown, when his brother stopped and put his hand on his back.

"Are you okay?" Zach asked. "What can I do?"

"Nothing," Evan said, standing straight and wiping his eyes with his sleeve. "I just had a whole bunch of emotions catch up to me, at the same time you actually caught up to me."

"We both know I've always been faster," Zach said, a hint of a smile on his face.

"In your dreams," Evan replied. "And besides, you burn out fast."

"Not anymore," Zach said. "Since I got healthy, I run further than before. It's therapeutic."

"I agree," Evan said. After a moment of hesitation, he gestured to the empty sidewalk. "Want to join me?"

"I'd love to," Zach said.

They set out, side by side, with just the sound of their sneakers hitting the pavement and their breathing in the air. In the silence between them, Evan finally found the peace he had been searching for.

***

When he let himself back into the house, it was still quiet. After letting Guinness out into the yard, he started a pot of coffee and then went to his office to check his email. By the time he went back to the kitchen, Finley was sitting at the table.

"Morning," she said, holding up the cup in front of her. "Thanks for starting this."

"No problem," he said. He dropped a kiss on her head before pouring his own. "I was up early."

"Everything okay?"

"I didn't sleep great," he admitted. "But I feel a little better now."

"You went for a run?"

"Yes," he said. "With Zach, if you can believe it."

"What? How did that happen?" She looked shocked as she asked.

"No idea," he said. "He just came up behind me. I invited him to join me."

"Wow," she said. "Did you talk at all?"

"No," he said, shaking his head. "But somehow, it was what I needed. A reminder that I can let him in a little, even if it's not all the way. At least not yet."

"Sounds like a good plan," she said, smiling encouragingly.

"I was thinking maybe we could go visit Edna Lee today?" he said. "Before we go to your parents. I checked, and she is at home now."

"Yes, that would be nice," Finely said. "Maybe we can bring her some flowers, or a meal."

"We can pick up a tray at Palace Plates," he suggested.

"Is that you insulting my cooking again?" she asked, clearly teasing him.

"Of course not," he said. "Just wanted to make sure you also had time to relax. We have a busier day than originally planned, I don't want to spring cooking on you as well."

"I appreciate the thoughtfulness," she said with a grin.

"Always," he said, smiling back at her. "I'll even let you shower first so you get all the hot water."

"You just say that so you can jump in halfway through," she said.

"I can't help my need for efficiency," he said. "I thought it was one of the things you loved about me."

"Sure, it is," she said. "Speaking of things I love about you, I know this experience with your parents is a stretch for you. But I'm proud of you that you're willing to try. I feel like I've pushed a lot of change on you since we started dating, and you've done it without hesitation."

"I would do anything for you," he answered her honestly. "You have my best interests at heart, and you can see things I can't. It may be uncomfortable for me sometimes, but the difference in my life is huge. I am happier, and that's because of you. Not just having you in my life, but what you've made possible for me here."

Her eyes looked like they held a sheen of tears as she smiled at him. "Okay, fine. If you want hot water that badly, I'm game."

He laughed and chased her up the stairs, only to run back down to let Guinness in when the dog let out a howl at seeing the fun inside. He heard the water turn on as he filled the dog's food bowl and was glad he had a smile on his face. The day had turned around just by being around Finley, and the chance encounter with his brother that didn't make him angry.

***

"Good morning, Mrs. Lee," Evan said as they walked into the living room of the older woman's house. She had been sitting with a volunteer from the church, watching the end of mass on television, when they came in. "I'm sorry we interrupted your service."

"It was over," Mrs. Les said. "And I'm so happy to see you both."

"We brought you a delicious casserole," Finley said, holding up the tray. "I can say that because I didn't cook it."

Evan winked at Edna. "She's right."

Edna laughed and waved to the couch. "Come sit."

The volunteer took the casserole to bring into the kitchen and offered coffee, which they both refused. "How are you feeling?" Evan asked.

"Better than I expected," Edna replied. "I feel like I should be lying in bed awaiting death, but I feel like a spring chicken."

"Good," Evan said. "There's no reason to think death is imminent."

"But you have people around me all the time," she argued. "Why the need for constant supervision?"

267

"I thought you would like the company," Evan said, shocked. "I didn't want you to be lonely."

"I'm not, dear," Edna said kindly. "And when the end comes, I'll be glad for the help. But I have my memories to keep me busy. I talk to my Hank all day, and these volunteers must think I'm going soft."

Evan laughed and looked around the small room. Everywhere he looked, there were pictures of Edna with her husband, Hank. On their wedding day, up until what was probably their last vacation together. "You look like you were very happy together."

"Yes," Edna said. "He's the love of my life. He brought me great joy, and he still does. I know he's here with me. And that's why I don't fear the future. I know we will be together again."

Finley wiped away a tear and sighed. "That's beautiful," she said. "I'm so glad you had that love."

"And now you two do," Edna said. When they looked at each other, she waved a hand. "Don't try to tell me otherwise. I've been around the sun enough times to know what I see. You're a perfect match. You're good for each other."

"Thank you," Evan said. He debated his words and chose to be candid with one of his favorite patients. "She's helped me a great deal."

"You're both healers," Edna said. "That's good. You'll nurture each other's hearts and be careful with them. You'll help each other grow. And you'll be wonderful parents, if you are so blessed."

"I hope so," Finley said. "If we could be half as lucky as you in love, we'd be doing good."

"Now, tell me all about what's happening," Edna said. "I've missed town gossip, and no one that visits me wants to talk about it. They all think I'm dying, after all, and should have bigger things to worry about."

Finley laughed and started to talk, but Evan squeezed her knee to indicate he wanted to go first. "Before we do that," he said. "I wanted to talk to you about another option. Would you consider moving to an assisted living? Then you'd have company when you want it, and a nursing staff that is available. Plus, your food and housekeeping needs would be taken care of, and we wouldn't worry."

"I lived in this house with my Hank," she said. "My father built it with his own two hands. This is where I want to be."

"But—"

Edna cut him off quickly. "I have some money put away, and the council on aging will help me get someone in to help with the chores and shopping a few days a week. I can also get a visiting nurse to check on me once a week if I need one. Although I hope I can count on you two coming by once in a while as well, even in an unofficial capacity."

"That might be okay for now, but what about down the line?" Evan asked.

"We'll deal with that when it gets here," Edna said simply. "What good is worrying about the next day when today is so beautiful?"

Finley leaned forward. "Of course we will be here often; you might even get sick of us. Now, about that town gossip," she said. "Top of the list that no one else knows, I'm going to be an aunt."

"Oh, how wonderful," Edna said, clapping her hands. "Which of your brothers made that happen?"

"JJ," Finley said. "Zoe told us on Thanksgiving. It's still top secret, so you're the only other person who knows."

"My lips are sealed," Edna said. "But I'll probably tell Hank."

"That's fine," Finley said with a smile. "Maybe he can put in a request for a girl. I'd love for my brother to have a daughter."

"He'd be a good girl dad?" Edna asked.

Evan laughed. "He'd probably lock her up until she's thirty," he said. "Even I got the lecture, and I'm only dating his sister."

"I'm about to take a back seat to his worrying," Finley said. "Girl or boy, that's what he's going to focus on now."

"JJ will look out for everyone," Edna predicted. "Just like you two are healers, he's a protector."

"I'm not sure what that makes Des and Colin," Finley said, looking at Evan.

"Colin is an intimidator, and Des is a jester," he said.

Edna laughed and shook her head. "Not quite," she said. "I think they both have great promise. Colin is mysterious, but you know what they say about still waters. And Desmond has to grow up someday."

They ended their visit when Edna was trying to hide yawns. One glance at his watch showed Evan that they had been there for hours and were due at JJ's house soon. Fortunately, his own exhaustion had been chased away with the positive spins the day had taken, and he was oddly looking forward to the time with his parents. Seeing them interact with Maggie and Tim, as well as Finley's brothers and Zoe, would be interesting at least.

Chapter 30

Finley gripped Evan's hand as they walked up to JJ's front door. "You ready for this?"

"Yes," he said. "I'm surprised by it, but I am."

"Good," Finley said. "I think we beat them here. I only see Colin's car, and he usually picks Des up."

Zoe was alone in the kitchen when they walked in. "Hi," she called out. "The guys are all out back if you want to go, Evan."

"I will, but first I wanted to make sure you were okay with my parents coming," he said.

"Of course I am," Zoe said. "I'm excited to meet them."

"Don't get too excited," Evan said, with a worried glance at Finley. "They're a little uptight."

"Give them a chance," Finley said. "Maybe around this crew they'll relax."

"Or see what a family actually looks like and spiral," Evan said.

Finley pointed at the back door. "Go outside and play," she ordered. Once he closed the door behind him, she turned back to Zoe. "How are you feeling?"

"Great," she said. "I passed the twelve-week mark, so I feel like I can relax a little."

"Are you going to find out the gender?" Finley asked.

"No."

"No? You're going to really make me wait six more months?" Finley cried out.

Zoe laughed. "You'll be fine," she said. "I'd rather be surprised on the day of. It gives me something to look forward to. Especially during labor, when I'll need an incentive."

"But we can talk about names, right?" Finley asked. "Give me something to work with here."

"JJ has some ridiculous ideas, as you can imagine," Zoe said. "We'll start to get serious about it soon."

The front door opened without a knock, and Maggie and Tim walked in. "You should have rung the bell," Maggie was saying to her husband. "We can't just walk in."

"Why not?"

"What if we were interrupting something?" Maggie asked. "Besides, it's not our house. JJ and Zoe deserve to have us knock, not just barge in."

"We don't mind at all," Zoe called out. She and Finley exchanged a look and laughed.

"I just walked in too, if that helps," Finley said.

"We all need to start using our manners," Maggie said. Just as she finished speaking, the doorbell rang, and she pointed at everyone. "See? That's the right way to do things."

"Do you want me to get it?" Finley asked Zoe. "I'm sure it must be Evan's parents."

"That would be great," Zoe said. She moved to the sink and turned on the water. "That will give me a chance to wash my hands. Should we tell the boys?"

"No, let's get them settled first," Finley said over her shoulder. She pulled open the door and smiled at Vicki and Bob, who looked nervous on the doorstep. "Hi! Welcome, come on in."

"Thank you so much," Vicki said. "We were worried we might have the wrong house, or that Evan might have changed his mind."

"We tried to text him," Bob explained. "Just to make sure."

"Oh, he left his phone in the kitchen when he went out back," Finley said, thinking back to when they had come inside. "I'm sorry. I wasn't paying any attention to it, and he didn't think to either."

"It's okay," Vicki said. "We're here now."

"Let me introduce you to my parents and my sister-in-law," Finley said, leading them into the kitchen. "This is my mom, Maggie, and my dad, Tim. And this is Zoe, the master chef who we tricked into marrying my brother so we could eat her food every Sunday."

Zoe hip-checked her as she walked past to offer her hand to both of Evan's parents. "So nice to meet you," she said. "I'm so glad you could join us."

"Yes, I'm so glad," Maggie joined in. "Come, sit down. I want to hear all about you both."

"What can I get you to drink?" Tim asked, looking between Bob and Vicki.

"We brought some wine," Bob said, holding up the two bottles he held. "To thank you for having us."

"Should we open one?" Zoe asked, reaching for the bottles.

Finley watched as her parents fussed over Evan's parents, getting them drinks and ushering them into chairs at the island. Zoe set out a tray of cheese and crackers for everyone to snack on and went back to what she was mixing in a bowl.

"You're from Georgia, Finley said?" Maggie asked.

"Yes," Vicki responded. "Not far from the coast."

"This weather must be a shock to the system," Tim said. "It took us a while to adjust, and we only came from Massachusetts."

"I didn't know cold like this happened," Vicki said. "I can't imagine how it is when winter really starts."

"We stay inside when it gets below negative forty," Tim said. "Once we get into the risk of frostbite, we prefer to stay by the fire."

"I'm sorry," Vicki said, holding up a hand. "Did you say negative forty?"

They all laughed and started discussing favorite warm vacation spots. Finley had briefed her parents on the situation earlier and asked them to help with neutral conversations. They had obviously come well prepared, and she could tell that Evan's parents were relaxing in their company.

The back door flew open, and the four men came in on an icy wind. JJ was in the lead, holding a football, and laughing. "Finley, you didn't tell us your man is fast," he said. "Poor Desmond might have pulled his hamstring trying to keep up."

"You joke, but I could be seriously injured," Desmond griped, just behind JJ.

"Lucky for you, we have a doctor in the house," Colin said dryly. "And he's used to dealing with medical emergencies here."

"Hey," Zoe called out. "No shots at the pregnant lady."

"Sorry, Zoe," Colin said. "It was meant to be a shot at Des. For being a wimp, if that wasn't clear."

Desmond pushed Colin, and they play wrestled for a moment, delaying Evan from coming into the house. When he did, he had a big smile on his face that faded when he saw his parents. Finely watched as his eyes quickly surveyed the situation, his shoulders tense, before he seemed pleased with what he saw.

"You made it," he said, crossing the room to shake his father's hand and drop a kiss on his mother's cheek. "Sorry, I was outside."

"Playing," Vicki said, looking amazed. "You never did things like that as a kid. It looks good on you."

"Trust me, we could tell he never threw a ball around," Desmond called from the other room.

"I'm going to tackle him," Finley declared, starting to storm from the room but stopped by Evan's hand.

"It's okay," he said. "He's right, I can't throw. But I caught just fine, and I'm much faster than him."

"And you don't get winded," Colin called out.

Evan quickly introduced his parents to JJ, Colin and Desmond before looking unsure of himself again. Maggie noticed and gestured toward the other room. "Go watch the game," she said. "We're fine in here."

Evan looked at Finley, then back at his parents. "Dad, do you want to come in? The game is about to start."

"I'd like that," Bob said, standing quickly before turning to his wife. "If you don't mind."

"No, you go," Vicki said. "I'll be fine."

Maggie immediately filled the room with her happy chatter, asking questions about life in Georgia and Vicki's work. Finley felt herself relaxing as well, grateful to her parents for making this so much easier on Evan. It was all still weird for him, and would take a lot of time, but they were on the right path.

***

Monday morning dawned too early for Finley, after a later than usual night at JJ and Zoe's. The two sets of parents had gotten along great, and Evan had relaxed enough to converse easily with them. Overall, it had been a fun night, but she was tired as she started getting ready for work.

Evan had already left for the hospital, wanting to get an early start, so she drove herself. Grabbing an extra-large coffee from the bakery that she hoped would get her through the day, she made it to the hospital just in time for her first patient.

"Want to get dinner tonight?" Audrey asked as they both sat down to do their charting.

"You don't have plans?" Finley asked, looking at her friend. "I'm surprised."

"My social calendar is sadly empty," Audrey said. "And it would be fun to catch up. I feel like I barely see you these days."

"Sure," Finley said. "Evan plays poker on Monday nights, so that's perfect."

"I'm glad you could squeeze me in," Audrey said, looking hurt.

"I'm sorry," Finley replied. "I didn't mean it like that. I'll always have time for you."

Audrey nodded, but Finley could tell her friend was still upset. She had been spending so much time with Evan, even Des had commented that he missed her. She needed to make sure she included time for her friends and family and didn't become someone who only cared about their partner.

"It's okay," Audrey said, softening. "I get it. The first few months are so exciting."

"It has flown by, to be honest," Finley said. "I didn't realize what a bad friend I've been."

"Good news for you, I've been distracted myself the last couple of weeks," Audrey said with a grin. "So, we're even. But I'm looking forward to a night out."

At the end of their shift, Finley tracked Evan down in his office. "Hey, you."

"Hey yourself," he said. He stretched and then stood up from behind his desk to kiss her. "How was your day?"

"Busy," she said. "Yours?"

"Same," he said. "I feel like I never stopped."

"You have poker tonight, right?"

"I do," he said. "Sorry to leave you to your own devices."

"It's fine," she said. "I was just reminded that I should spend time with friends too. I'm going to go out with Audrey."

"Oh, that will be fun," he said. "Will I see you later?"

"I don't know," she said. "I'm exhausted. If I feel too tired to drive after a drink, I'll just stay at my place tonight."

"Do you still have one?" He was teasing, but with a question in his eyes.

"For now," she said, winking at him. "We'll work on that soon enough. Unless you have an objection?"

"I did say that the next time I lived with someone it would be my wife," he said. His hands circled her waist, pulling her closer.

"Oh, yeah?" She tilted her chin up to look at him. "What does that mean?"

"I guess it means I should get shopping," he said. "Or get you on a plane to Vegas. I kind of like JJ's thinking on that one."

She laughed. "I'm my father's only daughter. If you think you're getting away without asking him for permission, or him walking me down the aisle, you're going to have a rude awakening."

"No, I would never," he said. "You think I'm scared of your brothers? That's nothing compared to how I feel about your dad. He's the type that will sneak up on you. All nice until you hurt his girl, then you'll just disappear."

She laughed. "I think that might be a stretch. I'd be more worried about hurting his feelings than anything else."

"Okay, we'll bring them with us," Evan said. "A quiet family wedding on a beach?"

"I'm sorry," Finley said, holding out her left hand and examining it. "I do not see a ring on this hand."

He laughed. "I'll work on it. As long as we're on the same page."

"You want confirmation that I'll accept?"

"That would be preferable," he said. "I'm a scientist. I don't like the unknown."

"Let's just say your odds are very favorable," she said, kissing him. "Hopefully better than they are at poker tonight."

"It's not that I'm bad," he said as she made her way out of the office. "But they must be cheating."

Finley had a smile on her face as she walked into the Palace a few minutes later. Desmond was behind the bar, flirting away with two young women, and Audrey sat towards the back. Only when she got closer did she see Cary was there, with the only empty seat on his other side. Which put her friend's new love interest smack between their girl's night, she realized. Reassuring herself that it meant an early night for her, she plastered a smile on her face and made her way to them.

"Hi," she said, pulling out the barstool.

"Oh," Cary said, jumping to his feet. "Want me to sit there? I didn't realize Audrey had plans to meet you. I just came in to grab some dinner."

"No, it's okay," Finley said. He seemed genuine, so she pushed her annoyance all the way to the back of her mind. "This way I won't be under pressure to be good company when I'm tired."

"Great," he said. He smiled at her, and something niggled at the back of her brain. She couldn't put her finger on it, but maybe it would come to her. She felt like maybe she had met him somewhere before.

"What can I get you all?" Desmond asked.

They all ordered drinks, and then Cary and Audrey put their heads close together, sharing a menu. Des leaned on the bar in front of Finley, talking so only she could hear. "You all alone tonight?"

"Yes," she said. "I'll probably be sleeping upstairs. I'm so tired."

"Want to order food so you can get moving?" Des asked, tilting his head toward the other two. "Looks like you're the third wheel tonight."

"No, she's not," Cary said quickly. "I am interrupting their night out. I should get food to go, and leave you to it."

"It's fine," Finley assured him. "I'll eat with you guys and then head upstairs."

"We'll have fun," Audrey said. "It's good to make new friends."

Once Finley had taken a few sips of her drink, she relaxed. Audrey carried the bulk of the conversation, telling Cary story after story of growing up in town. She seemed eager to impress him, and Finley had to stop herself from cautioning her friend that she was trying too hard. Cary was hard to get a read on, but seemed more distracted than interested, in Finley's opinion, anyway. It would be so nice if Audrey found her person at the same time she did, and they could do couples things together. She and Evan had been in their happy bubble for so long, it was time to expand and spend time with other people. Especially other happy couples who weren't her family. She didn't need every dinner to become a rehash of her most embarrassing moments, which is what it had been like since she first brought Evan home.

She let her thoughts drift to their conversation earlier. Were they really already talking about marriage? A part of her thought it was too fast, but then it also felt like the most right thing she had ever done. Loving him was as easy as taking a breath, and she could easily see doing it for the rest of her life.

Chapter 31

Patrick Burrows was hosting poker night for the first time, and Evan realized he had arrived before everyone else when he pulled into the driveway. The four-car garage was closed, and lights were streaming from the house, indicating that Patrick was home. Despite the weeks of getting to know the other man, he suddenly panicked. He wasn't the type to hang out at mansions. It was odd enough that he spent one night a week at a former NFL player's house, now a movie star?

Before he could convince himself to leave, a car pulled in, and he recognized Patrick's brother Jake behind the wheel. Evan climbed from his car at the same time the other man did and waited while Jake got his service dog from the backseat.

"Hey, Jake," Evan called out. "How are you?"

"Good," Jake replied, shaking his hand. "You?"

"I was about to run away when you pulled in," he answered. "This house is a little intimidating."

Jake laughed. "That's a compliment, believe it or not. I renovated this for him."

"Did you? It's amazing," Evan said. "Makes me want to buy a rundown place and let you work some magic."

"Anytime," Jake said. He rang the bell when they approached the door and turned back to Evan. "Patrick has to keep the doors locked. Otherwise, fans would try to just walk in."

"Really?"

"It's happened," Jake said as the door swung open.

"Hey," Patrick said. "Come on in."

"Thanks for having us," Evan said as he stepped inside. "I was just telling Jake how amazing your house is."

"Did he take full credit? Because he should," Patrick said. "I was everywhere but here when it was happening."

"Filming a movie?"

"Yes," Patrick said, nodding. "Luckily, Jake knew my taste."

"And he had me to add some more." Patrick's girlfriend Emma called over from the kitchen.

"All of the pillows are her idea," Jake said.

"Hey," Emma yelled. "I did more than that."

"Nat and Holly are coming over to hang out with Emma," Patrick told them. "Evan, you should have Finley come over."

"She went to meet a friend," he said. "Thanks, though."

"Next time," Emma said. "I'm looking forward to getting to know her better. We were all so grateful for what you both did for Stella."

"Just our jobs," Evan said.

Before anyone could respond, the doorbell rang again, and soon the room was full of his new friends. Patrick led the way to his new poker room, custom-made once he had taken up the habit with his brothers and friends. JJ, Dan, Liam and Mike rounded out the table, and the room was full of noise and laughter.

"No Colin tonight?" Evan asked JJ as they sat down. "Or Des?"

"Des is covering for someone at the bar," JJ answered. "And Colin was in a mood. I wasn't going to push it with him."

"What is his problem?" Dan asked. "I saw him in town today, and he looked like he could knock over a building."

"No idea," JJ said. "He wouldn't tell us even if we asked. He's just not the type."

"Overly emotional type, like my brother?" Jake asked.

"Hey," Dan objected. "Not me. Patrick maybe."

"There's nothing wrong with being in touch with your emotions," Mike said. They all turned to stare at the biggest man at the table, who shrugged. "Nat likes it."

They all nodded in understanding as Patrick started shuffling the cards. Once Evan had lost the first three hands, Liam shook his head. "You're either the worst poker player in the world," he said. "Or the best. I keep waiting for you to hustle us."

"No, I'm just this terrible," Evan admitted.

"He's a doctor," Patrick said. "He has to be bad at something."

"I'm sitting at a table with two movie stars and an NFL player," Evan said with a laugh. "I'm far from the most impressive person at the table."

"Don't forget a lawyer," Dan said. He pointed at Jake. "And retired military."

"And I could arrest you," JJ said casually, making everyone laugh.

"I heard your parents are in town," Dan said to Evan. "How's that going?"

"Better than expected," he said. "Thanks to JJ and his family. They could make anyone feel comfortable."

"Which brings us back to Colin," Patrick said.

An hour later, Evan was out of chips and yawning. After some ribbing about blowing it on purpose to see his girlfriend, he excused himself. If he left right then, he was sure he could catch Finley before she headed upstairs for the night. He slept better with her at his side, so if he could get her in time, that's where she would end up.

He drove slowly down the mountain from where Patrick lived and into town. Fortunately for him, there was an open parking spot right in front of the Palace. He parked and almost ran inside, so anxious to see her. How had he gone his whole life without this woman, and now he couldn't make it a few hours?

Once he stepped into the bar, he glanced around. Desmond was busy with a customer at the far end, and he caught sight of Finley near him. As he started walking in her direction, his steps faltered. Without thinking, he ducked behind the half wall that broke off a section of the room where comfortable furniture sat in front of a fire. Once he had his breath, he peeked out again and confirmed what he thought he had seen.

Finley was sitting, heads close together, with his brother. His mind was racing faster than his heart, and he waited until Desmond was back facing the other way before he ran out the door again. He got in his car before he let out a howl of pure rage. How had he been so stupid? To have this happen once was bad enough, but twice?

He drove home, barely seeing the road as he did. Once there, he clipped a leash on Guinness and headed back out, determined to walk until he could have a coherent thought. When the dog finally sat on the sidewalk and refused to move another step, he was forced to go home. There, he was relieved to see only his own car in the driveway. At least he didn't have to face Finley now. Although she didn't know that he had seen her, a fresh panic ran through him at the thought. What were she and Zach plotting while sitting at the bar?

His breathing more erratic, he sank to the floor in the kitchen. Guinness, as if sensing his panic, sat next to him. Only after a long time with the dog's solid weight reassuring him that he was alive did he feel safe enough to stand up. He spotted his cell phone on the table where he had dropped it and saw a text from Finley on the lock screen.

He debated not opening it but finally had to know if she would try to walk into his house. Thankful that it stated she would spend the night at her apartment, he dropped the phone again. For all he knew, Zach would be right there next to her. The thought had him rushing for the closest bathroom, his stomach revolting at the turmoil in his brain.

Once there was nothing left, he took a seat on the couch. There was nothing he could do until morning, and he expected a long, sleepless night ahead of him.

***

"Dr. Lincoln," the clerk at the bank called out as he walked in. He had been waiting outside until the doors were unlocked and was the first and only customer. Her nametag read Kate, and she had a cheerful smile on her face. "How can I help you?"

"Hi, Kate," he said. Before he could continue, another clerk appeared.

"Doc," she called out. "So nice to see you."

"Amy," he replied, nodding to her. "How are you feeling?"

"Alive, thanks to you," she said. "I get better every day."

"I'm glad to hear it," he said.

"I was just telling Mindy that you're the best," Amy continued, gesturing to the teller next to her.

"My dad had some unusual spots at the dermatologist," Mindy explained. "Amy was telling me how wonderful you are."

"Thank you," he said. His voice sounded off, even to his own ears, but he was doing the best he could. Just when he had grown comfortable enough in this small town to be okay chatting with the other residents, his whole world had to crumble down around him. On any other day, he would have even enjoyed the chance to chat with the bank staff, but his laser focus was making it difficult to form sentences. "Often times, the dermatologist can remove the area, and we never need to see those patients."

Kate smiled at him. "That happens to my husband," she said. "I tell him to wear sunscreen, but he doesn't listen. I should have you tell him."

He turned back to Kate, who had a look of concern now. "Are you okay? Would you like to sit down?"

"No, I'm okay," he said. "I just have a private matter to discuss, if it's possible?"

"Of course," Kate said. "Laura will get you set up with our manager; she can help."

"Good morning, Dr. Lincoln." Another woman smiled warmly at him as she walked around the counter. "Come this way."

He followed Laura, who ushered him into a small office, and was told the manager would be right with him. While he waited, he pulled out his phone to text Dr. Collins. Although he had called the hospital in the middle of the night to report he would be out sick, he wanted to make sure his boss knew. Within a minute, Neil replied, telling him to take the rest of the week off. He had vacation and sick time stacked up, so his boss said he should take advantage.

Happy to have that taken care of, he turned his phone off and put it away. He couldn't think about what he would say if Finley called him, so he wanted to avoid it if he could.

The manager came into the room and offered her hand. "Dr. Lincoln, I'm Erin Corshia," she said. "I'm the branch manager. I understand you have a private matter to discuss?"

"I do," Evan said, steeling his emotions. "I wondered if there was a way we could move or lock my accounts? I have reason to believe that someone may try to steal from them."

"Oh, no," she said. She opened a laptop on the desk and started typing. "Let's take care of this. Checking or savings? Or both?"

"Both, I'm afraid," Evan replied.

"The easiest solution from a bank perspective would be to open new accounts and transfer your funds," Erin said. "You're the only name on the account, so that's good. Does someone else have access?"

"I changed all my passwords last night," he said. "But I keep a checkbook and the savings account information in my desk. Not to mention my debit card. I have no way of knowing if they were accessed."

"I see," she said. "Opening new accounts will make the money secure, but any automatic payments that you have set up will obviously be impacted. Is that alright with you?"

"That's fine," he said. "I understand. I can set all of that up again; I just want to make sure no one can withdraw."

"Absolutely," Erin said. "And if anyone comes in to attempt a withdrawal or transfer, should we call the police?"

He nodded, the lump in his throat making it difficult to speak. If Zach repeated his same attack, the money would be simply transferred out of his account with no way of recovering it. He doubted that his brother or Finley would be so brazen as to walk into the bank and attempt to withdraw, but he had been fooled once. Never again.

After an hour with the helpful manager, he had moved all his money to new accounts and was back in his car with nowhere to go. Work was out of the question, since Finley would be there. He needed to leave town, he decided. Take his dog and go somewhere far, far away. Maybe back to Boston, where he could accept the position at Dana Farber that had been offered to him a year ago. Or further, somewhere in the Midwest where no one would know who he was.

The idea was forming in his head as someone knocked on his window, causing him to jump and hit his head on the doorframe. His father stood outside the car, looking at him with a frown. Evan rolled down his window, not willing to even get out of the car.

"What are you doing?" Bob asked. "Shouldn't you be at work?"

"I think I'll be leaving the hospital," he said, his voice sounding unfamiliar.

"What? Why?"

"Because once again, Zach has come along and ruined my life," Evan nearly screamed. His father took a step backward and stared at him as Evan fought to control his breathing. "I can't talk about this."

"I think we need to," Bob said, sticking his hand in the window before Evan could roll it up. "Come on. Let's go find breakfast."

"Can't you see that I'm falling apart here?"

"I can," his father said, nodding. "That's why I'm insisting. I wasn't there for you before, but I'm going to be now. If I have to force myself on you, I will."

"I just need to go," Evan said.

"Where?" Bob challenged him. "Run away? Leave this life behind? If your brother did something, I will have your back fully. But I need you to get out of the car and come and talk to me. Let me help."

Without thinking, he nodded. His father let him roll the window up and opened the door, leading him toward the crowded diner.

"Not there," Evan said. "Too many people."

"Coffee shop?" Bob asked, pointing across the street. At Evan's nod, he led the way, pulling open the door when they arrived. He glanced around and pointed to a small table in the back corner, far from anyone else. "Go sit there, and I'll get us some coffee."

Evan sat, head in his hands, until his father returned. He pushed a cup of coffee and a plate holding a muffin towards

Evan. "You look like you need to eat. And then tell me what's happening."

"How could I let this happen? Again?" Evan whispered, the words agonizing as he spoke them.

"What?"

"Zach," Evan said. "And Finley."

"What about them?" Bob looked perplexed. "I didn't think they had even met?"

"No, they didn't," Evan said. "At least I didn't introduce them. But they were cozy together last night when I was supposed to be at poker."

"Son, you have to be misunderstanding this," Bob said. "Finley loves you. And Zach is determined to make things right."

"All the easier to scam me, I guess," he said. "Tricks on him, though. At least this time, I found out before he cleaned me out."

"I said I would have your back, and I will," Bob said. "But first, you need to confirm that what you think is happening actually is. You're too rational to jump to conclusions like this."

"How could I believe anything they say?"

"Because you love her," Bob said calmly. "And from what I saw, she loves you. Don't throw that away, Evan. That's more valuable than anything else in the world. Trust me. I've left it in the rearview mirror so many times, and now I'm an old man, wishing I could go back and change it all. Don't end up like that."

"But how? How could I trust what she said? Or what Zach says?"

"Obviously, I don't know Finley well," Bob said, scratching his chin. "But she's from here. She has close family ties. I can't see her doing something to jeopardize that. And as for your brother, I witnessed firsthand how hard he fought to recover. And I know you don't want to hear it, but it's true. His one motivation through all of rehab and all these months of sobriety was you."

Evan tapped on the hard surface of the table, wishing he could feel as strong as his father did. He wanted to believe he was wrong, but how? What other reason would there be for the two of them to be together on the one night he was tied up elsewhere? "I have to think," he said finally. "I'm so tired."

"Come on," his dad said. "Let me get you home. I'll drive."

Walking back to the car with his father's arm around his shoulders brought Evan back to all the years he had wished for moments like this. When he got home, he let his father lead him into the house and tuck him in like a child, unable to fight the waves of exhaustion that overtook him. The darkness of sleep was at least going to be free from the thoughts that had chased him all night.

Chapter 32

Finley's day had been manic, from start to finish. Two new admissions, one medical crisis mid-treatment, and a chemotherapy graduation ceremony. By the time she finally sat down to do her charting, everyone else was almost done. She glanced around, realizing she hadn't seen Evan all day.

"Have you seen Dr. Lincoln?" she called over to Dr. Collins, who was at the other end of the desk.

"He's at home, sick," he told her. "Do you need something? I can help?"

"No, that's okay," she said. "I didn't know he was sick."

She pulled her phone out of her pocket and saw no missed calls or texts from Evan. Was he too sick to notify her? But he had obviously been in touch with Dr. Collins.

"I told him to take the rest of the week," Dr. Collins told her. "From what I heard, he called in the middle of the night and sounded terrible."

"Hopefully, he'll be better soon," she said. The doctor disappeared down the hall, leaving Finley alone with her thoughts. Why hadn't Evan told her? Was he planning a surprise, maybe? The proposal he had talked about the day before?

Feeling relieved and excited at the thought, she hurried through the rest of her work. After changing quickly in the locker room, she drove to Evan's house. His car was in the driveway, and she could hear Guinness barking out back at her arrival. As she approached the door, she was surprised by it opening and Vicki stepping out.

"Oh, hi," Finley said. "Nice to see you. I heard Evan might be sick?"

"He is, dear," Vicki said. "I think it would be best if you let him rest."

"Are you sure?" Finley asked. A pit formed in her stomach at the thought of being shut out. "I'm a nurse. I can probably help."

"No, that's okay," Vicki said. Her tone was firm and hard to read.

"I'm sorry, I'm just not understanding what's happening," Finley said. "Is Evan okay?"

"He will be," Vicki said. "He's resting, and then we'll get to the bottom of everything."

"Bottom of what?" Finley asked. Vicki simply stared at her in silence, unable or unwilling to answer. "Please, Vicki, tell me what's going on."

"I wish I could," she said, her expression softening. "Give him a little time, if you can."

"But why?" Finley felt like daggers were ripping through her abdomen, tearing her apart. The worst was the one she felt straight in her heart. "I need to talk to him. Is he asking not to see me?"

"He's asleep," Vicki said. "Other than that, I can't say much. Just give it time. I'll make sure he talks to you soon."

Finley walked back to her car, shocked to find she was still breathing. In fact, she was breathing too fast. What was happening? Why would Evan shut her out? Were his parents holding him hostage? These strangers had appeared out of nowhere, and now had her locked out of the house and away from him? Nothing was making sense; he had to be drugged or tied up to be ignoring her like this.

With that thought in mind, she raced down the street to the Sheriff's office, turning in on what felt like two wheels. JJ's two deputies, Jeff and Nick, were in the parking lot staring at her with wide eyes as she got out. "If anyone else pulled in like that,"

Jeff said. "I would either draw my gun or be writing a ticket. Are you okay?"

"No," she cried out. "Is JJ inside?"

"Yes," Nick said. "Can we help? Is someone chasing you?"

They were both scanning up and down the street, as if there were a physical threat to her being. Even though it felt that way, she shook her head. "I just need to talk to him."

She ran inside and didn't stop until she was in her brother's office, gasping for breath. He stood and closed the door, then grabbed her in a bear hug. "Slow down," he said. "You're going to hyperventilate. Slow down and tell me what's going on."

After a few minutes, she was finally able to do so. In halting sentences, she told him what had happened. "I think they're holding him hostage," she said. "Maybe they drugged him?"

"Let me do some digging," JJ said. He stared at Finley for a long moment before he spoke. "This doesn't feel like Evan. But it also doesn't feel like his parents," he said. "They seemed like normal people. Did anything happen last night? He was fine at poker."

"I didn't even see him," she said. "I had dinner at the bar with Audrey and her new friend and then went upstairs to sleep. I was so tired, I didn't want to try to make it to his house, and I didn't know what time he would get home. If I could go back, I would have gone there. Maybe this wouldn't be happening."

"We don't know that," JJ said. "You could have walked into a dangerous situation if you're right. I'm glad you stayed home. Now, who is Audrey's friend?"

Finley felt the same scratch at the back of her brain as she thought about Cary. What was it about him that set her off last night? She thought back to the encounter but couldn't come up with anything. "I don't know him," she said. "His name is Cary. I think he just moved to town?"

"Can you call Audrey?" JJ asked. "Let's cover all our bases."

She dialed the number on her cell phone, keeping it on speaker so JJ could hear. "Hey," Audrey said when she answered. "A night out and now a phone call, I feel special now."

"Audrey," Finley's voice broke as she talked.

"Oh, Fin, what's wrong?" Audrey's tone changed from light to serious. "Where are you?"

Finley was crying too hard to speak, so she looked at JJ. With a nod, he pulled the phone closer. "Audrey, this is JJ, Fin's brother. Mind if I ask you a couple of questions about last night?"

"Of course not," Audrey said. "Unless I did something wrong? Do I need a lawyer?"

"Not at all," JJ assured her. "This is unofficial; I'm just trying to help my sister figure something out. She said she was with you last night. Did anything unusual happen?"

"No," Audrey said, sounding more confused than anything. "I don't think so. She went upstairs a little after nine, I think?"

JJ thought back to the night before. Evan had been the first out and had left before nine to go home. He had said he was hoping to catch Finley before she went to bed, so he would have made it to the Palace in time. "Did you happen to see Evan there at all?"

"Evan? No," Audrey said.

"Who is your friend that joined you?"

"Cary," Audrey answered.

"Do you know his last name?"

"Actually, I don't," Audrey said. "I never thought to ask. He doesn't have social media. That's what he said when I asked to follow him. He's kind of kept me at arm's length, we've only hung out a couple of times."

"Do you know where he lives?"

"He mentioned he had been staying at an Airbnb, but he moved to a rental over on Casey Court."

"Great, thanks for the help," JJ said. "I'll have Finley touch base with you soon."

As soon as he hung up, JJ hit a button on the cell phone, and Finley heard it ring once before Desmond's voice came on the line. "What's up?"

"Hey," JJ said. "I'm with Finley. Talk to me about this Cary guy that was at the bar with her last night."

"He's new to town," Desmond said. "Quiet. Keeps to himself. I think Audrey just hangs out with him because she can talk as much as she wants."

"How did he pay?"

"Cash," Desmond said. "Always cash. Last night he paid for everyone, so I noticed. Normally, he just gets a soda, so it's a few dollars. Why?"

"Do you know anything else about him?"

"Dude, why are you going cop on me?" Desmond said. "Tell me what's going on."

"Evan won't talk to Finley, and I think maybe he saw her at the bar with that guy last night," JJ said. "The timing would work."

"Now that you say that, one of the servers said he came in and acted weird," Des said. "I was busy at the time, and then Fin went upstairs. I thought maybe they had a fight."

"He came into the Palace?" Finley asked, her voice breaking again. "And didn't talk to me?"

"I guess he came in and then left real quick," Desmond said. "I didn't see him, I only heard about it."

"Thanks," JJ said, hanging up on Desmond before turning back to Finley. "Who is this Cary guy?"

Finley shrugged, then gasped. "Oh, no. I think I know."

JJ stared at her. "Are you going to share with the class?"

"No," she said. "I think I need to go find him and talk to him."

"Not alone, you're not," JJ said. He pushed back from his chair and gestured for her to get up. "Let's go."

"I don't think I'm in any danger," she said.

"It doesn't matter," JJ said. "You showed up in my office hysterical, and now you want to go run off to find some mystery guy who is maybe causing problems. I'm coming."

***

JJ took a minute before they left the office to look at the addresses on the street that Audrey had mentioned. Within a couple of minutes, he had the number of a house that had been listed for rent a few weeks prior and was taken off the market. With it written on a Post-it, he grabbed keys from the front desk and led Finley to a Sheriff's truck.

"We could probably just go in mine," she said, pointing across the lot.

"No," JJ said firmly. "I want to make it clear who I am."

"The uniform isn't enough?"

"Nope," JJ said. He pulled out of the parking lot and drove the short distance to the neighborhood by the school. The street was lined with small, neat houses. Toward the end of the street, JJ pulled up to the curb in front of a one-story gray home. There was a car in the driveway with Georgia plates, so Finley knew she was right.

She took a deep breath and marched up the front walkway, surprised when the door opened as she raised her hand to knock. They stared at each other for a moment until JJ cleared his throat behind Finley. A glance back showed him standing with a hand on his service weapon and a no-nonsense look on his face.

"Zach?" Finley asked, her voice barely a whisper.

He nodded and gestured for them to come in. "Please, come sit down."

"Why did you introduce yourself as Cary?" Finley demanded instead, refusing to set foot into his home. "Evan calls you Zach."

"It's from my full name, Zachary," he said. "I panicked when we first met. Audrey told me you were nurses, and the chances of you knowing Evan seemed high in such a small town. I know how stupid it was, but I couldn't find a way to fix it without completely alienating Evan."

"Did you know who I was?"

"Not at first," Zach said. "But as soon as I figured it out, I knew I couldn't tell you. I swear I didn't have any ill intentions. But if Evan found out that I was even talking to someone he worked with, never mind his girlfriend, he would have shut me out completely."

"But now he shut me out," Finley cried. "You did this. Why are you here? How could you do this to him? To me?"

Zach took a step back and looked shocked. "What do you mean?"

"He won't talk to me," she said. "Your mom wouldn't even let me in the house. All because he saw me sitting with you last night."

Zach ran a hand through his hair and suddenly looked weary. "He must think history is repeating itself," he said. "I'll talk to him."

"Why would he ever believe you?" Finley spit out. "If he won't even talk to me, why would he talk to you?"

"I don't know," Zach said. "But I have to try. I'll make this right."

"No," she snapped. "You stay away from him. I need to talk to him, and I can't have you getting any more involved."

Finley started to walk away, but JJ stopped her with a hand on her arm. "Are you going to be a problem in my town?" he asked Zach.

"I hope not," Zach answered. "That wasn't my intention. I just wanted to fix things with my brother. I know that's hard to understand, but I'm lost without him. The biggest screwup in my life is how I treated him, not only when we were younger, but as adults. I did something unimaginable to him in the throes of addiction, and I need to make it right."

"And if the right thing is leaving him alone?" JJ asked, still not releasing Finley's arm.

"Then I'll go." Zach's voice sounded sad to Finley, and she turned to see the emotion on his face. "I don't deserve him. He's better than I'll ever be, and I will regret my actions every day for the rest of my life. But if it's causing him more pain for me to be here, then I'll leave."

JJ and Finley climbed back into the truck, and then he looked at her. "Where to now?"

"Evan's," she said without hesitation. "If you need to kick that door down, you're going to."

"Got it," he said, starting the truck. After a moment of silence, he spoke again. "He seemed sincere."

"Appearances can be deceiving," Finley said. "What if he's lying?"

"And what if he's not?" JJ challenged. "I'm a pretty good judge of character, and I don't see someone there who is destructive."

"But he blew up my life," Finley said, choking back a sob.

"Did he?" JJ asked. "Or did Evan, when he jumped to conclusions?"

The question rattled around in Finley's head, playing with her emotions. Before she knew what to make of it, or how to answer, they were in Evan's driveway. And she was far from prepared for the battle she was walking into, since she suddenly didn't know who the enemy was.

Chapter 33

Evan saw a Sherriff's truck pull into his driveway just after he stepped out of the shower and hurried to pull clothes on. He had slept most of the day away, a deep, dreamless sleep that left him feeling both refreshed and still tired. The headache that was splitting his head open didn't help matters.

He opened his bedroom door in time to hear raised voices from the hallway. It sounded like JJ arguing with his dad. "I need to speak to Evan," JJ was saying. "And I'm not leaving until I do. This is highly unusual, and I'm concerned."

"What's highly unusual? That his parents are trying to protect him?"

"That a grown man, who is a friend of mine and my sister's boyfriend, is suddenly behind a locked door that two other adults control," JJ said. "I need to make sure that he's not being held against his will, and that he's alive and well."

Evan heard a gasp that could only be his mother's as he hurried down the stairs. Before he got there, he heard her voice. "How dare you," Vicki cried. "We would never hurt our son."

Finley had her mouth open as he came into view, and he was glad he stopped whatever she was about to say. He had shared all his feelings with her about the hurt his parents had inflicted over the years, and she had been about to say that to his mother.

"I'm here," he said. "Come in."

JJ gave a pointed look at Bob, who stepped aside. He then waved for his sister to go in ahead of him and stayed by the door. In uniform, glaring at the room, he was making it very clear who was in charge, and not to mess with him.

"Evan," Finley said, her voice cracking. "We have to talk."

"Yes," he said with a sigh. "I guess we do."

"Can we talk privately?" Finley glanced at his parents as she asked, and he nodded, gesturing to his home office.

He took his seat behind the desk, which he could see hurt her feelings. But he needed that physical separation from her right now. The look on her face alone was almost enough to pull her into his arms and never let go, but he couldn't be duped again. The sleep had helped to make things clearer, but he had to make sure he was right before he did anything.

"I didn't know," Finley said. "I didn't know that was Zach."

"So, you know why I'm upset."

"Now I do," she said. "After JJ started asking around, it finally clicked. He smiled last night, and something was bothering me, as if I had met him before. He looked so familiar. But then, when JJ found out you had gone into the Palace and then left again, it clicked. He looks like you. Not a lot, but just a hint, when he smiles."

"And you had no idea who he was?" Evan challenged her.

"None," she said, her voice adamant. "He introduced himself as Cary. I honestly never paid him much attention at all, because Audrey was intent on getting his attention. I mostly just sat there while they talked, ate my food, and left."

"It was pretty late when I saw you at the bar," he said.

"It was," she said with a nod. "Later than I wanted to be there. But I hadn't been there in a while, and Des was introducing me to people. And I was having fun with Audrey and Cary. Or, really, Audrey. Cary, I mean Zach, kind of kept to himself."

Evan was in agony, which he was trying to keep inside. His heart was screaming that of course she wasn't involved with Zach, that it really was a coincidence. But his brain was telling him to be careful, that he had to examine this thoroughly before making a decision.

"You don't believe me," Finley said, her voice flat. She swiped a tear from her face, and when he looked at her carefully, he could see it wasn't the first she had shed today.

"I don't know what to believe," he said finally. Before he could say anything more, he heard voices raised again outside. He stood and pulled open his door, finding Zach toe-to-toe with JJ. "What's going on?"

"I was just telling your brother that he was not going to interrupt you two and he had other plans," JJ said.

"Evan, please let me explain," Zach said. "I don't want you to make a decision that could affect the rest of your life without hearing the truth."

Evan ran a hand through his hair and closed his eyes, wishing he were anywhere but here. Finally nodding, he gestured to the office. "Come in."

Finley looked shocked when Zach came in but didn't say anything. Evan went to resume his spot, studying the two of them. They really did appear to be strangers, and he was certain this wasn't planned out.

"I've made a lot of bad decisions, and done a lot of stupid things," Zach said. "I'm an addict. Or a recovering addict. That will never change. But what did change was my realization about how it impacted your life, and what I threw away. I came here to fix that, not to make it worse."

"Funny how that works," Evan said, instantly hating himself for his sarcastic words.

Zach stared at the floor for a minute, as if absorbing the blow, before continuing. "I should have told her who I was. Absolutely. I swear to you, she did not know I was your brother. We've only met twice, and I didn't find out that she was your girlfriend until after the first time. Last night, Audrey asked me to meet her there and said she was going to dinner with a friend. I was supposed to go later but figured I could grab a bite first. I didn't know they were going there, and I didn't know it was Finley she was going to be with. And when she came in, I was kind of hoping you would too. I thought it would be good for us to just hang out with no pressure."

"And when I wasn't there, you didn't think to tell her?" Evan asked, looking between them.

"No," Zach said. "I freaked out. I didn't know what to do, and I thought if I told her, it would backfire. She would tell you, and it would look bad. I had every intention of telling you today."

"And you didn't," Evan said.

"I tried," Zach insisted. "I sat out in the freezing cold all morning, waiting for you to go out for your run. I tried to call you, but the hospital said you weren't there, and you weren't answering your cell phone. Then I finally thought of asking Dad, and he said you were sick and sleeping. I had no idea it was because of me."

"You can see what this looks like," Evan said to his brother.

"Obviously," Zach replied. "It looks like history repeating itself. But it's not, I swear. Ev, if you knew how hard I've worked to get to where I am, you would know that there is no chance I would throw it away. I spent months in rehab, and it was the worst time of my life. Having to face all that I did, while feeling like I was dying, was like living in a nightmare. Then, when I left there, I went to meetings every single day. Sometimes more than one. And in each one, I made myself tell strangers what I did to my best friend. My brother."

Zach stopped talking for a minute and took a few deep breaths while staring at the ceiling. "I also went to therapy," he said. "I still do, once a week. That helped me realize I didn't resent you. I was jealous. And I think that because of that jealousy, I hurt you. I can't blame it all on addiction, because it came from something deeper than that. But it wasn't intentional,

I swear. My therapist has helped me understand the drugs made my jealousy even more severe. I felt bad about myself and what I was doing, and instead of trying to fix it and get help, I spiraled and made it so much worse."

"Does that mean I'm to blame, because I was successful? It's my fault for chasing my dreams?"

"No," Zach said adamantly. "Not at all. It's my fault, for not having the same drive. For wanting the easy way through everything. For accepting quick solutions rather than work. I look back at the first time I was offered drugs to try. I want to shake that kid and tell him not to do it. But he was a showoff, too full of bravado to say no in front of everyone. And then I was the party guy, and everyone thought I was so fun. I could have stopped it a hundred times over, but I didn't. And that's on me."

"I should have noticed," Evan said. His own feelings about letting his brother slide into addiction while he was so distracted with medical school were complicated. He was training to be a doctor and had missed what was happening right in front of him.

"None of it is your fault," Zach said vehemently. "Nothing. Not what I did, how I did it, nothing. It's on me. The only thing you can control, now or then, is whether you can forgive me."

Evan waited while Zach took a moment to compose himself. His brother was pacing in the small room. His emotions were so raw, it was like a physical being in the room with them. Finley was sitting in silence, crying as she watched.

"You were always so good to me," Zach said finally. "You looked out for me, protected me, helped me. And I returned the favor by stabbing you in the back, not once, but multiple times. I can never forgive myself for that. And I'm not even asking for your forgiveness. I'm just asking you to start over with me. Let me be the brother I wish I had been for all these years. I still go to meetings, and I will be sober whether you say yes or no. This was my doing. Falling back to rely on something to make me feel better isn't ever going to be my solution again. I just want to prove to you that I've changed."

"I don't know how to do that," Evan said. "Trusting you is going to be incredibly hard, and it's easier for me to say no."

"Please," Zach said. His voice broke on the word, and it tore at Evan's heart. "Could you come to a meeting with me? Or could we talk to my therapist? He offered to help, if you're willing."

"Do you swear on your sobriety that what you're saying about you and Finley is true?" Evan asked. He felt it in his bones that it was, but he needed his brother to say it.

"Yes." Zach met his eyes, and Evan could see the clarity and honesty there. "I promise, she never knew who I was, and it was two casual meetings with a mutual friend. And I would have told you about it today if I could have."

Evan was staring at his desk, trying to make sense of everything, when his brother handed him a folded check. "It's not everything," Zach said. "But it's a start."

"I don't want your money," Evan said, trying to give it back.

"No, but you're going to take it," Zach said. "I've been working and saving, just to pay you back."

"You can't fix it this way," Evan argued.

"No," Zach said, nodding. "But maybe it will help. Maybe you'll realize that I'm not following the same path. I'm not here to destroy your life or mine. I want to make things right in every way. Like with Mom and Dad."

"What about them?" Evan asked, looking away from the check to see his brother's face.

"I encouraged them both to get into therapy," Zach said. "I saw what it was doing for me, and I thought it would help them too. They also go to Al-Anon meetings and will sometimes come with me to mine. I was just hoping to fix my relationship with them, but somehow, it also fixed theirs with each other."

Evan nodded, unable to get into his parents' relationship at the moment. He needed to focus on his own, with the two people in the room. The ones who had been the most important to him at one time. Who still were, if he were being honest. Finley was studying him with an expression he couldn't place, and Zach looked exhausted. As if sensing he had said all he could, Zach headed to the door.

"I'm going to let you two talk," he said. "But I'm not leaving. I'll be out here, trying not to get killed by Finley's terrifying brother."

They both watched as Zach left the room, and then Evan returned his attention to Finley. She had found a tissue somewhere and was shredding it in her hands. He wanted to hold her with every fiber of his being and finally stood to move closer to her. When he reached for her, she held back.

"You thought I would do that," she said, her voice barely a whisper. "That I would cheat on you. With your brother. And probably thought we would steal from you. Right?"

He nodded, unable to form words. Fresh tears welled in her eyes and spilled down her cheeks, and a sob erupted from deep inside her.

"I can't do this," she said. "I thought something was wrong with you. I was scared you were being taken away from me in some horrible way. But this is so much worse."

"I'm sorry," he said. His own voice was hoarse, the weight of emotion choking him. "I am so, so sorry. I should have known better. And if I were rational, I would have. I was so exhausted, and the emotion of the last week just caught up with me. Having Zach reappear and try to get back into my life, and then my parents. Edna Lee's results and sitting with her. And all the things that I feel for you. I have no excuse. I'm just so sorry. And I love you."

"I don't know if that's enough," she said. "You broke us, Evan. You broke me. How can we go on if you don't trust me?"

She got up and walked out of his office, and possibly out of his life. He wanted to chase her; to make her understand how shattered he had felt all day. How the emotions and the exhaustion had combined to overtake his normally rational brain, making it impossible for him to see the difference between truth and misunderstanding. But instead, he was locked in place. She was the most important person in the world to him, and he had done this to her. The reality was paralyzing. How was he going to fix this?

Chapter 34

Three days passed with Finley prone on her couch or hidden under the covers of her bed before a sharp knock sounded on the door. She ignored it and pulled the blanket tighter around her but heard the creak of the back door as it opened.

"Finley," her mother's voice called out. A minute later, her bedroom door opened, and the covers were ripped off her. "Let's go."

Her mother was at her bedside, hands on her hips, with Zoe behind her. Both looked determined, and she had no energy to fight them. "I'm tired," she said.

"Get up, you're getting in the shower," her mother ordered. "Otherwise, we'll get one of your brothers up here to carry you in. Don't think they wouldn't love to throw you in fully dressed."

"Leave me alone," Finley muttered. At her mother's look, she quickly changed her tone. "Please."

"Absolutely not," Zoe said. "You wouldn't say no to the mother of your first niece or nephew."

"Should I get the boys? They're waiting right downstairs," Maggie said.

Finley threw back the sheet she had clung to dramatically. "Fine," she said, storming toward the bathroom. "Just a shower, though."

When she emerged from the bathroom, her bed had been stripped, and her mom and sister-in-law were waiting on the couch. Without the ability to fall back into her bed or lie prone on the sofa, she curled onto the loveseat.

"Talk to us," Zoe said gently.

"He didn't believe in me," Finley said, fresh tears gathering in her eyes. "He thought I would trick him like that. That I would cheat on him with his brother."

"Tell us from the beginning," Maggie said.

Finley walked them through the events of the last few days, stopping several times to cry. Zoe had moved to sit next to her, holding her hand through it all. "And then he told me he was sorry," she said in conclusion. "That he had just been so exhausted and overwhelmed, he couldn't think straight. He just reacted."

"He reacted to what had traumatized him before," Zoe said. "Not to you. It was about Zach more than you."

"But he thought I did that! How do I go back and assume that he would trust me? What if he gives up on me that quickly again?"

"All good questions," Maggie said. "I have one for you."

"What?" Finley wiped at her eyes while she waited for her mother to speak.

"Do you expect the relationship to be perfect from beginning to end? To never have conflict or moments of distrust between you?"

"Yes," Finley said, although doubt trickled in the second she said the word. Did she? Her own parents had fought over the years, and she had seen JJ and Zoe go through their own dark moments.

Her mother sat patiently, waiting for her to think it through, before she spoke again. "You know that's not true," she said. "No relationship is perfect. Part of the strength your father and I have is from those moments of trouble. Where we had to make a conscious choice to pick the other person and fight through what we were feeling."

"How do I do that?" Finley asked. "When he didn't trust me?"

"You listen to him," Maggie said. "Actually listen. Don't have your own mind made up before he starts to talk. And then you have to decide if you love him enough to move past it. To fully put it behind you and let it make you stronger, and to learn from it."

"If you don't," Zoe added. "You could miss out on the great love of your life. We've seen you together. What you have is real. Don't let this ruin you."

***

"Are you okay?" Desmond asked her later that afternoon. He had finished working his day job, which he did from a desk tucked into his bedroom, and was about to go down to the bar. In jeans and a T-shirt, his hair rumpled, he gave off the casual guy vibe. But his expression showed how concerned he was about his twin, and she knew he cared, despite disappearing earlier when she was ambushed.

"I hope so," she said. "Don't tell Mom and Zoe I said so, but they were right. I feel better after a shower and getting out of bed."

"What are you going to do about Evan?"

"I wish I knew," she said. "There's a lot going through my head right now. I've called in sick for the first time without actually being sick, and I feel terrible about that."

Des waved a hand. "People do it all the time," he said. "You work hard."

"I know, but I don't like abandoning my patients," she said.

"Then go back," he said. "You have the weekend to figure it out."

"I know," she said. "Part of me wonders if I should transfer to a different department."

"Does that mean you don't plan to make up with Evan?"

"Do you think I should?"

309

Desmond scratched his chin as he seemed to think about the question. "I can't answer that," he said. "What I do know is that you've been happier than I've ever seen you. And up until a few days ago, he treated you better than anyone I've ever seen you with. Is it worth throwing that away for one mistake?"

"But it was a big one," Finley pointed out, feeling the tears coming again.

"What if you made one? Would you want forgiveness, or would you understand if he walked away?" Desmond moved toward the door as he spoke. "I love you, Fin. You're one of the best people I know. But you are stubborn and used to being right. People make mistakes. It's how you handle them that should matter the most."

***

The sounds of happiness intruded her thoughts all night, as the entire town seemed to be below her celebrating the upcoming holiday season. She could hear the faint strains of music from the band that mixed pop hits with Christmas songs, and laughter as it drifted up. She finally went to bed, turning on a fan to block out the noise, so she was awake when the sun came up on Saturday morning. Not wanting to wake Desmond, she let herself out of the apartment for the first time in days, heading towards the coffee shop.

As she crossed the street, she heard the footsteps of someone running toward her on the sidewalk. Her legs suddenly wouldn't move, and her traitorous heart made her look, hoping for a glimpse of Evan. As if he were conjured from her dreams, he appeared, slowing to a stop when he saw her. They stood staring at each other, breath puffing out like white smoke in the cold air, for what felt like hours.

"Hi," he said softly. "It's good to see you. I've been calling."

"I know," she replied. "I didn't know what to say. Or if I wanted to talk to you."

310

"Does that still stand? Do you want me to leave?"

Her stomach flipped at the possibility of him walking away. Would that be it if she said yes? "No," she said without allowing herself to analyze it. "We need to talk."

"Want to get some coffees and we can go somewhere warmer? We can go up to your place," he suggested.

"Des is sleeping," she said. "But I don't want to do it here."

"Will you come home with me?"

The question hung in the air for a moment. She had gotten so used to his house, it had started to feel like she lived there. His phrasing of the question suggested that he thought the same. He didn't refer to it as his house, but home, and that's what it felt like to her.

"Yes," she whispered. Before she could say anything else, he held up a finger and ran inside the coffee shop, reappearing a few minutes later with two cups and a white pastry bag.

The walk seemed both endless and fast, and before she knew it, Finley was greeting Guinness. The dog was behaving as if she had been gone for years, and she felt that way. Evan put the bag and coffees down on the kitchen table and looked unsure of himself as she reunited with the dog.

"Do you want to sit in here?" Evan asked, gesturing to the table. "Or go out on the couch?"

"Here, maybe," she said. The couch held too many memories of nights spent cuddled up watching movies or binging TV shows. Then again, the kitchen table was where they had shared meals, played cards, and done puzzles. There wasn't a corner of the house that wouldn't remind her of better days, she realized as she sat down.

"I'm sorry," he said. "Before you say anything else, I want you to know that I am deeply, truly sorry. The biggest regret in my life is how I treated you. I was entirely to blame, and if there is any way to make it up to you, I'd like a chance."

"Why would you have even thought that?" Finley looked at him through a sheen of tears, her voice breaking as the pain ripped through her.

"I don't have a good answer," he said. "I was exhausted, and the emotion of everything with my family must have been more than I had realized. It wasn't a conscious thought, I promise. It was a raw, ugly reaction to seeing you sitting there with my brother."

"I didn't know who he was," Finely said. "Not until you wouldn't talk to me, and JJ started asking questions."

"And that was the first thing I should have done," Evan said, running a hand through his hair. "I should have walked right into the bar, right up to you, and asked what was going on. Instead, I panicked and ducked out like a coward. And then stayed up all night, so by the time any sense would have been clicking in, I was too tired to think. I was just sure that Zach was up to his old tricks, and that you had been pulled in."

"I would never do that to you," she said. "Or anyone, for that matter."

"I know that," Evan said. "And if I had taken even one minute to really think it through, I would have known it immediately. You're the kindest, most caring person I've ever met. Your heart is too good to ever do something like that."

"I don't think Zach was up to anything," Finley said. "I know I didn't get to know him well, but he was nice. When I figured out what had happened, he apologized and said he would do anything to help me fix it."

"He and I have spent a lot of time this week talking," Evan said. "You wouldn't talk to me, so I dedicated my time to him. We even went to therapy together. And I went to a meeting with him, and to an Al-Anon with my parents."

"Wow," she said. "That's a lot."

"It has been," he said. "All positive things, but I can't feel good about any of it."

"Why not?"

"Because you aren't in my life," he said. "If you give me another chance, I promise you that I'll do better. I can't say I won't ever make another mistake, or that I won't revert to my solitary ways when I am struggling with something. But I will promise to protect your heart and to communicate with you. I promise to finish healing myself, and my family, so that break doesn't impact our lives."

"I want to support you in that," she said, standing and offering him her hand. "Remember when you thought I was too full of hope? That's the only thing that has kept me breathing for the last few days. Hope that we could somehow find our way through this, and back to each other. I don't need you to be perfect, or to not make mistakes. I'll make them too. But we have to stick with each other and lean on each other. Especially in the hard times. Can you promise me that?"

"Absolutely," he said. "It's not always easy for me to open up, but you make me want to. You make me want to be the man you see me as, even when I have doubts that I can be that person. But will you promise me one thing as well?"

"Anything," she said. Her heart was beating so fast, the emotions of the last three days almost making her feel dizzy. She knew the hurt would linger for a little longer, and the fear that he would revert to his isolated ways, but she had to trust in their love. In the foundation they had built, that it would be strong enough to hold them up. "What do you need me to promise?"

"To love me forever," he answered without hesitation. Before she knew what was happening, he dropped to a knee on the kitchen floor in front of her. "To let me lean on you when I need to, and to let me be your strength when you need it. To be my partner, my best friend, my everything, for all of our days. Be my wife, Finley. Love me forever."

She gasped as he pulled a ring box out of his pocket. "How do you have that with you?"

"I've had it with me every minute of every day since I made the biggest mistake of my life," he said. "If I had the chance to fix it, I was going to do it right. But you haven't answered me."

"My dad—"

"I talked to him three days ago," he answered. "He gave me his blessing. Your mom approved of the ring. All three of your brothers welcomed me to the family, although Desmond also gave me some other advice that may or may not be true."

"Of course he did," she said, half laughing, half crying as she did. Tears were flowing freely now, streaking down her face and dropping onto his cheek below her. She reached down and swiped it away, studying him as she did. Raw love was shining from his eyes, a smile hinting at his lips.

"Will you marry me?" he asked again, opening the box to show her the ring. A single, beautiful round diamond shone on a thin platinum band. It was simple and perfect, and everything she didn't know she wanted.

"Yes," she said, her voice barely a whisper. Smiling at him, she said it again louder for good measure. "Yes, Evan. I love you, and I want to live my life with you. I'm sure we'll both make lots of mistakes over the years, but I won't give up on you again. I shouldn't have this time. I should have forced my way into your house and made you listen to me. And don't you give up on me, either."

"Never," he said, taking her into his arms. "You're everything I never knew I needed, and now I can't live without you."

"Even if I talk too much?" She couldn't help but tease him, seeing his expression lighten at her words.

"Even if I'm a grump," he said, teasing her back. "No matter what, I'm here. And I know I've found exactly where I belong, right here with you."

As he took her into his arms and kissed her, securing their future together, she felt the pieces of her heart becoming whole again. Their time apart had been painful, and she never wanted to repeat it, but it had been valuable. She had realized that she loved him more than she was hurt, and she would forever. Their love would be enough to get them through whatever lay ahead for them. She would take care of him and his heart, and trust hers with him, for the rest of her days.

Acknowledgements

As many of you know by now, I am a nurse as well as a writer. Although my field is not oncology, I admire the medical professionals who do this work, and I've seen their dedication when my mom was being treated for cancer. Nurses work harder than it appears, and we do get emotionally invested in those they care for. The doctors who I have gotten to know over the years carry some extra weight that comes with their title and work tirelessly to provide the best care. It's hard work, and can be draining, but it also brings joy. To all of you who work in the medical field, thank you for making our world a better place.

To my readers, I wouldn't be able to do any of this without your kind messages. You show up for me in so many ways, supporting me and motivating me, and I couldn't be more grateful. Even just thinking that I have readers is still surreal to me! You make me want to write faster, do better, and it keeps the words flowing. I am so grateful for each and every one of you!

I'm incredibly grateful for my friends and cousins (my cousins are also good friends!). The friends who were around before I started writing, the ones I reconnected with over the books, and the ones I have made through this new path I've started on–thank you all. You each support me in different ways, and I could not be happier to have you in my life. Whether it's making me laugh, being there when I cry, showing up at events, dragging me out to socialize, keeping me in line in a hockey rink, sending me messages of support, texting me and already knowing we are on the same page about something, or making plans to meet up after years of not seeing each other–you all keep me sane and happy!

My family makes it possible for me to do this, and shares in every accomplishment with me. My parents, Arlene and Jim, continue to approach strangers to share my books with them. I have never had a day in my life where I didn't know they were proud of me, but this really showcases it. Jeff and Danielle make time to show up for my events, even with three kids and impossible schedules. My nieces and nephews-Brendan, Conor, Timmy, Tessa and Emmy-make my world go around. Nothing can bring me out of a bad day faster than a phone call or text message from one of them.

Last but not least, my husband Tommy and boys Camden and Calum. Anyone who knows my husband knows he's not a reader, but he is excited and ready to celebrate everything that happens with the books. Our boys continue to make us proud parents, working incredibly hard in school and chasing dreams that others have told them are impossible. If my writing journey has taught them anything, it's that nothing is impossible. Chase those dreams and don't give up until you get them.

Up Next

Yes, I am staying in Windsor Peak until you all get sick of reading them! I have two projects that I'm working on now – a holiday Novella that I plan to release in November, and book 2 in this Monahan trilogy, which I'm aiming for February (but if I can get it out earlier, I will). Both are available for pre-order where you purchased this!

In the meantime, be sure to follow me on social media @deniselathamwrites, on Amazon or your favorite bookseller, and visit my website to sign up for my newsletter. Then you'll be in the know before the books hit the shelves!

www.deniselatham.com

Please continue sharing the books with your friends and family and leave reviews where you purchased the book and on Goodreads. I can't tell you how much it helps, and how much I appreciate it!